BEST
GAY
EROTICA
2006

BEST
GAY
EROTICA
2006

Series Editor

RICHARD LABONTÉ

Selected and Introduced by

MATTILDA, A.K.A.
MATT BERNSTEIN SYCAMORE

CLEIS
PRESS

Published in the United States by Cleis Press Inc., P.O. Box 14697, San Francisco, California 94114

Printed in the United States.
Cover design: Scott Idleman
Cover photograph: Celesta Danger
Text design: Frank Wiedemann
Cleis logo art: Juana Alicia
First Edition
10 9 8 7 6 5 4 3 2 1

For a tenth time
for Asa Dean Liles—
now almost a Canadian

CONTENTS

ix Foreword • RICHARD LABONTÉ

xiii Dangerous and Lovely • MATTILDA, A.K.A.
      MATT BERNSTEIN SYCAMORE

1 In Bed with Allen • MARCUS EWERT

9 Stephen • KIRK READ

23 They Can't Stop Us • TIM DOODY

34 Fucking Doseone •
    RALOWE TRINITROTOLUENE AMPU

52 Site 1: from *The Sluts* • DENNIS COOPER

69 All the Creatures Were Stirring •
    ANDREW SPIELDENNER

76 Gender Queer • PATRICK CALIFIA

91 From *Sexile* • JAIME CORTEZ

105 Best Friendster Date Ever • ALEXANDER CHEE

119 Marcos y Che • SIMON SHEPPARD

130 Garlic • BOB VICKERY

139 Electrical Type of Thing • SAM D'ALLESANDRO

145 The Pancake Circus • TREBOR HEALEY

165 DogBoy and the BetaGoth • NADYALEC HIJAZI
     AND BEN BLACKTHORNE

187 From *What We Do Is Secret* •
     THORN KIEF HILLSBERY

205 Lizard Killing • JULY SHARK

211 Too Far • KEVIN KILLIAN AND THOM WOLF

233 Jailbait • DARIN KLEIN

236 Depression Halved Production Costs •
     SAM J. MILLER

242 Now Fix Me • DUANE WILLIAMS

254 Half-Eaten Lollipop • BLAKE NEMEC

259 Trouble Loves Me • STEVEN ZEELAND

279 About the Authors

286 About the Editors

FOREWORD

Richard Labonté

The *Best Gay Erotica* series is eleven years old with this edition—and this is the tenth volume in the series that I've edited: many thousands of stories read, several hundred of them enjoyed, a couple of hundred "bests" selected by a distinguished array of guest judges, from Douglas Sadownick in 1997 to, this year, Mattilda, a.k.a. Matt Bernstein Sycamore.

As with every judge, she—think gender fluidity, eh?—brings a unique sensibility in story selection. Every year, I cull a few dozen stories from the many, many submissions, searching not for a unifying theme, but rather for overall excellence and intriguing original-ity; what sets each year's *BGE* apart from the erotic anthology hordes, I believe, is that each edition, year to year, reflects the ultimate taste of writerly intelligences: Christopher Bram and Felice Picano and D. Travers Scott and Neal Drinnan and Randy Boyd and Kirk Read and Michael Rowe and William J. Mann—like Sadownick, all past judges—epitomize queer quality; what they write and how they write are markedly different in voice, and each of them stamped their year of *Best Gay Erotica* with a distinct style.

Just so, Mattilda—in a young lifetime a lusty hustler, an able editor, a fierce activist, and a gifted writer—brought a number of newer writers to my attention, encouraging them to submit stories. Not all of them made my cut, but it's a pleasure this year to include new fiction by Ralowe Trinitrotoluene Ampu, Tim Doody, July Shark, Darin Klein, Sam J. Miller, and blake nemec—I hope their appearance between the covers of this collection of "bests" is as good for them as it is for me. Ditto for the writing partners Nadyalec Hijazi and Ben Blackthorne, whose rambunctious story came my way through one of the several online journals that have matured into fecund homes for new writers.

Anthology virgins they are not; newish (and sometimes youngish) they are. Count Marcus Ewert (with a story from *Beatboy,* his memoir-in-progress), Kirk Read (author of the memoir *How I Learned to Snap*), Alexander Chee (*Edinburgh* and the forthcoming *The Queen of the Night*), Trebor Healey (*Through It Came Bright Colors*), Duane Williams, and Andrew Spieldenner among writers whose prose I'll read anywhere, anytime, and whom we feature most enthusiastically in this year's collection.

Older by a writing generation or two—though none is nearing any sort of dotage, of course—are contributors Simon Sheppard, Patrick Califia, Bob Vickery, Kevin Killian (with coauthor Thom Wolf), and Dennis Cooper: writers whose work has almost nothing in common with the others except for stylish strength, daunting depth, and immense intelligence. Sheppard, Califia, Vickery, and Killian are *BGE* veterans, writers whose work, erotic or not, is always at its best; this is Cooper's first *BGE* appearance, with an excerpt from *The Sluts*, an uncommon, uneasy, and unsettling read that explicates depravity with an astonishing blend of dark humor, potent truth, and spooky realism.

Somewhere in the middle, as generations go, are Thorn Kief Hillsbery, with an excerpt from *What We Do Is Secret*, and Steven Zeeland, editor of five best-selling military-sex books from Haworth Press.

And Sam D'Allesandro—well, his writing transcends generations. He died in 1988, even before his first collection *The Zombie Pit* (Crossing Press, 1989) was published; "Electrical Type of Thing" is from *The Wild Creatures* (Suspect Thought, 2005) a collection that reprints stories from *The Zombie Pit* and adds work from writing he left behind, shepherded into print by his literary executor, Kevin Killian. Twenty-five years after AIDS began to kill off a generation of gay writers and editors—Bo Huston, Joseph Beam, Stan Leventhal, Essex Hemphill, Allan Barnett, Steven Corbin, Robert Ferro, Michael Grumley, Melvin Dixon, Paul Monette, Steve Abbott, so many more—there is a grace about bringing writing from a melancholy past into the vibrant present.

Mattilda and I both wanted to feature graphic narrative in *BGE06*. Rounding out the selections this year is the first-chapter excerpt from Jaime Cortez's dazzling graphic biography: *Sexile*, based on interviews with Adela Vazquez, showcases how beautifully art and words can fuse to tell a tale.

And that's the book. I'm celebrating my tenth anniversary with one of the best of the *Bests*, a collection with literary astonishments and erotic eclecticism aplenty.

Thanks, as always, to Frédérique Delacoste and Felice Newman, consummate publishers; to Diane Levinson and Chris Fox, who round out the Cleis empire; to Ottawa book-seller David Rimmer, who points me to new smut on the shelves of After Stonewall for my annual consideration; to book collector extraordinaire Bryan Wannop and his partner in dusting, Frank Kajfes; to old Canadian friends Andrew Currie and Nik Sheehan; to old American friends Justin Chin, Lawrence Schimel, Ian Philips (and, though we've never met, his husband, Mr. Greg Wharton); and to Shane Allison, whose story didn't make it into *Best Gay Erotica 2006*—but he's a writer of poetry and prose to watch out for.

Richard Labonté
Perth, Ontario
August 2005

DANGEROUS AND LOVELY:
AN INTRODUCTION

Mattilda, a.k.a Matt Bernstein Sycamore

I was thirteen the first time I had sex in a public bathroom. Or maybe I was fourteen, but anyway it happened at Woodie's—not the bar in Philadelphia, but the department store in Washington, D.C.—or actually at the Friendship Heights branch literally steps across the Maryland state line. I was on the way to my father's office after school, so that he could drive me home. I stopped at the Woodie's makeup counter to look for a suitable base to cover up my acne, and the salesperson asked if I was shopping for my mother. I could feel my face turning red. The only thing I could bring myself to ask about was the Evian Brumisateur, spring water in a metal can with a nozzle that sprayed out a fine mist. I bought some: Gay consumerism hit me early.

But back to the bathroom, I stood at a urinal right next to someone, which made me nervous but my father was always yelling at me to get used to it, what was I so afraid of, any normal kid would just pull it out and piss. Normal kids had been calling me faggot since I could remember, way before I knew what it meant. I'd go home to my father screaming at me about everything else. He didn't even know that I jerked off to pictures of guys in onionskin shorts, that I planned to live in an East Village commune, that at thirteen I already searched frantically for the right cream to eliminate the bags under my eyes.

But back to the urinal, I was staring straight ahead at the wall so that I wouldn't get accused of looking, but I could still see what was next to me, which was this guy's dick sticking straight out after he dropped his right hand. My heart started pounding, I didn't know how to breathe. My dick got hard and I covered it with my hands. I stood there for a while, facing straight ahead with my eyes looking diagonally down to the left. I didn't know what to do. I dropped my left hand.

I reached over to touch this guy's dick, and he reached for mine. Someone came in, I stuffed my dick into my pants and practically ran. Never again, I promised myself. Never again.

I was back a week later, then several times a week throughout high school. Woodie's Friendship Heights, Woodie's downtown, Mazza Gallery, Georgetown Park, Georgetown Public Library, Bethesda Public Library. Always promising: never again.

I want to say that every time I came, it was an explosion of unbridled passion. I want to say that every time I looked into the eyes of some old guy with pasty skin standing next to me, tongue flicking in and out of his mouth in anticipation of my eager erection, I was in heaven. I want to say that every time I saw some man shaking out of fear and longing, sweat appearing in the armpits of his starched shirt, I wanted to hold him.

The truth is that I grew up in a world that wanted me dead, in a family that was ready to kill me, except then who would be around to carry on the family name? Kids had been calling me sissy for so long—I knew about gender deviance, but I didn't know how to claim it. What I knew is that I didn't want to feel, that if I just kept going back to the bathrooms, holding my body shut while men opened their mouths down there, then maybe I would win.

Winning meant defeating my father on every front—doing better in school, going to a more prestigious college, getting a higher-paying job. This was the '80s, not the '80s we now see on the fashion runways but the late-'80s that seemed like the tail end of a decade of greed (little did we know what was to come). And winning also meant learning not to feel, because then I wouldn't have to remember my father splitting me open, over the sink in the basement, with all that mold entering my nostrils, when I was a broken toy. I'd already blocked that out, now I just needed to conquer my desires and then no one would be able to erase all my accomplishments with a single word.

Faggot. My sex life started with guilt and shame and grabbing that guy's dick in the Woodie's bathroom, it felt so huge and warm and spongy. My sex life started with the urinals, usually me and some old white guy with puckering lips or a business type with a briefcase on the floor between us. Was I attracted to them? I was hard, I wanted to come, I didn't want to feel it.

I graduated from urinals to stalls after this one guy waved me in; when I pulled down my pants he put his hands under my shirt. Someone entered the bathroom, this guy sat on the toilet and pulled me onto his lap. *Shh,* he said. He hugged me and this flooded me with so much sensation. But I could feel his dick pressing up against me, I was afraid that it would get inside, that I would get AIDS. When the other guy left, I slid away, pulled up my pants, opened the stall door, and hurried out. Soon I heard the guy behind me, looked back to see his curly hair and glasses, black overcoat with brown leather shoulder bag. I literally ran—out the door and through the parking lot, up the hill and over to my father's fateful fucking office.

Okay, so you're wondering about all this seriousness in a porn anthology, but I just stopped writing to jerk off. I kept spitting on my hands, and there was a little bit of food residue in my mouth; now that I've switched chairs I can see little spots all over the pillows where I was just sitting. I could say: You made me jerk off so hard that my hands are burning, forearms tight with exertion, shoulders aching. Go ahead: Shoot your load too, smear your come all over this paragraph and then make all your boyfriends peel the pages open. Or better yet: Send it to me, pages stuck together—I dare you.

Or I could say: I have such terrible, chronic pain that even jerking off makes my body hurt. I still want to come, I just called the phone sex line and was about to hook up with some guy who sounded hot and was only seven blocks away, but he needed twenty minutes to leave the house and it was already 4:12 A.M. though now it's 4:32. I could be fucking that guy's face, instead of just jerking off and hurting, which is what I'm doing now. I'm jerking off while I'm writing this—voice activation software has some advantages, though it's not helping my jock itch. Okay, my dick is shining with spit, I'm rolling my ergonomic desk chair over to the mirror so I can watch myself, the curve in my dick that used to make me think that I couldn't get all the way hard. But now I know better. I'm hard, staring at the vein on the bottom of my dick in the mirror.

But let's return to the bathrooms, which were my first safe gay spaces—or not safe, really, but more comfortable than the rest of the world. I discovered a hidden culture of foot tapping and notes written on toilet paper, wrapped around pens, and passed underneath stall walls. I imagined entire worlds around shoes and socks and ankles, the texture of hands, the skin underneath wristwatches, the pattern of hair on thighs. I pressed my body against metal partitions while guys on the other side offered hands and tongues and lips and mouths.

I grew bolder, cock against cock or my hand cupping his balls. At the Georgetown Public Library, I would kneel on the floor when no one was around and inhale the smell of stale piss. I came all over the floor of the bathroom at Mazza Gallery, right in the center of the room, halfway between the stalls and the sinks, and left it there. I led guys into stairwells and parking lots, I jerked guys off in the safety of their cars. One guy wanted me to meet his wife, another handed me his business card: Capitol Hill. Just after I learned to drive, I picked a guy up at a gas station, by leaving my hand at my crotch a little too long and then moving my gaze to the hill across the street. It wasn't a hill, really, just some landfill between buildings, but we jerked each other off in the sun anyway. He pulled way too hard.

And yes, every time I promised: never again. Until I got away, not from the bathrooms but from high school and my parents and Washington, D.C., and then farther away after a year at some fancy college still trying to outdo my father. I decided, instead, to beat him on my own terms. I cruised bathrooms and sex clubs and beaches and alleys, phone sex lines and backrooms and more bathrooms and backrooms and sex clubs and beaches. I want to say that I reveled in indecency, that I embraced sluttiness with a passion. And I did. But I also found myself in a sexual world that worshipped the masculinity I despised, elevating it to a preeminent space in the pantheon of the gods.

I longed for something else, but I took what I could get. I discovered a whole universe of shaking and moaning and panting and groaning, so much sweat and spit and come on my face and my chest, in my hands and my clothes. Boston's Fens, in the middle of a freezing winter, with the reeds cut down so that no one could hide—fifty guys in a circle just grabbing and holding and petting, gripping and pumping and shaking and grinding, somehow I was close to the middle, almost getting squashed, just feeling it. Or San Francisco's Buena Vista Park, with the trees tossing in the wind and making strange screeching sounds, the fog tinting the sky pink, and I'm standing up into so many guys' arms. Or the backroom at The Cock in New York, kneeling on the floor and sucking one cock after another, there's no use trying to stop because if you stand up then you're pushed back by the crowd pushing forward; finally you do it anyway and find yourself up against this one guy hugging you with his dick angled right at your asshole.

But back to the disease of unquestioned masculinity—in 1996, I got kicked out of a sex club for delivering unrepentant queeniness with integrity and charm. This was at Blow

Buddies in San Francisco: A friend and I pulled open a curtain to glimpse two steroid-pumped manimals humping, a third specimen bent over with his ass in the air, and I guess they didn't want us in their Gymlandia because the guy doing the fucking rudely pulled the curtain shut. We thought this was the funniest thing, and pretty soon we were cackling at every he-man trying so desperately to shun our sisterhood. Someone summoned the door guy, who told us we were being too loud, which made us louder, yelling with more testosterone than he could handle: Yeah, suck that dick man, yeah!

We were hastily ushered out, and I promised myself that I would never enter that corral again. But nine years later, I find myself desperate. Public sexual spaces have been depopulated by the Internet. I go to Buena Vista Park at 1:45 A.M., and there's no one there, I mean not a single person—this used to be prime time. I wait a half hour and then go home. Most of San Francisco's backrooms have been shut down to make way for Tiffany wedding bands, and the Power Exchange, the sex club I usually go to, has always been tweaked out, but at least people used to have sex there—now they just walk in circles like they're at some demented mall, or lock themselves in cubicles and dream of bedrooms. When people do have sex, they stare at each other with computer screens in their eyes—Kirk Read calls this "two-dimensional sex," the crap you have when you hook up online, and everything is scripted to avoid any intimacy or even passion.

Of course, guys have been figuring out ways to avoid intimacy in public sexual spaces for generations, but there's something more brutal and dehumanizing about the calculated hyperobjectification of the Internet. I've been a whore for more than a dozen years, so I'm aware of the ways in which reality desperately strives to imitate fantasy, but at least a trick who's paying generally wants some intimacy, or the illusion of intimacy. But the Internet intensifies all the worst aspects of gay male sexual culture: A ruthless search for the perfect abs or ass or cheekbones or cock becomes an all-day obsession, scorn becomes "just a preference," lack of respect is assumed, lying is a given. The Internet makes it safe for corporate lawyers to go on three-day crystal barebacking binges and rationalize the weekend by assuring themselves: At least no one knows.

But back to Blow Buddies, where I returned after a nine-year absence—I figured it had to be better than the Power Exchange. Military aficionado Steve Zeeland claims he's celebrating masculinity in order to destroy it, and I'm skeptical but not entirely innocent either. I've learned to negotiate the hallways of sexual longing with just the right combination of studied innocence and discreet charm. Sure, I still smile way too much, but I can press silently against you for just the right amount of time to get your dick into my throat.

So at first, Blow Buddies was refreshing. Guys were sucking cock and jerking each other off in the open, but maybe I was accustomed to the Power Exchange, because I kept walking around and around until there was almost no one left. I eyed this one guy sucking a thick dick through a glory hole, looked up to see a hot guy with a shaved head, just the right amount of stubble, and the perfect scowl, I was practically drooling. The cocksucker kept choking, until he actually turned to me and asked if I wanted to take over—manners! Then I was the cocksucker, even though at first the guy's dick tasted like a not-too-delicate mixture of liquor and digestive enzymes. I figured I'd just keep sucking and eventually it would taste better, and I was right, pressing my lips up against this guy's groin and wishing I could get closer to the rest of him.

I looked up and saw that the guy was watching me, so I reached up to grab his neck, and then he was pulling at my armpit and pumping my throat really hard and I was taking it like I live for, and he grabbed my head with the other hand and I was in homo heaven, sucking and slurping and aching for that load. And then he pulled away, shook off his dick, zipped up his pants, and walked off. And here I am now, still salivating over his masculinity, jerking off as I write this, aggravating my jock itch and teasing you with my flaming tendonitis.

But back to Blow Buddies, I stumbled upon some guy's stretched-open shaven asshole pushed into a glory hole like a toothless mouth with big big cheeks. I thought: If sex is gonna imitate porn, then porn's gonna have to become a whole lot more creative. Which brings us to the volume you have in your hand—the hand that's not squeezing your cucumber, grabbing your peppermint stick, massaging your glo-snake. This book is dangerous and lovely, just like you.

IN BED WITH ALLEN

Marcus Ewert

In 1988, when I was seventeen, I flew out to the Naropa Institute in Boulder, Colorado, with the express purpose of sleeping with Allen Ginsberg, the world's most famous living poet. To be more specific, I wanted to sleep with Allen so that I could join my life to his, thereby speeding up my own ascent into personal and artistic greatness. At the time, Allen was sixty-two years old, and I knew from reading his poetry how attracted he was to teenage guys. In the following true story, I have just introduced myself to Allen, and we've agreed to meet later that same afternoon, with the understanding that we are going to have sex.

After a desultory meal of fried tempeh in a bun—my stomach's too jumpy for me to do much more than pick around the edges—I head back towards Allen's. I mount the stairs and knock on his front door; he lets me in. Once again, Allen's dressed in blowzy, white, pajama-like clothing. Stepping further into the apartment, I see that it too is suffused with whiteness: the sunshine of high noon slicing up the living room into a thicket of angles, as it streams in through the plate-glass windows.

Allen looks at me questioningly and cocks his head in the direction of the bedroom, upstairs. "Well, shall we?"

"Okay."

And then it's like a wind is pushing us up up up the staircase—a hastening of the narrative inevitable. Allen leads the way. He's holding both my hands, clasped in a lovers' knot.

The bedroom is primarily bed—a broad, king-sized mattress neatly made up with clean white sheets. A writing desk against one wall displays a ream of blank paper, one of those school composition journals with the mottled, black-and-white covers, a clutch of fountain pens, an ink bottle, and a box of Kleenex. Above the desk, the room's one small window stands open. Through it, breezes bat like kittens' paws, catching and belling the short curtains; warm puffs of air fragrant with the smells of summer: grass and pine and sun-baked soil. Allen unclasps his clunky wristwatch and drops it on the desk, causing a few pens to scatter. He faces me expectantly. I guess I'm supposed to take the lead now.

I guide Allen to the foot of the bed, and gently push him onto his back. He sighs and shivers with delight...so let's be a bit more daring. I hop onto the bed behind him and cradle his head in my hands. I give his skull a little tug so that his neck will fully extend, which seems like the kind of thing a sexy...*masseur*-type guy would think of. Once Allen's neck is unkinked, I carefully rest it, head back down, on the pillow. Then I worry: *Did I go too far, just now? Is pulling on his head too weird?*

But Allen's looking up at me with the starry eyes and blank smile of a baby with gas. An expression which in this case, unfortunately, seems a bit cutesy and self-satisfied, as if Allen were thinking, *Aren't I amazing, to let myself* FEEL *pleasure so deeply?*

On the other hand, *I'm* beaming right back at *him*, intoxicated myself that I seem to be playing the part of young swain so successfully. To an outside observer, we'd no doubt look like lovers gazing at each other raptly, but actually we read in each other's expressions only signs of our own depth and goodness. Oh well.

However, as I peer down at Allen—intent as the mother in a Mary Cassatt painting—I *do* take the opportunity to really *look* at him for the first time...and am rewarded with a flush of physical attraction that I wasn't expecting to feel! *Wow,* I think, *he's actually really handsome, kind of!*

Supine in the sunlight, his head has a craggy dignity, like the face of a god on an ancient coin—Zeus or Dionysus. And he's definitely got the lusty, bearded satyr-thing going for him....

The moment I establish a lineage for Allen, a historical precedent for the way he looks, any remaining doubts about having sex with him fly right out the window. Don't I want to be a part of history, too?

"You're very handsome, Allen," I tell him. "You have a kind of...noble, heroic look to your face."

"Yes-s-s-s," says Allen slowly, astonished by my sagacity, "you're right, I *do* look noble and heroic. How intelligent of you, to notice that! Most people your age wouldn't have!"

Time to distract Mr. "Ego Unbound"! Glancing at Allen's forehead, I suddenly remember how my Dad would tickle-torture me when I was a kid—pinning me down and blowing tightly focused little breaths on my head until I'd go crazy.—Ah ha!

Just as Allen is drawing breath to say something else, I cover his eyes with one hand. Gamely he goes limp, and shuts up—happy once more to concede control. I hover over him and purse my lips. Then, I graze his brow with zephyrs.

Allen groans! Twitches! Shudders! "*Ohhhhh!*" he moans. "*Angel* kisses!"—Nice.

I continue tickle-torturing him until I start to hyperventilate, then I flop down beside him to catch my breath. After a moment, Allen leans over and tells me eagerly, "Do you know that when you were doing that it's like you were blowing directly onto my *brain?*"

God, I'm such a good lover all of a sudden—it's like I can do no wrong!

Let's up it another notch: kissing.

I haul myself on top of Allen, push-up style. His lips are firm and puckered, emerging from the crinkly hairs of his beard like what I imagine a vagina to look like. I lower my face down to his, exquisitely slowly, so that we can really FEEL our energies mingling—bringing my lips down so that they just barely brush his, not even a kiss yet, just...contact. My eyes are closed. I keep us suspended there, right on the edge.

And then I part my lips, and fuck his mouth with mine.

Allen returns the fervor, doubled, which spurs me on further. His tongue is bumpy and slabby; visually, it looks like square pieces have been sliced from it at random. And on his tongue's left side, my own tongue encounters a hard, raised nodule, like the pellet from a BB gun embedded in there—what is that? None of this is gross, though, it just adds texture. Allen's mouth tastes like some sort of mouthwash too, kind of old-fashioned and medicinal, but not unpleasant.

After several minutes of hard-core frenching, Allen pulls himself free. "Oh!" he cries, unable to constrain the urge-to-describe a moment longer: "*Candy!*"

Wow, I think, *he really is good with words!* "Candy!" *The perfect way to describe kisses from me: a mouthful of sweet, youthful innocence....*

Emboldened, I begin to take off his shirt. Suspensefully, I undo each plastic button: striptease. I slide my hands under the shirt flaps and splay them open, baring Allen's torso as if shucking an ear of corn. I skate my hands up his chest—the skin is cool. I place a hand over his heart and pause dramatically, as if calling upon the spirits to help me pump cosmic energy into Allen's body. Cupped in my hand, his breast is soft and quivery, like a pudding with little hairs on it. Inside its cage of bone and flesh, I feel his heart softly juddering.

My turn for a little wordplay. Remembering a term I once came across in Tolkien, which always sounded cool, I say, "Allen, you are a *greatheart*." I enunciate the unusual word carefully: "You are a *greatheart*, Allen."

He looks at me like I'm the rooster who quoted Shelley. "Yes-s-s," he says, with wonder, "yes-s-s, you're right! I *am*, I *am* a great heart!" He makes it two words. Gazing off into distant realms of Destiny, he says, "And that's what I try to be in the world—a *great heart*." Then he brings his attention back to the here and now, and looks at me again, still marveling. "How *wise* of you, to see that!"

I pause respectfully for a beat, then change subjects by putting my hand on his crotch. That quiets him. Through the fabric of his pants I feel his erection, a short hard rod that I knead with the heel of my hand. I unzip his fly and withdraw his dick. It stands up proudly, perpendicular to his belly, just three or four inches tall. Not *too* threatening....

Still, looking down at the swollen head, I ask myself if I'm really going to go through with this. But the skin looks so tight and glossy, I *do* wonder what it would feel like against my lips.... Hmm, smooth. Well, while I'm down here, why not pop the whole thing in my mouth, see what *that* feels like? Hmm. Kinda filling, in a satisfying sort of way....

Gee, I guess I am going to blow him after all.

I suck Allen's dick for several minutes and, really, it's not that bad. On the other hand, I *am* getting light-headed. I find that breathing while giving head is difficult, plus, the intense self-consciousness of the last forty minutes—"*In Bed with Allen Ginsberg*"—has really worn me out. I just want to get off and go to sleep. God, I'm so selfish!

I stop blowing him, and lie back to rest. Allen doesn't chastise me, but instead transitions himself from passive to active. He ministers to my body, doing a lot of the things to me that I did to him—like the blowing on the forehead, and the portentous hand-over-the-heart thing—but he's not as good at them as I was, he's kinda half-assed. On the other hand, the moment he gets my dick in his mouth, I know that I'm hopelessly outclassed. He blows me with one hand wrapped firmly around my cock, sluicing me up and down while his head bobs frenetically. After a few minutes of me bucking and thrashing in pleasure, Allen glances up.

"If you use your hand like this," he explains, coming off my dick and showing me the wet sleeve he's made with his fingers, "you keep your lover's penis covered the *entire time* you blow him, so that it never gets cold. Also, this way, there's never a moment in which his *entire shaft* isn't receiving stimulation of *some* kind…which demonstrates mindfulness and compassion for your partner.

"Now you try," he adds.

Ugh, I'm so *tired!* Plus, I absolutely HATE the fact that now there's *technique* involved, a right way and a wrong way to do things. I *knew* sex couldn't be that easy. I *knew* I'd fuck everything up somehow….

Deeply depressed, I try to blow Allen like he blew me, but—sure enough—my timing and coordination are totally shot. Instead of the fluid, synchronized movements that Allen used, my mouth goes up when my hand goes down and vice versa, and I'm almost in tears. Plus, I'm gagging really badly. Allen cheerfully calls out blowjob suggestions, but they only confuse me more. Finally, I just give up.

Thankfully, Allen doesn't seem too upset. Still chipper, he resumes blowing me as if there hadn't been an interruption, until he brings me to a truly shattering orgasm. My eyelids seek to drag me down into sleep, but it's only common courtesy to help Allen get off, I've screwed up too much already to shirk now. Allen pumps his dick with gusto and asks me to pinch his nipples, cup his balls, and look into his eyes while I kiss him, all at the same time. This seems physically impossible, but somehow I manage it, and Allen finally cums. I'm sure his orgasm was a lot less fun than mine, but he's sighing happily, so I guess everything's okay. We wipe ourselves off and then curl towards each other, ready to nap.

Just before we both drift off into pleasant, afternoon dozing, Allen bestirs himself. "This," he says, indicating our quiescent, satiated forms, "is the ONLY way to teach. Just like this—one on one, in bed. The ancient Greeks knew it. That was how all the great philosophers instructed their pupils—after sex, when the mind and the heart are more open.

"Whatever I do out there," he continues, waving his hand in the direction of Naropa, and the world at large, "the things I say in class? That's not teaching, those are just *words*—the neurotic chattering of the ego.

"*Real* education only happens between two people," Allen tells me. "Through intimacy."

STEPHEN

Kirk Read

Andy's words are italicized because hookers speak Italics.

[Notes to aspiring hookers are in brackets in roman typeface.]

Hooker phone: Andy's client Stephen

—Hey Andy, it's Stephen. Are we still on for tonight?

—*Sure.*

—Can you bring some of your toys? I wanna try something different. You can just run the whole evening.

—*Okay.*

—Two hours, okay?

—*Call when you check into the hotel and give me your room number.*

—Will do.

—Also, if you could call down to the desk and ask them which exit it is from 101, that would be great.

Voice mail, received during a class discussion of Raymond Carver (which Andy thought got a little out of hand, what with all the flagrant worship)

—Hey guy, it's Stephen. It's the Millbrae exit, then you cross the freeway and go right on Airport Road. Pass the Hyatt and it's all the way at the end. You'll see it—the Crowne Plaza. Okay. I'm looking forward to seeing you. I want you to take charge.

Hooker phone: Andy's friend Doug

—...I think children are used to further this notion of sex as terror. Adults assert their kids as an excuse to repress everyone else. It's the ultimate double bind for people who care about liberty. How do you bring a child into this over-populated planet—I mean, it's already problematic on an ecological level—and not just put them in front of Disney videos? I mean, can it be subversive or are we deluding ourselves?

—I agree. What did you do today?

—Just got home from Harbin Hot Springs. I'm on my way to see a client.

—I thought you might be driving.

—I'm turning into the parking lot of the hotel.

[Early in your sex work career, this is an exotic thing to say to a friend on the phone.]

—How are you?

—Good. Went to see Tori Amos last night, U2 Thursday. Got three shows this week.

—*I thought you were on a budget! I'm gonna do a seminar on how to be poor.*

—Well, once I sell the book I figure it'll change around. Something has to.

—*Honey, I just can't imagine myself being anything but poor. Then I don't get disappointed.*

—You going to see anyone this week?

—*Gang of Four. You should download their album* Entertainment! *From BitTorrent or something. They're really important.*

—When were they important?

—*The late '70s and early '80s.*

—I usually like the bands that sound like the important bands.

—*Well, that's the thing. Every band is derivative of Gang of Four these days. Michael Stipe and Bono stole every messianic lead singer move in the book from Jon King. Flea learned to play bass listening to Gang of Four. Andy Gill's angular guitar? Forget it!*

—What's angular guitar?

—*Download Gang of Four, on either BitTorrent or Acquisition.*

—What's Acquisition?

—*It's like LimeWire but it's a more graceful application.*

—I'll give it a shot, but are they like Television?

—*What do you mean?*

—Does every band in the world claim to have been influenced by them?

—*Yes, they're just like Television.*

—Okay, I better let you go.

—*Okay.*

—Have fun.

Lobby, Crowne Plaza Hotel

People smile. A fat man with two cell phones on his hip leers at Andy in front of the elevator. What would it be like to go to a hotel lobby with no appointments and just see what happens? Andy has too much Scottish blood for that. He's too practical. Time is money is money is time.

Room 813

A soft knock. Andy always wants to knock with a car key, just to scare someone, the way maids do it in cheap motels. Click click click. *Housekeeping!*

—Hey guy.

They kiss. Andy sets down the bags: a black duffle bag full of sex toys. He sees four hundred-dollar bills fanned out on the desk. It's the first thing he looks for. Stephen wants adventure this time. Usually he spanks and fucks Andy, but this time he's flopping. Andy sits down on the couch. It's a *suite*, not just a room. Stephen must be there for a conference. He only says *meetings*.

[Businesspeople either are too ashamed of the boredom they endure to fully reveal what they're doing all day, or they can't conceive of any escort's having been to a conference.]

Stephen calls it a "leadership seminar," which translates to an excuse for men to drink together in hotel lobbies that could be anywhere. Cleveland, Phoenix, Atlanta. The carpet is the same toasted almond medium pile no matter where you go. These guys are at an airport hotel for three days and they will only go into the city once for dinner. That is really the end of the line.

Couch

Andy pulls Stephen's fat ass over his knees so Stephen is lying across his lap. He spanks him through his shorts. Andy usually warms up a person's ass so the spanking will be mystical. When Andy first moved to San Francisco, he saw a daddy on a regular basis who lit dozens of candles and spanked him with dazzling mastery. There was an entire ritual to their evenings together. For hours, the daddy would gradually warm up Andy's butt and give him a case of "hungry butt." The slightest touch felt like an emergency room cardiac jump start. Andy would be squirming.

[You must learn the difference between play and work. Both realms must be distinct and exquisite. Find a man who hates overhead lights and takes his time.]

It was the closest Andy ever came to being Catholic. Going to this man's house was like going to Mass. This is where Andy learned to spank. This daddy was the Obi-Wan Kenobi of spanking. The next day, Andy would cry from yearning— that awful dilemma boys have when they're handled well.

[You'll know it when you feel it.]

All weekend, Andy had been soaking in hot water with hippies and doing yoga twice a day. Despite these pacifying measures, Andy wants to skip the warm-up and really hurt Stephen.

—*Get on the floor.*

—Yessir.

—*Take off my shoes.*

—Yessir.

INSERT FACE SLAP

—No marks....

—*Okay.*

INSERT FACE SLAP—LIKE, TEN OF THEM
—Now my jeans...socks...briefs. Just sniff it. Don't touch it. Close your mouth. Sniff it.

Andy lets a few drops of piss shake onto Stephen's black shirt. He wonders if this is his only casual shirt. Will this be traumatic for Stephen? They've never done this. Andy does it anyway. Some of the piss falls onto the carpet and the couch.

[Be mindful of where you sit in hotel rooms. Cleaning is cursory at best.]

Bathroom
—Lie in the tub. Open your mouth.
—Not in my eyes.
—Shut up.
—Careful.
—Here.
INSERT TOWEL DRYING FACE
—Never done that with you. I've thought about it.
—How are you doing?
—Good. That was hot.
—If we go anywhere you don't feel comfortable, just say so. Even when we're playing with dominance, you should be able to stop it if you need to.
—Okay.
—Take a shower and come back to the bedroom.

Bedroom
Andy tells Stephen to lie on the bed face down. The window faces the freeway, eight floors up, so no one can see in. It's a

sheer white curtain at 6:30 P.M., so there's plenty of light out. Andy has never tied Stephen up. He chewed half a Viagra so it would work faster, and that shit makes him aggressive.

[If you chew Viagra (and sometimes you must), then chase it with something strong like cranberry juice.]

Andy takes out two fifty-foot lengths of rope from his bag, then attaches polyester fur-lined leather cuffs to Stephen's wrists and ankles.

[Not all hotel beds are good for bondage. Many have solid wood bed frames. What you want is a cheaper bed with four wrappable legs.]

Andy runs the rope through the metal hook in each of the cuffs, then uses a slipknot to secure each of Stephen's append-ages flat to the bed. He craves no movement.

[If there's a knot that doesn't work, it's better to untie it and start over. Otherwise there'll be a mess afterward and it'll take forever to clean up. You want to leave quickly so you'll be invited back.]

[Don't do psychedelics when you're playing with bondage. All it takes is one experience seeing snakes and spiders, and the concept of rope will never be the same for you.]

The first toy Andy uses is a ten-inch rubber line of beads. Kind of like a stack of chocolate eggs, increasing in circumference. He pushes it in Stephen's butthole, then pulls it out. He spanks Stephen's ass with a black leather paddle until Andy sees the beginnings of a blister. (*No marks, Andy*, Stephen says.) Andy starts to feel the aggro of the Viagra. Viaggro is what they should call it. He puts a rubber ball in Stephen's mouth and pulls the straps tight so Stephen doesn't make too much noise. He pushes the balls all the way in—slowly, because he knew the toy's curving into Stephen's colon. When he pulls it out, there's shit covering the first four balls. Stephen cleaned himself out, but probably with a single squirt of a Fleet enema. That's not enough to get this far up. Andy takes the toy to the bathroom and washes it off, then leaves it in the sink.

[Teach your repeat clients to wash themselves with a Fleet enema bottle. This is also helpful for straight guys who want to get their prostates touched: Empty out the saline solution in the Fleet bottle, fill it with warm water, then squirt it up there and sit on the toilet. You don't really gain anything by holding the water. Remove the nozzle, then blow air into the bottle as if you're playing a trumpet. Fill and reuse. If you wash your nozzle, you can reuse your Fleet. Each client's bottle should be tossed after each use. They're recyclable, by the way.]

Andy comes back from the bathroom and sees Stephen's ass—how it's bright red and has a few white patches where it would be really tender later. Stephen would think of this when he was in his leadership meetings. Stephen hadn't requested this much domination. He had spanked Andy a bunch of times early on in the dot-com years when Andy started working. At one point in late 2002, Andy decided he needed to take care of himself and not let Stephen spank him because Stephen didn't understand pacing and warm-up.

[You don't just hit someone. Spank them lightly through their jeans, then lightly through their underwear. Finally, approach their bare ass gingerly and take cues, unless you want to hurt them, which is also valid.]

Stephen has a really fat cockhead and never waits long enough before pushing it into Andy's ass. There's never enough time to prepare. This doesn't bother Andy as much as the spanking. It's not like it triggers childhood memories of abuse. There was no childhood abuse to prepare him for this. That's the point. He wasn't trained as a child for any of this careless touch.

Andy notices that Stephen has spit out the ball gag.

—It's hurting my jaw.
—*Okay, then let's take it out. We don't want that.*

Andy puts on a condom and lubes up. He knows it's going to be a dirty fuck because of the toy. He puts some Wet Platinum in the tip of the condom because he wants to enjoy this. [Nobody should buy Eros. It's German and expensive.] Andy keeps it in a Nalgene bottle that he got in a variety pack of empty plastic bottles at REI, the camping superstore. This is the capitalist product placement portion of the story. Even anarcho hookers can't escape capitalism. *The fanned hundred-dollar bills, the fanned hundred-dollar bills.*
INSERT INSERTION
—Wait, wait. That hurt.
Andy pulls out and lets Stephen settle. Pushes in again. Slow.
—Fuck me, guy.

Andy does this. Andy was never very interested in dirty talk. He likes hearing it but doesn't like doing it. He'd tried reading Carol Queen's book *Exhibitionism for the Shy* and even read the appendix on "talking hot" or whatever it's called, thinking maybe it was an issue of available vocabulary. Still, it wasn't happening. Andy shifts to fuck Stephen sideways. He moves to navigate Stephen's big ass. Ten minutes of fucking is all Stephen can take. Andy keeps going.

—I'm worn out.

—*I don't care.*

—I need to stop now.

—*I want you to beg me to stop. I want it to hurt.*

—Please stop, sir.

Andy thinks of the time he was dating a guy who had a boyfriend and several regular play buddies. It was early in his San Francisco years—1999. They were exotic to each other. The man was trying to negotiate a consensual nonconsensual whipping scene with Pat Califia. This was before Pat became Patrick. That's a big thing to ask of someone: to keep going, once there's blood and genuine resistance, to push past a real live "No."

—*I'm not done fucking you.*

—Please, sir. It hurts.

—*Good.*

There was no safeword. Andy thinks of the joke about Jesus: Crucifixion is what happens when you don't have a safeword.

—Please.

—*I want it to hurt tomorrow. You're gonna think about this.*

—I can't take any more.
—*This is the part you'll jerk off to later.*
Andy pulls a pillow out from underneath the comforter.
—*Bite on this.*

Stephen daintily closes his teeth on the edge of the pillow-
case. Andy stuffs a mouthful of the pillow into Stephen's teeth
and keeps fucking. Stephen struggles in earnest. It's a good
thing he's so well tied. It's a good thing Andy had gone to all
those knot-tying seminars. This is where Stephen had miscalculated. Andy had been to plenty of conferences and meetings
and even leadership seminars. He knows all the language.

—*I'm gonna fuck you as long as I want. I could really hurt
you right now.*

Andy almost says, "I could just leave you tied up like this
and go home," but stops himself. That might be the end
of everything between them. As it is, Stephen might be too
freaked out to ever let Andy tie him up again. Andy pulls
out, sees the shit caked on his dick, and pushes it back in. He
spanks Stephen's ass as he fucks him, so the white patches rise
again between the mounds of bright pink.

—*I'm gonna fuck you up.*
—Please stop. I mean it.
—*No.*

[If you can't sleep, especially with an overnight client, keep
melatonin and Ambien in your bathroom kit. This is occupa-
tional health and safety.]

Later that night, Andy will have a dream about screaming
NO MEANS NO at his mother, because she was asking an Army
general, "When's he coming home?"

Ten more minutes. It's 7:46 P.M.—almost time to leave.
There is time to shower and gather toys.

[Often, clients don't figure the shower as part of your time together. Play this by ear. If he's at your house, stop ten minutes before the hour's up. If he wants to lie there for a bit and shower, you could end up going fifteen minutes into the next hour. You'll know which clients do this. Adjust your timing accordingly. You'll be able to spot these guys because they'll talk to you as they put their socks on and it will take forever.]

INSERT EVACUATION

Andy goes to the bathroom to get a wad of toilet paper. He wipes the shit and faint traces of pink blood from Stephen's ass. He unties all the ropes, then climbs on the bed and holds Stephen to his chest. Three minutes. Andy thinks maybe Stephen will fuck him quickly and squirt his load. That's always how it went. Maybe Stephen will just want him to leave. Andy doesn't know. Stephen abruptly stands up at the end of the bed, then goes to the bathroom to look for a condom.

—*I've got them right here.*

—You want Daddy to fuck your ass?

Stephen is saving face. He pushes in hard, as usual. Andy cleaned out twice and lubed up well in preparation for that. Behavior change takes a long time.

—Yeah, fucking your ass, boy.

Andy squeezes his ass muscles together and Stephen shudders. It doesn't take long at all.

7:52. Digital clocks have bright red numbers. Andy strokes up his load and shoots all over the hotel comforter.

[Word to the wise: They only wash hotel comforters every few weeks or so, if ever. It's a mystery.]

By the time Stephen gets back from his shower, Andy has

packed his bags. Stephen asks him some questions about what he's been doing with himself and Andy sort of answers, but it's obvious that he's on his way out. Andy flushes the condoms and takes a shower. He wonders about the environmental impact of that sort of thing. What could he do instead? What do permaculturists do with used condoms?

—Did you get your money?

—*Yes, thank you.*

—I'll call you when I'm coming back to town.

—*Okay. Take care.*

Andy is able to use his cell phone in the elevator. That's not always the case.

Hooker phone: Andy's mother

—*Hey Mom, it's me.*

—I can tell.

—*How are you?*

—I mailed those packages, all your empty CD cases. Angela told me to send them Media Mail.

—*Oh, great. How much did it cost?*

—Six dollars for one, eight dollars for the other one.

—*That's so cheap. I'm relieved.*

—There are still three other boxes. I'm looking for the right boxes. I had to tell the post office they weren't empty, that there were CDs in them. So I could get the cheap rate.

—*Good for you for lying. Lying saves money.*

—You should get them in a few days.

Parking lot

—*We had a great weekend sitting in hot water.*

—Oh, good. Was it a retreat type place?

—*Yes, kind of a hippie spa.*
—Good. Do you feel relaxed?
—*I do, yes.*

Car

—What was that sound?
—*Oh, I just undid the car alarm.*
—You're driving?
—*I'm getting in the car.*
—I don't want you to have a wreck.
—*I won't.*
—Call your aunt. She's just out of surgery.
—*Okay, I will.*

Andy gathers the parking ticket in the car caddy and three dollars from the ashtray. They always make you pay for the third hour even if you're only a few minutes into it. When he drives up to the gate, the orange and white bars are already lifted. Parking is free tonight. Andy puts the money back in the ashtray and rolls gently over the speed bumps on his way out of the parking lot. Three dollars. What a relief.

THEY CAN'T STOP US

Tim Doody

I'm waiting for the sun to set, for my shift to
end, so I can pedal into my favorite part of
Manhattan, an emerald oasis right in the center of all the concrete canyons. But I'm so not
there yet. On Broadway, I steer my road bike
between columns of men (and some women)
doing the black-suit-shuffle, cut west to pick
up my thirty-fourth package of the day at the
World Financial Center, turn east to drop off at
120 Wall Street, and then north to an alley in
Chinatown where I climb the stairs to the second floor and hand over a manila envelope to
a man who kneads his hands behind a counter.
As I wait for his signature, I inhale the incense
from a candle-lit Buddhist shrine. Behind him,
several rows of women move fabric through
the stabbing needles of sewing machines.

I plummet back down the stairs, skipping over every other step, and ponder the sheer number of daily encounters in this city, their anonymity and intimacy, how cultures clash, cavort, merge. Then I'm back in the streets jostling with vendors and taxis and tourists, everybody staking out a claim to space. Sirens scream. New sweat drips down the old sweat that's caked to my face from the last seven hours of exertion and summer heat.

Sometimes, I hate that I get CEOs what they need, when they need it, in death-defying time, for semiadequate wages. Maybe that's why I scream a war cry as I near a crosswalk filled with commuters moving against the light. My voice and my barreling bike part the commuters so fast that one guy's knees jerk up high enough to almost touch the tip of his nose. It takes me ten minutes to stop laughing.

Once I get through Midtown, weaving between cars that stop and go and shift lanes, I drop off my last parcels, radio in to say see you tomorrow. I turn my bike from the four lanes of 59th Street into Central Park, where the noise of the city subsides to a hum. A dozen blocks later, on a footpath, I unhitch the Kryptonite chain from my waist and wrap it around the bike frame and a bench. Finally.

I peel off my sweaty T-shirt, stuff it into the messenger bag that's still slung over my right shoulder, and plop onto the bench to watch the sun crouch down behind the Beresford, the twin-towered San Remo, and the other buildings of the Upper West Side. Then I slink along the dirt paths of the Ramble, around its oaks, maples, and glacial rocks, and stop near a footbridge spanning a brook. The minutes slip by, taking the last bit of natural light with them.

A clear night here turns strangers into silhouettes. But on

a cloudy night, like tonight, the eternal lights of New York City are captured and then refracted in an orange glow that peeks under tree tops and reveals glimpses: shiny Adidas pants with racer stripes hugging boy hips; a nipple ring glimmering in the light down of a defined chest; a knit cap above a square jaw.

Two guys stare each other down like gunslingers about to draw. I hear footsteps. I glance behind me, see tousled hair and lips forming a soundless *coo*.

Punks are so hot, the guy I'm looking at says in a voice as serpentine as his fingers sliding through my bleach-blond dreadlocks. His hand doesn't stop at my shoulders, where my hair ends, but meanders around my messenger bag and then traces down my lateral muscles. I suck in summer air, arch my back. He slips his fingers inside my spiked belt and combat pants, snapping the band of the neon yellow spandex shorts beneath.

He leans in closer, till his chest hair tickles my back. I smell sandalwood and sweat. I turn toward him.

Like what you see? he asks.

He steps into a shard of that orange glow: stubbly cheeks, the indent of tight abs above his profiled hips. He's Middle Eastern, maybe Latino. It's too hard to tell out here. He wears jeans and, like me, no shirt.

I nod.

I reach down, feel along the zipper of his jeans. The bulge beneath pushes back. It's never hard for me to get laid out here. I mean, I might gorge on a pint of Ben and Jerry's for breakfast but I burn it off before noon and don't have an ounce of fat on my body, and all the biking has hardened my calves, my thighs, my ass. But still, this guy—Snake Boy, that's what I'll call him on account of his voice and fingers—he's so fucking hot.

We step off the path, back up against the bark of an oak, and I'm rubbing his rounded biceps. They're so slick with sweat that my hands glide. I lean in and exhale heat into his ear and massage it with my tongue. He moans and says, I love your pink nipples. He clenches down on one of them, shakes it around in his teeth.

I unzip his jeans and he tugs down my combat pants, which land on the ground with a metallic *thunk* 'cause of the spiked belt. His cock bounces out and mine is still sheathed beneath the spandex until he reaches in and swings it around, my cock head brushing against the fabric for two seconds of too much sensation before it's free. And there's that feeling of being naked outdoors, my hips so sensitized to the slight swirl of breeze.

Snake Boy licks my neck, looks up into my eyes, and maybe it's the darkness but his black lashes look like eyeliner.

Here, he says, breathe. He holds a small bottle to my nose. When I inhale, the pungent chemicals burn my nostrils, everything melts, and I'm just a flushed face and a beating heart. And a stiff cock. Which he slides a hand up and down. I'm jerking him off too. With my other hand, I probe the spot right behind his balls. I'm sucking his tongue and the whole world is reduced to me and him. We're pulsing flesh, a single heartbeat.

Suddenly everything turns bright white as if the sun has risen to its zenith. But it's nine o'clock at night. When my eyes flash open, I see that the light emanates from what must be an electric cop car, the kind with a silent engine. I yank my pants up as fast as I can. Too late, way too fucking late.

My hands shake. Red and blue lights flash behind the white. Snake Boy grabs my hand and says Run, and he runs and I stumble and then run. Next thing, sirens scream and hard-shelled feet clomp the earth behind us and our hands break apart so we can run faster—through brush, I feel stings, know my calves just got shredded, but it doesn't even hurt; up over this steep knoll and slipping, tumbling down the other side; into more brush, Snake Boy's still right in front of me. We're long-stepping rock to rock along a narrow stream and then running on the other side. We duck down into a gully. Angry voices, radio static, the crunch of foliage. These sounds get louder. And recede. My arteries throb, my chest heaves, and Snake Boy has his hands on his knees as he draws in ragged breaths. We stay crouched for fifteen minutes until he says he knows a place where they won't find us.

A year ago, when I was twenty-five, I first stumbled into the Ramble. Since then, I've made it the finale to my evening commute. The Ramble is a micro-forest in the heart of Central Park. Paths grip cliffsides, double back, and meander along slopes. The dense brush and trees provide an infinite variety of alcoves. At its southernmost point, this cock-shaped peninsula projects into Azalea Pond, a topographical totem to the men who have been coming here for over a century. And still they come: uptown boys in do-rags, downtown artists wearing paint-spattered pants, even middle-aged men from the Upper East Side. Just trees and rocks and sky and us.

And, obviously, cops. They patrol in vehicles or wear plain-clothes to try to surprise us. Queers scatter under the beams of headlights or, after a big bust, line up in handcuffs.

It's not like I wouldn't have run. I just got totally startled. I mean, you should've seen what I did to the cops last month after they fucked with me. I had just walked down the gravel path of the peninsula. At its proverbial head, this cop shined a light in my face.

Did you lose your dog? he asked me.

I saw a poodle around here somewhere, another cop said.

I turned around to leave and they got into their souped-up golf carts and followed me, the headlights blazing on my backside. My face burned, not with shame but rage. They finally swerved away and the night draped back around me.

I remembered reading about a tactic that eco-warriors had used to save national forests. They dragged fallen trees and other objects from the forest floor into the logging roads, creating blockades. The logging trucks backed out; the forest lived another day.

So I began dragging rocks, branches, and decaying tree trunks into the paths. Some queers looked over at me with raised eyebrows or walked a wide U around my mounting fortifications.

We have to bash back, I said. Fuck Giuliani. My exhortations were accompanied by the sound of long branches splashing through fallen leaves.

A queen in a leather trench coat and a shaved head stopped and smiled. Girlfriend, she said, you bangin' on the wasps' nest tonight, ain't you?

I prayed no undercovers would see or hear me, but I didn't stop. Not until I had erected three barricades along a path that was several feet wider than a car. Unplanned, the barricades went from smallest to tallest. The tallest was over eight feet (a fallen tree with an umbrella of intact branches provided the base). Behind it was the gazebo, the place the cops most love to surprise us—that's where group scenes often happen.

Five minutes passed. Some cops in an electric car drove in to start another sweep of the area. They pulled up to the lowest of the barricades and…a crash, a scraping of rock and wood on metal.

Their lights started flashing and the vehicle remained stationary for a full minute before continuing forward. They were heading toward the next barricade.

Other queers stood in clumps, watching, waiting. Some of them snickered.

The cops hit the next barricade without seeing it, the sound of damage much louder. This time, the car didn't move. One of them hit the sirens and must have radioed for backup, because an SUV spun down another path, headed toward the gazebo, lights flashing. The driver slammed the brakes right before the third barricade.

Within five minutes, a sea of red and blue lights pulsed along the peripherals of the Ramble as dozens of backup units arrived. I unchained my bike and pedaled out, laughing. Even if I'd fucked up everyone's cruising for the night, I still felt freer than when I'd arrived.

I keep telling Snake Boy—actually, his name's Ahmed—Thanks man, really, thanks so much, I just totally froze back there. He smiles and rubs my arm and says he's happy we got away. We creep through the shadows. Luckily, so many guys are wandering down paths or moaning in the woods or standing there rubbing their crotches that we should be able to blend.

We walk across an elevated footpath with metal hand

railings. Then Ahmed points down into the ravine on the left, and after my eyes adjust, I see, just barely, a steep staircase gouged into the cliffside. We hop the railing and descend the steps into the darkness. At the bottom, we're alone, obscured from almost every angle.

I pull my messenger bag over my head, set it on the moist ground. Then I slide Ahmed's shirt up, suck one of his tight, hard nipples. He massages my scalp, says Oh baby, you're so pretty, look at that hot ass of yours. I trace the back of his right thigh and he grins.

So it's not too long before I'm practically crawling on top of him. I'm chewing his lips. He unbuttons the top of my pants and pushes them down, and there they go again, landing with that same *thunk,* and even in this ravine, the warm air brushes my pelvis and my skin feels so new.

Pebbles tumble down near us. We jump like we just stepped on a live wire with bare feet. The sound of falling pebbles turns into the unmistakable even rhythm of footsteps coming down the staircase. Fuck, fuck, fuck. Pants. Up. Button. I can't get the fucking button to—

I jerk my head up, see a mahogany-skinned man with baggy jeans so low that the fly of his boxers peeks out. His shirt is hooked over his head, bunched up along his shoulders, exposing his worked-out chest muscles.

Keep about your business, he says, reaching up and adjusting the black bandana he wears with the knot tied above his forehead, gangsta-style. I see another guy behind him who's chubby and cute, like someone's kid brother. He wears a football jersey that hangs to his knees.

I glance toward Ahmed and he looks down for a second and then shrugs a Sure, why not. My fingers unclench and my pants, since I never did get them buttoned, drop for the third time tonight. Just have to be more careful, I promise myself. The yellow spandex shorts glow in the semidarkness.

Then the guy with the black bandana saunters toward me and nudges Ahmed away. He reaches out to the small of my back, grabs a fistful of spandex, and tugs it up until I can feel it burrowing into my asscrack. I turn my head to get a better look at him. Up close like this, I can see the details of his tattoos: Christ on a cross, left bicep; a dragon stretching from right pec to over his shoulder. He pulls down his checkered boxers and his cock springs out, pops up once, twice. I swear, even in these shadows, I can see its ropey veins throbbing. Nobody's speaking.

Black Bandana grabs a handful of my dreadlocks and pushes my head forward till my chest is lying against the warm rocks of the stairs and my ass is pointing into the air. He slaps his cock on my lower back several times.

You like that black dick? he says.

I hear the crinkle of plastic and turn around to see him rolling a condom down his shaft. He slaps his cock on my back again and then spreads my asscheeks and runs it up and down between them. The guy with the football jersey moves a hand around the outside of my hole and I feel the cold jelly wetness of lubrication, so much of it that it oozes down my legs.

Black Bandana smacks my ass. I gasp. My chest stays flat against the staircase. He sticks his cock near my hole and I feel rabbit-thrusts, him just toying with the idea of fucking me. I breathe deep again. He pushes for real this time, but even with all the lube, it's too big. I cry out, forgetting about the cops, the breeze, the other guys around me, everything but that bull's-eye of pain and him saying, Come on, nigga. Open that ass. Open. That. Ass.

I'm white as white but it's so hot that he says that and I don't know why it gets me off but it does. He slides his cock in slow, prying me open, and I'm clenching my asshole, trying to resist 'cause it does hurt but then his pelvis is flush against me. He's in.

My cock lifts and lands back on the stone. I reach down to stroke it but Black Bandana grabs my arm, stops me.

He tightens his abdominals harder and then his thighs start smacking into my ass and my whole body jolts with each smack. Manhattan still hums somewhere in the background and I add my moan to its incessant drone.

Ahmed walks around us, up to the rock stair that my head hovers above. He sits there, legs on either side of me.

Come on, suck it, he says. He sticks his cock in my mouth and I slurp. He rubs the tops of his fingers along my cheek. My body keeps rocking to the cadence of Black Bandana's thrusts. I can't get my mouth moving to the right counter-rhythm. So Ahmed grabs the back of my head and jerks it toward him each time his hips push forward.

I roll my eyes to the left and see the guy in the football jersey jerking off.

My cock is so hard but I still can't grab it 'cause Black Bandana keeps my right arm behind my back and I need the other to stay propped up. My knees feel like they're bruising.

Yeah, nigga, yeah, Black Bandana says. I don't hear anything else anymore and my ass doesn't hurt, it's warm ripples spreading all the way to my head and then even further outward, it's tingles so strong my toes curl, I breathe heavy and steady, and my eyes seal tight like I'm seeing into the beyond.

Ahmed keeps rubbing the back of my head and fucking my face. I hear sirens from far away and they're getting closer but we don't stop. I taste the pretzel salt of pre-cum. They can't stop us. They never could.

FUCKING DOSEONE

Ralowe Trinitrotoluene Ampu

For Dax Pierson, my sexy one-time assigned processing correspondent

Doseone said something really weird and homophobic at an Anticon show when he was freestyling. It was at 26 Mix. It made me really angry. I keep talking about it. I get so emotional. As a rapper, I feel like I need to create my own history: points in a time line of some personal significance, the way De La Soul tried to manufacture a consumer history on *Stakes Is High* by opening the album with the question, Where were you when you first heard "Criminal Minded"? I went to this fateful Anticon show around when I first started rapping seriously, and Dose was one of the first real rappers I'd ever met. I ran into him at Amoeba Records on Telegraph Avenue in Berkeley. I suppose he still works there. I was browsing when I saw him out of the corner of my eye. White boy. White T-shirt. Glasses.

I grew up in Ventura, in an all-white suburb of Southern California, a sprawling, desolate expanse of tract homes. I lived there for twenty-one years and it made me really angry. Telegraph Avenue near the UC Berkeley campus reminds me of Ventura. And Dose reminds me of the white boys across the street who used to call me *nigger*. They were the first kids I made friends with.

I'm wandering around Telegraph when I start writing about desire, or maybe childhood. I see a group of young, pouty white boys fully nigga'ed-out in saggy sweat suits and I imagine their dicks in my mouth as they cast shady glances at me, just barely giving me enough sidewalk. There are also mall boys, with asymmetrical rocker hair, wearing Leon Neon bracelets and sports coats, angel blue eyes wracked with pain. Looks like they've just gotten dropped off by their parents. There's a feeling of a constant sea of frustrated desire. My pornographic imagination is utterly overloaded by the ebb and flow to and from the Berkeley campus.

Dose was superfriendly. My hand was hovering above MF Doom, and Dose came over and was all, like, "That's a good album," then produced another from a row of CDs. "This is, too." Then, "Actually, this is *my* album. Hi, I'm Adam." When I realized I had seen Doseone perform before at Rico's in downtown San Francisco, I said, "Your stuff sounds like Solesides," and Dose said, "Lyrics Born was one of the first rappers that opened up to me." I told her I was in Deep Dickollective, a black gay rap group, and I gave her my group's URL, and she gave me her email at Dirtyloop. I ended up at Amoeba the next day because my friend Lyndon wanted to shop for CDs and I ran into Dose again. I was, like, "Hmm, you work a lot." She asked me again what I meant about being in a gay rap group. The concept seemed to evade her. Doseone had listened to a D/DC EP, and was perplexed by our apparent homophobia, demanding to know, "Are you gay?" and I said for the third time, "Yes." I didn't realize that Dose might be indicating an insight into the fallacy of D/DC's hypermasculine performance; I was also caught up in it.

Doseone's show began with a freestyle battle where Sage Francis and Pedestrian abandoned their "conscious and experimental" rap style to imitate the homophobic remarks of ignorant rappers. At that time I was too stunned by the literal homophobia in it to register that it was also obviously racist. Then Doseone did "Spin Classes" and "innovation in the field of breath" and her verse from the second side of *cLOUD-DEAD apt. A,* and I thought it was the most amazing thing I'd heard in my life. He was combining the dark, bleak insanity of early Tricky, the insular self-sustained inventiveness of De La Soul's first albums, and raw Freestyle Fellowship improvisational shit straight out of the old Good Life Café open mike in South Central Los Angeles. He took these and infused them with his own particular experiences, creating something I'd never heard before. His delivery was completely inconsistent and unpredictable. He sounded so vulnerable and effeminate, performing the exact queer rap style I'd been cultivating. But then Dose freestyled in this weird mannish voice: "I've been to college / did my four years / it's like a penitentiary / except no queers...." I mean, he actually said that.

There are queers at colleges. I've had sex with them in the bathroom at Cal, right up the street from where Adam "Doseone" Drucker works.

Up Telegraph from Amoeba Records, go through Sather Gate across the bridge, and on your left stands Dwinelle Hall. Downstairs in the men's bathroom there's a stall from which one can see anyone entering the bathroom. There's a flood of human masturbation material making its way to the basement between classes. It's funny to speculate which people have the weakest alibi for coming into this particular remote bathroom. There are two or three bathrooms on every floor of Dwinelle. Can this many obvious faggots all have to pee here at the same time? And these girls are not closet cases, but, like, straight-up *Queer As Folk* wannabes. They give something away in their overdetermined attempt to identify as casual when peeing. Once, I saw a very proper queen wearing a tear-away snap-up sweats athletic ensemble, pretending to be jockish. I cruised her with no subtlety at all. But I didn't allow her any space for pretense, so she lost sexual interest. She had her long, permed hair in a bob. And she had a fat cock with a thick head. I didn't get a chance to taste it.

Another time, I saw spiky, dark-haired twins with really beautiful eyes and pretty, reddish pink lips. Nothing makes me cum harder than boys' lips. I have an early memory of being repulsed by a kiss on the cheek from some random matron at my church. That repulsion swelled when my next-door neighbor (and best friend), a white boy named Steven, tried to kiss me on his front lawn. I pushed him away. His family moved to Taiwan shortly afterward and I never saw him again. I've spent the rest of my life overcompensating. Maybe I'll find him, and his lips, here. My ex-boyfriend Jo-ey had really full lips that would engorge when he was aroused; when I masturbate, thinking about the sex we used to have,

I recall the soft fleshy cushion of his lips as we kissed and jerked each other off. So I fantasize kissing and jerking off with these twins, whose lips are delicate and shaped like a dove's wings. Actually, I don't think they were cruising, but that doesn't stop me from imagining that their erect cocks are the same color as their lips, and I want to watch them 69-ing each other.

Time passes. Enough time for the smallest details to become exaggerated to manic-depressive extremes. Feelings of rejection seem like a well-grounded justification for suicide. Why am I participating in this hunting range of masculinity? But then a stern, frumpy white boy stands at the urinal with his eyes fixed on mine, through the crack in my stall door. I stand up to get a better look, with my cock in my hand as the blood that was trapped in my thighs by the toilet seat circulates from toes to head once more. I open the door with my pants unzipped so that my hard cock juts out, and I walk over to a urinal a couple down from this boy's. His face is pale and his lips are pink-rose colored and fixed at an attitude that's a mixture of pride and bewilderment. His thick glasses stand on the end of a pointy nose. His cock is of a compulsive-masturbating-nerd thickness, with a beautiful veiny shaft, and his cockhead is throbbing. I'm in love. I move to stand next to him and we start jerking each other off.

Someone comes in and we snap back into place apart from each other and pretend to finish peeing. The intruder is in his mid-forties, dressed like she's getting ready for a hiking trip through leather country with the Sierra Club; she's a regular whom I recognize immediately. The frumpy white boy zips his hard-on away, a huge and conspicuous bulge in the crotch of his pants, and leaves the bathroom in embarrassment. The way he knew precisely where to look into my stall convinces me that he's only pretending to be embarrassed. I follow her out of the bathroom and can't figure out which way she went, so I guess. I leave Dwinelle and I spot the boy by the library. I trail him past the clock tower and toward buildings I don't recognize, while maintaining what I feel to be a discreet distance. I assure myself that I'm not stalking her. She's going to show me another cruise spot and then we'll have the most amazing sex of our lives. But I lose her in some kind of science faculty building. On this occasion I don't feel suicidal because I'm not really depressed, since she hasn't actually rejected me. Just to be sure, I check every bathroom in this new building. I convince myself that this guy's locked away in his professor's office, leaking semen from his pulsing fire extinguisher cock while surfing porn online at an old wooden desk, and shooting all over his own face and lips. I wonder if he takes his glasses off first.

Back at Dwinelle, the air is calm, at a nearly *in utero* temperature. The fluorescent lights buzz dream-like, and there's all that tile. When you get a stranger's grooming habits, moisture, and intent stuck under your skin, it's really hard to shake loose. I'm sitting in a stall trying to either meditate or go into hibernation when the stall door next to me opens and closes. I peer through the hole where a bolt once held the toilet paper dispenser in place, and see a hot, skinny gay boy, wearing sports vintage, furiously stroking his cock. His arms are lean and toned and I think I see a couple of circuit tats peeking gingerly from under the sleeve of his off-yellow T-shirt. I get on the floor and stick my hard pre-cum-slicked cock underneath the stall partition and he starts sucking me off—just above par. I fuck his mouth but someone enters the bathroom and we both hop onto our respective thrones until it's clear, and then start again, until he stands and strokes his fat cock while watching someone else enter. After they leave he continues to stand, and I can see from his shadow that he's stroking his cock wistfully. This strikes me as forlorn.

I look under the partition at him to let him know that I want to suck him off. His petite features suggest to me that he's mixed race, perhaps with a little black somewhere, who knows, also thick eyebrows and a very blank gay lifestyle expression on his young face. He crouches and begins to lay his cock on my lips when someone else enters the bathroom. This happens several times. I spot drool below the partition of the stall wall. It registers that it's mine. Or maybe his? I look through the bolt hole and see him dabbing spit on his cock, or maybe tasting his own pre-cum; I can't tell which. She stands up again, stroking her cock, watching someone who's now at the far urinal. I sit back on my toilet seat and try to see who it is. It's another gay boy, Latino I think, with extremely present thick-lashed brown eyes that are intensely affecting innocence. She has full, florid lips parted in a las-civious attitude, lips that she alternately licks and bites in a roller-coaster–riding fashion. He has a crew cut and strikes me as beefy but in a jock sort of way and she's also wearing a bright red long-sleeved T-shirt that says, "I'm a Pepper!" between erect nipples across her broad chest. She stands back and starts stroking a surface-to-air missile-shaped dick with a bright red tip shooting from the fly of her unbuckled jeans after we—that is, the gay boy in the stall next to me, and I myself—simultaneously open our doors so that he can see us stroking our cocks. I notice that his cockhead is pinker than his lips, more the color of his tongue. And then *someone else* enters the bathroom. Busy afternoon. I slam my door as the new person walks to the sink.

I peek through the crack. It's another gay boy, brown hair and blue eyes, with maybe freckles and an abrupt set of lips. He has a patient look. He's wearing a blue lacrosse jersey. I'm not sure how I know at first that it's a lacrosse jersey, but then I realize everybody is wearing Abercrombie. The gay boy with the red Abercrombie shirt is cruising the gay boy with the blue Abercrombie shirt, who starts rubbing a bulge in the baggy crotch of his Abercrombie cargo shorts. I open my stall door and find that my neighbor, with her yellow Abercrombie tee, has opened hers too.

My revulsion at being so breathlessly aroused by not just gay boys, but by gay boys wearing Abercrombie, starts fucking with my head. I find myself stroking and squeezing my cock just to continue appearing aroused. I start having a panic attack and faintly notice the sound of pants being ankle-dragged across the floor. I look down at the blue Abercrombie shirt gay boy's shoes. I divert myself with objective class analysis, to cool my panic attack. The other gay boys' shoes are new and sporty, but blue is going in the other direction—his couture is not as new or together as the other boys' mall ensembles. I observe that she has the sensible yet unfortunately unkempt dark brown hair of someone who doesn't like thinking about it. She's dressed like someone would want to dress if they aspired to dress just like someone who's part of the universal Caucasian-gay-person standard for the ruling class working at being working class—and therefore bound to a conservative utilitarianism that only hints at originality, because perhaps his resources aren't adequate to acquire the correct brand of boring shoe, so she could only get that which was within reach, so that his shoes are only almost (but not yet completely) boring.

At last I admit to myself that nobody is paying attention to me, or my runaway class analysis. I leave the bathroom.

After I rapped with D/DC at Wesleyan, I went from Connecticut to Pittsburgh with DDT. I played Greenthink and cLOUDDEAD for her. She was a fag, and thought it sucked. Now she likes it and tells me she appreciates their playful and inventive dissonance. At that time, working with her did not go as planned. After she told me I had no rhythm, I wandered around an area of Pittsburgh called Oakland and went to a cruisy business school auditorium basement bathroom and saw a tag that read *Dose-1* in blue marker. It was like Dwinelle, but even busier. I noticed that here too there were more gay boys than people who looked like they were in the closet. When you entered the bathroom there was an anteroom and another door. This door led around a bend to a row of urinals. Next to that was a row of toilet stalls in a corner of the bathroom that seemed intentionally to not be as well lit as the rest. I came through briefly and fell in love, like, six times, but had to hurry to go see a nice distracting Hollywood movie with DDT since I had abandoned any hope of collaborating with him.

However, I remembered the tag. True, it could've belonged to anyone. But I know that Dose went to business school. I wrote lyrics to it in the song I made with DDT right before he decided that I had no rhythm.

Bathrooms, bathrooms. So imagine my shock when Dose starts talking from behind me in the john.

"Is this an oblivion check?" I coo.

Okay, hold on a second....

I can tell you're wondering if I'm going to fuck Doseone. Well, I'm not sure. I remember the time before this that I ran into him. Eric was there. Eric is white and in Gay Shame with me. Eric and I were standing in front of Modern Times Bookstore in San Francisco after our Saturday Gay Shame meeting, and we were processing how she was upset about the Queer Anarchist People of Color group's having a meeting at the same time as ours, and spreading too thin the identical group of people who do radical queer direct action, and not wanting to be in a group without people of color. Doseone walked up with his friend. He was wearing camouflage cargo shorts. I hate camouflage and I hate cargo shorts. He said hi, and I was *so* not in any kind of space to deal with Dose at that second because I was really concerned with the issues that Eric was raising. What was so striking about this moment was that symbols for everything in the world that I felt strongly about were intersecting and converging with astronomical intensity. So I was taken aback. Dose asked what was going on and I said that Eric and I had just come out of a Gay Shame meeting. Eric later scolded me for saying to Dose that Gay Shame is a radical queer direct action group that focuses on "homophobia and assimilation in the gay community," when actually our focus is a lot broader than that, but I was panicking. As I fucked up my explanation of what Gay Shame was about, Dose interjected his opinions: when I said "homophobia," he said "and nonhomophobia?" in an oddly contentious manner. This was as close to a free-style battle as I'd ever want to get into with Doseone. So while talking, I was also thinking: *Oh shit, Dose is going to serve me on this curb.* But I didn't have the presence of mind to turn to Doseone and say: "Dose, I was really annoyed about that song where you talk about the city—you appear to have no interest in the real systematic and historic dynamics that create divisions among people and cause tension in urban settings. I find it really problematic to suggest that all that oppressed and disenfranchised people in the city need to do is say, 'Let it be said dead butterfly' and 'Where's the love?' and then all these larger issues will be solved. But you mention nothing about these larger issues. Like, never in your music. Anywhere. Why?"

I did have the presence of mind to notice that Dose had not introduced his friend, a woman. She watched our interaction with a staid but not unpleasant expression. I snatched the opportunity to introduce myself to her, in an attempt to expose what, in all fairness, could have been either social awkwardness or male chauvinism...or maybe male chauvinism masquerading as social awkwardness. Then Dose disappeared into the store with his female companion.

But back to the bathroom.

"Is this an oblivion check?" I coo.

Dose asks, "So, you're still making music with Gay Shame?"

"Gay Shame doesn't make music. That would be Deep Dickollective. And no. I do solo stuff. D/DC has no politics."

I hate being black.... Dose senses my energy. I interpret something in the rhythm of his pauses and the direction of his attention as some type of contentious male competitive athlete drama. It's a rapper thing. It's a performance cue. Our interaction, my instincts tell me, is probably not going to be conducive to any preperformance preparation rituals

Dose may have…. Searching his eyes, I find myself wondering about how I read paragraphs in *The Brothers Karamazov* and imagine that Dose has read the same shit. And I want to talk to him about the book for hours. Shrug and lie around devouring poetic discovery, holding each other, kissing in Ventura, or something….

"Yeah…they're really liberal."

"I guess you think I'm liberal, too," Dose says.

"Yes, I do."

My hands drop and I sputter.

"There's no soap."

"I think you're supposed to just scald them, then."

"Ah, c'mon. Don't. That seems judgmental."

"Of course it is. Judgment is a function of intelligence."

"Why're you so mad all the time?" Doseone says, and then I'm, like, well…. I do the thing I do when I turn tricks. I'm unexpectedly calm. It's a new feature of my reasoning. I'm looking at the surface of Dose's mouth, and I'm imagining something outside the arty white-trash-chic unseemliness of the press photos, or accidental passings on the sidewalk. His lips look like desiccated bus bumpers, I imagine from years of unchecked alcohol and ecstasy consumption. Suddenly his flesh is demystified and it's just flesh. And then I start thinking about how something standing still can turn into something else. I want to vitiate the spirited message board claims—oh, there was quite an uproar on the Anticon message board, now defunct, on the subject of my outcry against the 26 Mix incident: claims that all my noise was nothing more than reaction to my spurned, star-crazed love for Doseone.

I'm watching for what Dose decides to do, feeling not so much cornered as completely blank and ready. I mean, if there's anything you want. If I give it to you, that doesn't make you a thief. Does it become less interesting? The me-offering-it part? Examining the rest of his body, of nearly identical stature to mine, how it would look contorted in the act of coming, contorted like when he performs. "Yes, y'all. If you got the cock I got the balls." I'm eager to be present for whatever happens in this bathroom at the LoBot Gallery in West Oakland. The idea gets me off. I do want to fuck Doseone. Out of spite for the bathroom in the basement of the David Lawrence Auditorium at Pittsburgh University where I saw *Dose-1* tagged next to a glory hole. In the song I wrote with DDT, I confused Pittsburgh U with Carnegie Mellon U. Both are in Oakland, PA, not to be confused with Oakland, CA, where Anticon is now based. The *Dose-1* tag struck me because there were no other tags next to it.

I wandered around the Pittsburgh campus using an online tip. Being from California and really bad at geography in general, I didn't realize that Pennsylvania was sandwiched between Ohio and New Jersey. Doseone met up with Odd Nosdam and Why? in Cincinnati to collaborate on Greenthink and cLOUDDEAD. Doseone writes about growing up in New Jersey. I didn't really realize where I was. I've always kind of wondered if the tag was really Dose's. And what was he doing in that bathroom?

The bathroom in the basement of David Lawrence Auditorium was really busy when I first passed through, but when I came back it was dead. I was hurrying out the door from using the sink when a boy zipped past me, meeting my eyes. I paused before the stairs leading up into the main lobby of the auditorium. My eyes were drawn to a poster about something Islamic plastered on the fake wood paneling; my mind danced elsewhere, wondering about the boy. I returned to the bathroom, imagining that if I walked a certain way he wouldn't know by the sound of my footsteps that I was the same person. He was alone in the toilet stall with the glory hole and Dose's tag. I shuffled to the stall next to his. Through the glory hole, I could see his arm moving up and down and then stopping. I was crazy hard. I unzipped my fly and pulled out my cock. Its tip was shiny.

Instead of entering the other stall, I peeked through the crack of his door. His head was down. He seemed embarrassed. I stood back and displayed my rigid pulsing cock, swinging it until he looked up. His face was pudgy and cute. He appeared to be half Asian, half white. His lips were small and angular. His eyes were wide, looking first at my cock then into my eyes, then back. I pulled my shirt up and tweaked my nipples. He opened his legs and sat back on the toilet, stroking his cock anew. He stood and moved his backpack from the hook on the stall door and set it on the floor. He pulled his shirt over his head and opened the stall door. I stepped closer, squeezing my pre-cumming cock. Something about the earnest artlessness of his red mohawk suggested to me that he wasn't a gay boy just yet, but had been reading a couple of books on gay theory while listening to downloads of Tracy and the Plastics. His cock was medium sized, pointy, and uncut, with a shiny bright-pink hammerhead. I leaned over and sucked the salty, sticky dripping pre-cum collected under his foreskin. He panted, frantically bucking his hips into my face. His cock throttled in my cheeks and I grabbed his ass to force it deeper, to choke me. I exhaled and I stood up and we kissed, stroking our cocks together in saliva and pre-cum.

I liked how his body was pudgy and not gym-toned to death, in contrast to an actual gay boy's. I did frown at the spiked belt, which to me seemed to hint at the misfortune to come. We shot at the same time, spraying both the glory hole and Doseone's tag.

But back to the bathroom at LoBot Gallery in West Oakland.

Doseone is wearing camouflage again, which I deplore above all things in the world; this time it's a camouflage trucker cap. How can Dose have any antifascist critique in his work while unthinkingly choosing to adorn his person in the costume of the military? Here I could win an argument about the ineffectiveness of a liberal ideology. I look at Dose and feel so utterly self-conscious about my art. I remember doing the new listening stations at Amoeba that played *Deep Puddle Dynamics* and feeling every strained syllable of my D/DC delivery and body language on stage, how I would channel Dose's inflections. Then I remember the past. Taking my ex-boyfriend to the Imusicast show. Sure, Jo-ey was cuter than Dose—because clearly Jo-ey's lips were at that time a great deal more hydrated and healthy than Dose's chain-smoker lips—but I think how an obsession with intention and technique had half-filled the time since I last had a boyfriend. Planning my alibi as the Black Doseone, the triple irony of a black person impersonating a white person impersonating a black person.

So we're letting the silence pass in the bathroom and I'm witnessing the impression of Dose's nipples rising up through his nonsweatshop Subtle T-shirt. It's so hip-hop to wear a T-shirt with your band's name on it that's the same as the one you sell.

"I wanna suck your cock," I finally say.

"You should come to the after party," Dose says without a beat.

"Now."

"No sex before the show."

"What kind of a rock star *are* you?"

"I'm not a rock star. I'm a poet."

"Rock star poet."

"No sex before the show," Doseone says again, and leaves the bathroom, just as someone enters.

I retreat to the handicapped stall. I think: *Freedom penis dipping in a toilet of tears.* It's the hot white boy I saw on his cell phone in the street coming to LoBot. Where do these people *come* from? This one has sideburns. I've been especially enamored of sideburns lately. You know, I had a dream about this white boy before. In it he's peeing and glances around to find me looking at him. He slips into the stall next to mine. I look under the stall wall at him and he starts jerking off. But I came before he got there, just from looking at him, so it's too late, and then I wake up.

But this hot cell phone white boy has come into the bathroom to gaze into the mirror. Using the mirror takes her a long time. On the back of her baggy T-shirt is a picture of Bub Rubb going "Whooooo-whoooooo!" White boys love their Internet objectification of black people, don't they? I find my cock tender and semihard as, for an improbable duration, this boy preens herself in the mirror, just for me. I masturbate, studying her from inside my stall while she anoints her insanely smooth and clear face. She has such good skin. "The no-place of an ache dangles body all around it," Dose wrote. The sordid and masochistic suburban identification...a body in a mirror. "See me," I think, as finally being seen feels as close as touching a streetlamp light bulb from a seat on the train poised on the aerial track over a neighborhood in West Oakland. He'll see me in five seconds. I'm lost because all I can think is, "She'd come into the stall next to me in a split second if I was white." Conqueror. The giving is dripping off every muscled hormonal gland and pore in my feverish, abject flesh. Or: "He'd kiss me if I was white." I'm giving every part of my sweaty, mathematical lucubration, tightening around a pencil to go over some really pornographic diagnostics of what it is to want to slide into some skin with a couple of years knocked off mine, to feel whatever unthinkable thing is happening between self and image; to be taking careful stock of all the bone-structured angles that have never experienced worry, never drifted, never been alienated out of the confines of their own extravagant symmetry. Whiteboy: check! Hegemony: check! It's there...yet remote, desirable. "It's the boy in me that binds a worldly, gutted man's angst to change. Celebratory delta paints shit-eating grins on what you and mirrors think my face looks like." New clothes, she puts her camouflage trucker hat on, slightly off center. They must be giving them away tonight. I hate being black. I do. My cock, trembling hard, continues to drip, and my sense of history numbs. All I can see is locked suburban rooms in rows by the thousands, TV sets, a breathing semidark, and hard white cocks and faces flushed the same color. "Johnny Cock Rocket!" I recite. Skateboard, a doll-like face with impossibly blushed blood-colored lips and ocean-colored eyes...and what I do with my dick disappears into a racial Ventura rewrite, history is traded for a second of an orgasmic pang of oppressive escapism, hardening my resolve to unmake the world like a slap in the face. For exactly one instant it occurs to me that I know the precise and obvious words that would unmake the world. The moment fades. It takes me, like, two seconds to come.

SITE 1: FROM *THE SLUTS*

Dennis Cooper

REVIEW #1
Escort's name: Brad
Location: Long Beach
Age: 18?
Month and year of your date: June 2001
Where did you find him? Street
Internet address: no
Escort's email address: none
Escort's advertised phone number: not
advertised, but try 310-555-6112
Rates: I gave him $200
Did he live up to his physical description?
Did he live up to what he promised?
Height: 5'11"?
Weight: 150 lbs.?
Facial hair: no
Body hair: pubes only

Hair color: blond (dyed)
Eye color: hazel
Dick size: 6 inches?
Cut or uncut: cut
Thickness: couldn't tell
Does he smoke? yes
Top, bottom, versatile: bottom
In calls/out calls/not sure: not sure
Kisser: yes
Has he been reviewed before? no
Rating: recommended (see review)
Hire again: no (see review)
Handle: bigman60
Submissions: this is my seventh review
URL for pics: no

Experience: There are usually a few street hustlers working the blocks around a local bar here in Long Beach called Pumper's. That's where they like to hang out and play pool between tricks. It's a pretty sad scene, so I couldn't believe my eyes when I saw this beautiful, skinny kid with a backpack who told me his name was Brad. He didn't look a day over fourteen, but his ID said 18 so I'll let it stand at that.

I took him back to my place. He was very quiet and didn't seem to want to talk. He wouldn't give me a price or say what he was into. He also had a slight twitch where he'd crane his neck and open his mouth. I took that to be a drug reaction since he was obviously on something. There were warning signs everywhere but Brad was so hot that I just ignored them. I'm glad I did, but keep reading.

He asked if I had any alcohol. I thought he was high enough already, but he said he had to be "fucked up to do it." So I gave him some whiskey and he proceeded to get quite drunk but not loud and obnoxious. If anything he got even quieter. He still wouldn't talk money or specifics. He gave me the impression that whatever I wanted to do and pay him was fine. After about thirty minutes of steady drinking, I decided to make a move.

Here's the thing. The sex was unbelievable. Brad will do anything as far I can tell, but he's definitely a bottom. He never got hard, but he sure acted like he was into it. He has the hottest, sweetest little ass, especially if you like them a little used like I do. I must have eaten out his hole for an hour. I got four fingers inside him. I couldn't fuck him hard and deep enough. I spanked him, and not softly either. I pinched and twisted the hell out of his nipples. Nothing fazed him. All the time his cute boy face looked at me with his mouth wide open and made these sounds like he was scared to death and turned on at the same time. I came twice, first in his mouth and then up his ass. I should say that I never practice unsafe sex, but I just couldn't help it. I'm HIV–, however.

Here's where the problems started. He didn't want to stop. It's like he couldn't get himself out of whatever zone he was in. I was afraid he'd lost his mind. It was very spooky. I didn't know what to do with him. I let him sleep over because he didn't seem dangerous, but I fell asleep to the sound of him whimpering and thrashing around. I left $200 for him on the dresser, and when I woke up, he and the money were gone. There was a note from him with his phone number on it saying to please call him or tell my friends about him. Overall, it was great, but once is enough for me.

You: I'm a middle-aged, overweight top into teenaged street trade, the cuter and skinnier the better.

REVIEW #2
Escort's name: Brad
Location: Long Beach
Age: 18 (LOL)
Month and year of your date: June 2001
Where did you find him? on this site
Escort's advertised phone number: 310-555-6112
Rates: whatever you want to pay him. I gave him $150
Did he live up to his physical description: yes!
Did he live up to what he promised: fuck, yes
Height: 5'9"?
Weight: 145 lbs?
Facial hair: no
Body hair: no
Hair color: blond
Eye color: green
Dick size: don't care
Cut or uncut: don't care
Thickness: don't care
Does he smoke? yes
Top, bottom, versatile: bottom
In calls/out calls/not sure: out
Kisser? don't care
Rating: what do you think?
Hire again? fuck, yes
Handle: llbean
Submissions: this is my first review
Experience: The earlier review of Brad seemed too good to be
true, but I called him anyway. It turned out to be the phone
number of a homeless shelter in Long Beach. I left a message
for Brad not expecting to hear back, but he called me a few

hours later. He sounded unfriendly and bored on the phone, but I told him what I was into and he said that was fine. I offered to call him a taxi, but he said he wanted to walk. It must have been a good ten-mile walk to my house from that location, so I figured right then that he was a little strange. He arrived maybe two and a half hours later. I opened the door and couldn't believe my eyes. He seriously looks about fourteen, and they don't get any cuter.

Brad looked and smelled like he hadn't showered for a while, but from the earlier review I'd expected as much. I personally like my boys a little lived in. I met him at the door with a bottle of Jack Daniels, and he just took off the cap, and chugged about half of it down while I stripped him. He has a very tight, adolescent looking body with long, skinny arms and legs, and the smallest ass and about twelve pubic hairs. The earlier review stated Brad was spooky, and he has some mental problems for sure, but I'm not into being some kid's father, so I could care less.

I don't have the space to go into everything we did, so I'll cut to the chase. Brad let me handcuff him to my bed and I went to work on his ass. I gave him a good finger stretching then started burying bigger and bigger dildos in his ass. I got a fat, two-foot-long dildo all the way inside and he let me churn and pound that ass like I was making butter. The whole time, he screamed like he was dying, but his dick was always rock hard. When I finally got around to fisting him, his hole was so hot that I came within a minute, then sucked the sweetest, biggest load of come out of him that I've ever tasted.

It was clear that he could have gone on all night if I'd wanted. I did have to order him to leave, and he was very out of it and acting pretty strange. But let me tell you, he's worth it. I'll be hiring him again for sure.

You: Leather daddy type, mid-50s, into restraints and heavy anal sex with young-looking bottoms.

REVIEW #3
Escort's name: Brad
Location: Long Beach
Age: 18?
Month and year of date: July 2001
Where did you find him: on this site
Rates: not applicable
Height: 5'9"
Weight: 130 lbs.
Facial hair: no
Body hair: no
Hair color: brown
Eye color: blue
Dick size: don't know
Cut or uncut: don't know
Thickness: don't know
Does he smoke? yes
Top, bottom, versatile? don't know
Rating: not applicable
Hire again: not applicable
Handle: JoseR72
Submissions: This is my seventeenth review
Experience: Call me a caretaker if you want, but after reading Brad's reviews, I couldn't help but feel concerned about this troubled young man, and angered by the callousness with which the previous reviewers have treated him. I work in the mental heath industry in Orange County, not far from Long

Beach. I made an appointment with Brad in order to encourage him to seek treatment, although he didn't know my intentions until we met.

Regular visitors to this site know that I'm not against hiring escorts. I will even admit that Brad is my type and that meeting him involved a high degree of self-control on my part. Something the previous reviewers are right about is that he's extraordinarily cute. Brad is one of the cutest twinks I've ever seen, in fact. I don't know how a boy as cute and young as Brad ended up in the low end of his profession, but it's wrong to exploit him. He deserves better.

I had a long talk with Brad. It took him a while to open up to me, but he did. My knee-jerk diagnosis is that Brad is probably schizophrenic with an untreated chemical imbalance. He might also be suffering from a mild neurological disorder, as evidenced by the physical tics that the first reviewer mentioned. He allowed me to drive him to the facility where I work and enroll him in an outpatient program. I set him up to live at the home of a female acquaintance of mine. He is no longer at the phone number posted here and with any luck, you have heard the last of him. Shame on you.

You: Hispanic male in my late 30s.

Brad responds: Don't believe this guy. He's a prick. I have a new number. It's 310-555-9876. Call me if you're a generous man. I'm up for anything. I need a place to live too. This guy's a fucking prick. I don't need help. He's a liar. I'm writing this on his computer. What does that tell you? Guys like him are the worst. They promise you shit and they don't mean it. Don't call me if you're like him.

Webmaster's message: My repeated attempts to contact JoseR72 and have him confirm this review have been unsuccessful. Until further notice, I strongly advise all of you to stay clear of Brad.

REVIEW #4
Escort's name: Brad
Location: Los Angeles
Age: 18
Month and year of your date: July 2001
Where did you find him: this site
Escort's advertised phone number: pager 310-555-9876
Rates: $500 overnight
Did he live up to his physical description: yes
Did he live up to what he promised: no
Height: 5'10"
Weight: 130 lbs
Facial hair: no
Body hair: pubes
Hair color: dirty blond
Eye color: hazel
Dick size: 6 inches
Cut or uncut: cut
Thickness: less than medium
Does he smoke? not with me
Top, bottom, versatile? total bottom
In calls/out calls/not sure: out with me
Kisser: yes
Rating: not recommended
Hire again: no
Handle: bizeeb7
Experience: I read the warning on Brad, but I was in the L.A. area on business and decided to take a chance. I called the

number expecting a pager but Brad answered. Despite what has been said about him, he was quite talkative, too talkative if anything. I suspected he was on drugs at the time, but in retrospect I think he was in the manic phase of whatever mental illness he is suffering from. I offered to pay for his taxi ride to my hotel near the LAX airport, and he said he wasn't far away and would leave immediately. I waited for him in front of the hotel for more than two hours, then gave up and went to sleep after trying to reach him by phone with no luck.

At about 3:30 in the morning I was woken up by a call from the lobby saying a young man was here to see me. I asked the concierge if there was a taxi waiting, and he told me there was. I asked him to pay the driver and charge it to my bill and send the young man up to my room. Big mistake. When I let Brad in, he was a very agitated state. He wanted alcohol but I told him there was none in the room, and that room service was closed. He seemed extremely upset by this and sat on the bed and began crying. I was half-asleep, naked, frightened, and wondering what the hell I'd gotten myself into. I suggested that we go try to find an open liquor store, but he said no. I offered to call him a taxi and even pay him the full, agreed upon amount if he wanted to leave, but that just made him even more upset. He started saying, "Don't you like me," and things like that, which I have to admit I found rather heartbreaking.

I didn't know what to do, but I told Brad that he could go ahead and get undressed and that we'd give sex a shot. I really wasn't in the mood, but I thought he might be carrying a knife or something, so it was more of a safety precaution at that point. When I said that, he calmed right down, and took his clothes off, and even made a few jokes about how crazy he'd been acting. Like the other reviewers said, Brad is an extremely cute boy. Without his clothes on, he took my breath away. If it weren't for his height, I'd guess from his body he was no older than thirteen or fourteen. He has a slim, slight build with tiny nipples and the most precious little ass. It was just too arousing, and I decided that I had to indulge myself a little.

Brad didn't so much suck my cock as open his mouth and let me pound his throat as deep and hard as I wanted. Previous reviewers mentioned Brad's poor hygiene, and while he certainly wasn't the cleanest escort I've ever been with, he smelled and tasted like a boy should. Rimming him seemed to drive both of us out of our minds. As soon as I started eating his hole, he had almost what seemed like a seizure. His whole body spasmed violently, and his mouth opened wide, and his eyes rolled back in his head. It sounds frightening, and it was, but it was also incredibly hot to see a boy that cute lose control. I knew from the earlier reviews that Brad could be barebacked, and that's a huge fantasy of mine, so I fucked him condom-free and had two orgasms inside him before I felt too exhausted to continue. Still, I was dying to taste his come. He was still seizing and shaking all over, so I jerked him off and felched his hole until he shot, then licked up his delicious load.

As soon as Brad came, his seizure seemed to come to an end. He was drenched in sweat, and looked disoriented and exhausted. I suggested we get some sleep, as I was very spent by that point. That's when things suddenly went bad very fast. Brad started yelling and screaming at the top of his lungs that I was a sicko who'd had unsafe sex with him against his will. He was out of control, and soon enough there was a loud knock at my door. It was the hotel's manager and a couple of employees. He took one look at us and told me to either get the boy out of the hotel immediately or I would have to leave. I asked him to call Brad a taxi and that I would have the boy downstairs ready to leave in a minute, and he agreed and left. (God knows what would have happened if the manager hadn't been gay!) Brad continued to scream at me, one minute saying he was sorry and to please let him stay, and the next minute telling me he was going to tell the police I raped and tried to kill him. I just kept begging him to get dressed and leave, and he finally did, but not before calling me every terrible name in the book.

The nightmare didn't end there. About half an hour later he started calling my cell phone, begging me to come get him, and that he didn't know where he was, and that he was scared. I tried to reason with him, but he got more and more upset, threatening to kill himself. He told me there was someone who wanted to kill him, and that if I didn't come get him, he was going to go over to this person's house and let himself be killed, and that he didn't want to die, but he was afraid he would do that if I didn't stop him. After about five calls from Brad, I turned my phone off. I don't know if he's alive or dead, or if he was just trying to fuck with my head. I've never had anything like this happen to me in all my years of hiring escorts, and I thought I should warn others interested in Brad that, as cute as he is, he is definitely not worth it.

You: Asian-American man in my early 30s, like to try new things, into young guys, generally a top.

REVIEW #5
Escort's name: Brad

Location: Los Angeles
Age: let's just say 18
Month and year of your date: ongoing
Where did you find him: here
Internet address: bdax@hotmail.com
Escort's email address: bridax@hotmail.com
Escort's advertised phone number: 310-655-0033
Rates: Available on request
Did he live up to his physical description? if you hurry
Did he live up what he promised? and more
Height: 5'10½"
Weight: currently 150 lbs.
Facial hair: no
Body hair: no
Hair color: dishwater blond
Eye color: aquamarine
Dick size: 6 inches
Cut or uncut: cut
Thickness: medium
Does he smoke? not anymore
Top, bottom, versatile? bottom
In calls/out calls/not sure: in or out
Kisser: depends
Rating: highest
Hire again: ongoing
Handle: brian
Submissions: this is my first
URL for pics: no
Experience: I read with great interest the most recent review on Brad. I believe I'm the man Brad mentioned who "wants to kill him." Let me explain something to you all. Both of

my parents died of brain tumors. After reading the first three reviews of Brad, I was convinced that his physical and behavioral problems were the result of an undiagnosed brain tumor. I arranged a date with him, but instead of bringing him back to my place for sex, I took him to a hospital and paid for him to have a series of tests to see if I was right. It turns out that Brad does have an advanced, inoperable brain tumor and will die from complications resulting from the tumor within the next six months. That night I moved him into my house and he has been living here off and on for the past few weeks. I am paying for all of his medical bills, as well as his day-to-day expenses. He is on a medication that greatly reduces the severity and frequency of his seizures, although the side effects cause him to be very fatigued and irritable. For two days earlier this week, Brad went off his medication and disappeared, and this is when and how the previous reviewer had the date with Brad that he described. Brad is now home and on his medication again and doing as well as could be expected.

Before you decide that I'm a saint, I should explain that my all-time fantasy is to murder a boy during the sex act. I've had sex with a number of boys who were perfectly willing to be killed, but something always stopped me from going all the way. Brad provides me with the ideal situation, and, except for our disagreement earlier this week, he is also sexually aroused by what we both have agreed will happen. If all of this seems hard to believe, maybe it would help to know that in addition to his fatal condition, Brad suffers from severe bipolar disorder. He grew up in foster homes and has been emotionally, physically, and sexually abused his entire life. He will tell you himself that since he moved in with me, he has felt security and contentment for the first time.

When the day comes that he is so disabled that sex with him is no longer exciting to either one of us, I am going to end his suffering. In the meantime, I will allow him to do escort work on a limited basis. Anyone interested in seeing Brad can email or phone me, and arrangements will be made.

You: none of your business

Webmaster's comments: On July 16, reviewer JoseR72 was found severely beaten in his apartment. He remains in a coma. While there is no evidence to suggest that Brad is responsible, I nonetheless urge you to stay away from Brad. However, due to your overwhelming interest in the Brad saga, I will continue to post any reviews and updates that come in. Let me also say that because "Brian" has never posted on this site before, and because a new review of Brad that I will post in the morning throws the veracity of "Brian's" post into question, his claims should be taken with a grain of salt.

REVIEW #6
Escort's name: Brad aka Steve
Location: Long Beach
Age: 20?
Months and year of your date: July, 2001
Where did you find him? Pumpers
Rates: $400
Did he live up to his physical description?
Did he live up to what he promised? yes
Height: roughly 6 feet
Weight: maybe 165 lbs.
Facial hair: no
Body hair: pubes, ass crack
Hair color: brown

Eye color: blue
Dick size: 7 inches
Cut or uncut: cut
Thickness: medium thick
Does he smoke? like a chimney
Top, bottom, versatile: top for rimming only
In calls/out calls/not sure: out
Kisser: no
Rating: overpriced
Hire again: maybe
Handle: baglover
Submissions: This is my third review

Experience: Not that the Brad story needs another wrinkle, but here's mine. I hired "Brad" about three weeks ago. I question how much of what the two previous reviewers wrote is true. I suspect the reviews were written by Brad/ Steve himself. I went looking for Brad at Pumpers in Long Beach after reading the first review. It turns out that I'd seen him there a number of times drinking and sometimes playing pool or pinball. I had been told by the bartender that his name was Steve. He stood out because of how young he looks, but apart from being cuter than your usual street trade, I wouldn't say there was anything supernatural about his appearance. He had a reputation among the regulars at the bar as an arrogant creep who charged a ridiculously large fee ($350) to sit on men's faces and masturbate. That was the extent of his services, and even getting him to agree to that meant buying him many drinks and waiting until he was in the mood, which could take hours. Need I say that this "Brad" is a very different character from the boy described in the recent reviews? The only things that match are his young appearance and the facial tics and body twitching that everyone describes.

I had a couple of drinks and decided to ask this character if he was Brad. He looked shocked but he said he used that name sometimes. I explained that I'd seen a review of him on this site. He said he knew nothing about the site, and had never even used a computer much less surfed the Web. I used his curiosity to get him to agree to go home with me, telling him I'd show him the review on my computer. Maybe I caught him off guard because he seemed like a nice enough boy at the time and even agreed to let me top him. But after a few more drinks, he started acting in what I would call a bizarre and aggressive manner. He changed his mind about coming to my place and insisted we go back to his place instead, which I agreed to. It was hardly a homeless shelter. It was quite a pricey, upscale apartment an hour north in Los Angeles. Let me say for the record that there was no sign that anyone else lived there, so it wasn't the home of the self-styled murderer Brian. (He also had a very expensive G4 computer in full view, but he didn't seem to care that I'd caught him in a lie.)

As soon as we arrived, he became very cold and matter of fact. He told me to sit on the couch then pulled his pants down and sat on my face. I rimmed him for a few minutes until he came. I hadn't come yet, since I was expecting to top him, but he refused to continue, although for an additional $50 he did agree to sit on my face for another couple of minutes. I will say that if your fantasy is to rim a decent looking piece of jail-bait, he's quite satisfactory. He has a delicious, baby soft ass with a talented hole that he genuinely seems to enjoy having eaten, but whether it's worth the money is up to you. Clearly what the previous reviewers wrote about Brad is a bunch of lies and nonsense. BTW, he still hangs out at Pumpers. I saw him there two nights ago.

You: Good looking, early 30s, keep myself in shape. I'm a top who loves to rim young guys.

Brian responds: While Brad is in no condition to respond personally at the moment, I'm almost sure I know this lying asshole. First of all, if I'm right, it was my condo. I was there in the room watching the entire encounter. Brad had just moved in with me the day before, and he was at Pumpers only to tell some old friends there about his diagnosis and say good-bye. Brad says this guy badgered him for sex the whole time he was there. He finally agreed and brought the guy back to the condo. Brad has always been a bottom who will accommodate any scene for a price. This guy offered Brad $300 dollars to rim him. That was his request. Brad accommodated him. During the scene, he decided that he wanted to eat shit out of Brad's ass, which cost him an additional $100. He also drank Brad's piss for no extra charge. Since that night he has hounded me, asking to come over and eat Brad's shit, and on three occasions we accommodated him. He's obsessed with Brad, and ultimately I found his constant phone calls and emails tiresome and stopped accommodating him. This is undoubtedly the reason that he has chosen to lie about Brad. Even his physical description of Brad has no resemblance to the reality. This guy is just an ugly, fat pedophile and scat queen who got his heart broken. End of story. Let me add that Brad is available as a WS, scat, body fluid top, or bottom if you're interested....

ALL THE CREATURES
WERE STIRRING

Andrew Spieldenner

For F. D.

I was never one of those kids who rattled the
box for a clue or tried to peer through loose
wrapping paper corners. The gift was the
same, whether uncovered a day early or not.
I'd like it or not, would have begged for it or
not, would appreciate my refugee mother's
and working-class father's ersatz interpreta-
tions of Christmas wish-lists or not. Even celebrating the birth of Christ grows stale, year
after year: putting up the same decorations
and lights in the same places, wearing the
same seasonally outrageous clothes, making
the same recipes from the same combination
of homemade touches and the contents of
tin cans, singing the same songs, and watching the same repeated television specials and
church services. The droning gets so loud,

it drowns out the lessons of the winter solstice; the buzz of commerce so pervasive, mall after mall, that the only way to remember what it is to be human, connected, a community, is to break yourself open like overripe fruit and begin anew with someone else's hand in yours.

2003 was a lean year both for me and for many of my friends, and the holidays held no promise of relief. It meant that we had to—yet again—defy the basic tenets of the American Dream: We would not stand apart and pull ourselves up by our bootstraps, but we would huddle together for warmth and food; we could not gauge happiness by a mountain of *things*, instead we forgave each other our glaring lack of purchases. Poverty altered the appearances of the holidays so completely that I didn't realize Christmas Eve was upon us. 2003 would become known for me, not for the opening of presents, but for the first time I fisted someone I actually liked.

When I was a teenager, a few men paid me to slam my fist in their ass. Each provided long surgical gloves, and I'd lube up and start punching. I didn't know what to do; they didn't think to instruct the street hustler. The johns were always on a random and somewhat obscene assortment of liquor, powders, and pills, screaming *Harder! Faster!* with their asses up in the air. This violence was their fantasy; I looked away to the clocks or the porcelain foreign princess doll collections or the ice melting in the Scotch or the straight porn. It was all blood and shit and over in ten minutes. Generally, they'd give me a bonus bag of coke. I would have to puke and scrub my arm in hot water three or four times before I could go anywhere.

Ten years later, I meet a formidable man, F. D., who gets me hard just thinking about touching him. His muscles writhe under a covering of tattoos. He's bald, and black, with a closely shaved beard and moustache. Pierced through his nipples, his dick, and the skin between his balls and ass. He demands that I fist him on our first encounter. The decade between That Me and This Me doesn't seem to stretch quite so far. I'm still at a loss. He isn't; he knows how to teach.

We smoke some crystal first. A friend is over too—K. T., another impressively built black man—and the three of us talk, dealing out the obligatory introductions between puffs on the glass pipe. We talk about the tattoos marking us. K. T. sneaks his interest in body piercing into the conversation. Soon, K. T. exits to the other room and I am left with my newfound friend and the daunting face of his desire between us.

We smoke some more. We start talking about things we wanted to do in our lives. We strip, licking at lips, nipples, and groin. He mentions bondage; I find a rope. He secures it to the bed; I wrap it around his wrists. He lies there, pulling to make sure I've gotten the knot right.

He wants me to put his piercing in. I'd met some Prince Alberts before, but this was new—finding the hole in his flesh, unscrewing the metal piercing, and pushing it in, pulling it out the other side, watching his skin work against the silver, feeling the drag of his dick as I push the heavy ring through. I get erect.

It's easier to put on his cock ring, wrapping it twice around his balls. Familiar territory, and the action lets me play with his dick and balls, getting lost in the licking and slurping. Luckily, he likes it that way.

Both of us look mischievously at the door. We know K. T. is too shy to take part with me around, but my new friend looks at me and says with perfect practicality, "Don't you think your friend wants to see my Prince Albert?" I smile and open the door. K. T. sits in the other room, trying to focus on the computer screen. He barely resists jumping up when he hears, "You want to see the ring?" All too eager to see the Prince Albert, sliding the ring around and full of "does THIS hurt?," "what's this feel like?," "how long did it take to heal?" while holding onto F. D.'s dick and ballsac.

F. D. wants to smoke more, but the ropes prevent simple access. Between the three of us, we manage. K. T. holds the glass pipe to the bound F. D.'s mouth. I suck on F. D.'s nipples, his six-pack, his nuts, his thighs, his long smooth feet and toes. K. T. leaves when he sees that we are proceeding to sex, but his curiosity is piqued.

I mess around with my newfound friend and prisoner, for a while, getting comfortable with our positions. I fuck him, force him to suck my dick, pull on his piercings, worship his balls, lick him all over, use a dildo in his ass. I lose track of time until I need a pee break. We smoke more, and I go next door to ask K. T. to fill in for a bit. This is new ground, and K. T.'s painful shyness prevents him from releasing the *Hallelujah* that crosses his face. This is what he wants and did not know to ask, had no idea that the rules of *please* and *thank you* could apply. I find other things to do for twenty minutes.

When I come back, K. T. glows in sweat. He towers over F. D.'s still-restrained body, trembling with the power he feels. I was ready for more; K. T. excuses himself. F. D. and I play until day comes up and we're still wired, and talking, kissing, fucking, sucking, licking. I hit him when I fuck him, my fist resounding loudly against his muscular chest. He asks for more, and I stand to let a dribble of piss land on him. He smiles.

K. T. comes in and out a few times to get more crystal and

watch us. Eventually, he leaves on his own adventure. Then F. D. and I are alone. My prisoner/new friend looks at me, and asks, "So, you ever fist anyone?" My embarrassment makes the silence stretch until I'm sure all my insecurities show. "Don't worry, I can talk you through it." I want him to see me as a wicked man of experience, not a fumbling and unsure kid. "Just do exactly what I say." I untie the rope. "We'll go slow." I find more lube and a towel. "I want you so bad." We smoke some more; his cock ring snaps off and I remove his Prince Albert. We begin.

He pulls his legs back, all the way, as if he was in stirrups. He glistens, every muscle tight and gleaming. He breathes slowly. I begin with a few fingers of my left hand, opening him up and feeling my way around comfortably. Inside, he is a new space, welcoming my hand. He enjoys it; asks for more. I get the other fingers in next, pushing until all five are in, leaving the knuckles out.

The first ring is hard. I have to reposition my hand until I have just the right angle. At some point, I don't think it'll go in at all. And then it does. He has me push my leg and right arm to help hold his legs back. He breathes carefully, deliberately. I move my fingertips inside him, and manage to get my whole hand in. I can feel his heartbeat surround my fist and I hold it there until my breath and his, my pulse and his, match.

We kiss. "Pull back slowly and push up slower." I obey, wiggle my fingers to help get further up. His body shakes, like he's cumming inside. His dick leaks pre-cum, trickling against his leg, sliding down his crack. It tastes like gym sweat and orange rinds.

The second ring is harder. My left hand seems to hold up

his two hundred pounds all on its own. I pull back and push in. I wiggle my fingers. It is slow moving. My phone rings; so does his. The sun comes up, and the woman selling fresh tortillas announces her presence on my block. We barely notice.

I stare at my hand lost in his hole, and I don't think any more will fit. His throbbing asscheeks feel like they're smashing my hand together. I don't know what to do. He smiles. "Wiggle around some more, then pull almost all the way out, then push in. Slow." And it works. More and more of me slithers up his anus. The second ring opens suddenly and I am stunned by the heat of him, the pounding of his heart gripping my fist. He is all around me.

We lie there in each other for a second. We kiss. I almost start crying at the gift of this man, heavy on my hand. I realize how precious this is. He shakes, asks for more. And I push on.

The third ring is like a wall. Every millimeter is a struggle where we breathe in complete synchronicity, fully aware of the other, wrapped up so completely in this shared trip. It's like picking lychees all day in the Florida sun with your mom. At first, it starts okay, then shame grows, frustration at the tedious labor and the stickiness coating your hands, the smell of it, wondering if anyone sees you, uncertain of your own skill and pissed to even worry about it: You crack bad jokes to hide the other feelings. Finally, you get to return home, where your mom will have a bowl of fresh lychees chilled on the table the next day and you will happily devour them until the taste of them sickens you. He is that twenty-four hour stretch with my mom picking lychees, that maddening, that refreshing, that alien from everyone else's day. I want to open him up.

At one point I prod in the wrong direction, by the littlest

bit. His whole mass shifts and he nearly yells. "Careful! Whoa! Slow, baby." He grits his teeth and tries to smile. I want to apologize but I know it's the wrong thing to do. I am an inch past my wrist in him and just noticing the danger permeating us.

The third ring takes a few tries. I wiggle the tips of my fingers, I pull back almost all the way and push in, relishing each moment when the weight and heat of him surround me. Finally he takes a deep breath and somehow my hand slides further in, and we stay there. His whole pulse shakes me, holds me halfway to my elbow. Never have I been more inside somebody. Never been deeper.

It's like love—our version of giving birth. My fist deep in him, his legs up and back, heavy controlled breaths, life connecting us. And we stay there, on each other's breathing, both of us working together to keep him open. He trembles and moans.

I pull out. And we hold each other until unfamiliar juices and oozing push us to the shower. My left hand is numb from his throbbing, pinpricks of pain jabbing through every tiny bone with any movement. In the shower, he shoves me to my knees and baptizes my back with a hot stream of urine. He smiles at me, and I look down, grateful for him. He scrubs me, and I wash him. We're like new.

It's Christmas morning.

GENDER QUEER

Patrick Califia

Carleton was still trying to get his strawberry-
blond cowlick to lie down when the doorbell
rang. He gave his too-thin, five-foot-eight
body a critical glance in the full-length mirror,
threw the tube of styling gel back on top of
his dresser, sighed, and went to get the door.
At least he had a suntan and his calves were
showing some muscle from all that bike riding. He had eaten both breakfast and lunch,
and planned to eat dinner as well. He was no
longer the anorexic teenage girl who'd had to
be hospitalized twice. Testosterone and the
free weights in his bedroom were sculpting his
arms and torso into a body he could accept,
maybe even love.

The local FTM group had almost a hundred people on its mailing list, but the typi-

cal meeting was less than a dozen guys. Tonight, by the time he'd admitted the last arrival, there were only six others than himself, so everyone fit comfortably in Carleton's living room. The red recliner he usually claimed for his own had been occupied by a new person, someone he thought he recognized from the audience at one of his more horrendous speaking engagements. She looked ready to bolt, so he didn't ask her to move. The regular guys already had places on the three-seater sofa and the room's other two chairs. A tower of large paisley pillows resided in one corner of the room, so he dragged two of them into the circle, wedged one of them up against the bookshelf for whatever it was worth as back support, and sat down, legs crossed, to see who would start the meeting.

"I guess I'll go first," Bear said, in a voice that had only recently stopped cracking like a teenage boy's. Bear was the biggest guy there, a wide and tall Latino who had his own gardening business. He had good news: a letter from his psychiatrist and an appointment with a doctor who would do the chest surgery he had been saving to afford. Everyone was excited for him except Greg, who had spent a summer in San Francisco, avoided any gendered pronouns, and called himself "no-ho, no-op." Carleton had engaged in some behind-the-scenes diplomacy to keep the other guys from asking Greg to leave the group. "He doesn't even call himself an FTM!" Lou (who still tended bar at the local lesbian dive) had objected. "What is all this 'gender queer' shit? Either he wants to transition or he doesn't."

"Come on," Carleton had retorted, "how long did it take you to make up your mind? Let him take his own path. We get enough judgment from the outside. If he can be happy in his own skin without taking testosterone or getting any surgery, who are we to make that decision for him? Our web-site says we are for anybody who: (a) wasn't born male, and (b) has questions about their gender."

After everybody had high-fived Bear, Lou wanted to bitch about his lesbian girlfriend and fantasize about the perfect straight girl he would never be able to date until he got his phalloplasty. Carleton wondered, not for the last time, what he was doing providing a haven for a bunch of straight men. He was the only self-proclaimed bisexual in the group, and there wasn't much empathy for the problems he had getting up the nerve to go to a gay men's sex club downtown.

The others kept glancing over to the short-haired woman in Carleton's recliner, waiting for her to introduce herself or add some comment that would help them to understand why she was there. When they weren't giving her pointed looks, they were glaring at Carleton. As the unacknowledged leader of the group, he was supposed to facilitate such awkward things for them. Tonight he refused to do so, because the only time he had looked directly at the rosy-cheeked butch, he had seen the silver sheen of silent tears coursing down her face. Partly because he was in no mood to entertain, the guys left fairly early, planning to continue their conversations at a diner owned by two retired gay men. "I'll catch up with you later," Carleton said to their suggestion that he join them.

When he shut the door, the new group attendee was right behind him. "You're not going anywhere," he said firmly, and led her into the kitchen. Her. What a fucked-up language English was. What the hell did he know about this visitor in his home? Nothing. Well—she had been pretty nasty to him when he gave his talk at the community college's Psychology 101 class. "Aren't FTMs just butch dykes who gave up because it got too hard to be queer?" she had demanded. "Why do you think there's anything radical about claiming male privilege?"

"Tea?" he asked, pulling out a chair and moving a plate of cookies closer to her. The kitchen had big windows, and he'd painted it a soft yellow, then painted his kitchen furniture white and made delft blue cushions and place mats. "You've got a choice between Earl Grey and peppermint."

"I think I could use some caffeine," she said shakily, and picked up a peanut butter cookie.

"Baked those myself, I did," Carleton said in his best Eliza Doolittle Cockney accent. "I'll make someone a luverly wife someday."

She smiled. "I didn't know we were going camping," she quipped.

Carleton laughed a little more than the shy joke deserved. The electric kettle had the water boiling quickly, and he was soon able to bring a tray to the table with mugs of black tea, a creamer shaped like a black-and-white cow, and a beehive sugar bowl. The spoons were not alike. He collected antique silver at garage sales. It was a poor substitute for sucking dick, he reflected, but one claimed one's fag identity however one could in the Midwest.

Before picking up the tea, she faced him bravely. "I owe you an apology."

"No," he interrupted, wanting to put his guest at ease. "It's okay."

"No, it's not, and I can't accept your hospitality until I tell you I'm sorry for heckling you when you came to our class. I appreciated the fact that you didn't blow up at me. You spoke with a lot of dignity and courage, and after you left, I went and got every single book on that reading list you handed out. I've been so messed up, it's like I can't think my way out of all of the memories and fears that keep coming up for me. I'm really scared. I think that's why I wanted to tear into you. Looking at you, I felt—I wanted…"

Her voice trailed off into a whisper. The tears were back, and her shoulders were shaking. "What?" Carleton asked gently. He put his hand on top of her own, stroked it lightly.

"You looked so fucking happy and I wondered what it would be like to be you, to stand there without these sandbags strapped to my chest, and feel my body straight and strong and free. I wanted to know how it felt to shave my face and walk out my front door whistling. To have the guy at the gas station call me sir and not have anybody give me a second look. But how can I do that, how can I even think that?"

Carleton had a sip of his own tea to calm the pounding of his heart. How well he remembered his own version of this woman's angst. His ex-lover had not spoken to him for eight long years. Nor had he seen the twins that he'd helped her to conceive. A mutual friend sent him photos of the children and news about them. If Deborah ever found out that the woman who had broken her heart by becoming a man had even that much contact with the kids, Carleton didn't like to think about what she would do.

"There's nothing wrong with how you feel," he said. "You can't help it. You've probably always felt this way." His guest nodded, and he handed her a tissue. "What's your name, buddy?" he asked.

She hesitated. Carleton thought he knew why. "No, don't tell me your girl name," he said, just a shade impatiently.

"It's the only name I've got," she confessed in a wobbly

voice. "But I hate it. I hate it so much I don't even want to say it out loud."

Carleton fortified himself with a large bite of cookie washed down with tea that was still too hot to gulp. "Well, we can fix that," he mused. "I was an only child, and I always wished I had a little brother I could climb trees with and take camping. I even had a name all picked out for him. Moss. Isn't that a funny name?"

"I like it," she whispered.

"It goes with your green eyes," he commented, then blushed. What was he doing looking so closely at her olive-skinned face and the soft shine of her black hair? "So, Moss," he said, suddenly all business. "You don't exactly like being a woman, but you're not sure you want to be a man. And there's no safe place to talk about these things. You have trouble even thinking about them in the privacy of your own mind." She nodded. "I wish I could give you a desert island where you could change into a boy and see if you liked it, and then change back if it didn't make you happier." He smiled. "But we just don't get any holidays from gender, do we?"

Moss shook his head. Carleton appraised his guest. "Your chest isn't that big," he said. "I can show you how to tape yourself down. I think I've got my old binder around here somewhere. Want me to dress you up, little brother?"

"Sure," Moss said, throat dry. She decided to let this slight, bossy-but-kind stranger proceed. If she went home now, she might lose herself looking for the bottom of a bottle. There had been too many nights of drinking and not enough honesty. She had promised herself to stay clear-headed long enough to think this frightening conundrum through.

Carleton led him to the bedroom, stopping in the bathroom

to get some tape and bandage scissors. "Off with your shirt," he said, turning his back to rummage through a plastic storage bin in the bottom of his closet. The binder was, of course, the last thing in there, all the way at the bottom. He resisted the impulse to tidy everything up and shut the closet door. He would show Moss how to do the things that he had only been able to read about in Lou Sullivan's book about how to pass as a man. Making things easier for new guys was one of the ways Carleton exorcised the pain of his own coming out process.

Moss was standing straight, arms at his side. What a cute boy he would make. "Is it okay if I call you 'he'?" Carleton asked, pulling off a strip of tape, then tearing it with his teeth. Moss's only response was a tight nod. Then Carleton set to work taping down his little brother's chest, hoping that his touch didn't intensify his new friend's shame about his body.

As if he could read Carleton's mind, Moss said, "I like the way you touch me."

"And normally you don't like being touched?" Carleton asked softly.

"That's right," Moss affirmed. The tape was unpleasantly sticky, but it was good to have those breasts removed from view. "I love breasts," he said thoughtfully, "but only on other people."

"I'm right there with you, buddy," Carleton said, and smoothed down the last strip of tape. "Is that too tight?"

"I wouldn't care if it was," Moss replied. Carleton held up a length of putty-colored elastic cloth that looked kind of like a girdle, except for the two shoulder straps. "Put this on," he instructed, sliding it up Moss's arms, "then I'll fasten the hooks and eyes up the front. You can do this yourself if you've got a mirror. But wait, I don't want you to look yet."

Over the binder went a black T-shirt. Then Carleton turned Moss around to see his new silhouette.

The difference was shocking. "But nobody would think I was a boy," Moss said. "I couldn't pass. Could I?"

"Please, Mary, I can make anybody look like anything," Carleton lisped, and ran back to the bathroom. He returned with makeup sponges and a few pots of color. By carefully dabbing at Moss's cheeks and upper lip, then dotting his skin here and there, he created the impression of a five o'clock shadow. "My man, you been working out!" Carleton exclaimed, circling Moss's upper arms with his hands. "But that haircut has gotta go. No self-respecting gay boy has a mullet." Moss did not protest, so Carleton got out his electric clippers and proceeded to give his little brother a proper fag buzz cut. "Now look at you!" Carleton exclaimed, proud of his handiwork.

"Do I really look like a gay guy?"

"Yes. We could go barhopping right now."

"But what if somebody gropes me?"

"Hmmm. Do I have a spare packer?" Carleton opened the drawer of his nightstand. "It's chocolate brown," he said. "The only color they had the first time I went to the sex toy shop. I'm not a racist, but I kind of thought a white boy should have a peach-colored packer."

"I don't care," Moss said, laughing. Carleton dropped the spongy little cock with its two small balls into a women's nylon kneesock and tied a knot in it, then clipped off the excess stocking. He approached Moss, undid his jeans, and noted with approval the Y-fronts he found underneath them. "Been cross-dressing long?" he asked, tucking the small cock into the fly.

"Ever since I could buy my own underwear," Moss said seriously. He had expected to be repulsed by the dick. But it felt right having a bulge to fill out his pants. There was something else that felt even better. Carleton was close enough for Moss to smell his aftershave. A muscular, tanned arm was thrust down his shorts, and Carleton's flat chest pressed against Moss's artificially tamed torso. Moss said, "Can you move that a little to the right?" then took Carleton's face in his hands and kissed him.

Carleton almost swooned. How long had it been since a man had explored his mouth with his tongue? Moss was a good kisser, thorough without being sloppy or pushy. He wasn't sure what to do with his hand and almost withdrew it, but Moss clamped his legs together, trapping it there.

They moved toward the bed, but Moss's courage gave out when they reached the edge of the mattress, so Carleton helped his brother up and onto its surface. "Relax," he said, laying at his side, one arm across his chest. "We don't have to do anything that you don't want to do."

"Can I see your chest?" Moss asked.

Carleton hesitated, then unbuttoned his Oxford shirt and pulled it out of his pants. He doffed the T-shirt underneath it. Moss explored his scars with gentle fingers, then sucked his nipples sweetly, kissing them alive. Before Carleton could become uncomfortable with that much attention, Moss began rubbing his back, encouraging him to come close for another kiss.

They embraced with growing passion. "I love how strong you are," Moss gasped. "And I love it that I can use all my strength with you. What can we do? Can I touch you? Will you touch me?"

"Anything you want," Carleton promised. "But if I take off my pants, I better get at least a hand job. My dick is so hard it hurts."

"Sure," Moss said bravely. "Let's see your equipment."

Unzipping his khaki pants, Carleton said, "You just have to promise me that you're not going to think I'm a girl once you see me naked."

"No," Moss said, appalled at the very idea, then quietly freaked out at the idea that she—no, he—she? he?—was affirming someone's manhood. "Carleton. You're my big brother. I know you're a man. You're the best man I've ever met. The cutest one too."

Carleton said, "Aw, shucks," and tossed what remained of his clothes off the bed. It felt weird to be the only one who was naked, but he hoped to remedy that situation soon. In the meantime, he hadn't been lying about his hard-on, which desperately wanted some of Moss's attention. The younger guy was quick to kneel at his side, then lie down between his legs to get a better view.

"Wow!" Moss said. "Hormones did all that to you?" Carleton's clit had become a ruddy appendage that looked like a small cock head. Moss experimentally put his fingers on either side of it and moved the hood/foreskin up and down. Carleton gasped. Without thinking, Moss reached down for some moisture to ease the jack-off. Carleton stiffened, then rolled over and retrieved a bottle of lubricant from the nightstand. "Use this," he directed, and Moss silently cursed himself for an insensitive fool. Of course Carleton didn't want anyone to touch his vagina.

"Oh! God!" Carleton gasped as lubricated fingers circled his sensitive dicklet. "That feels great."

"What does this lube taste like?" Moss wondered, then answered his own question by putting his mouth over Carleton's cock. The very shape and size of it warned him that he should not lick it the same way that he would lick a girl's clit. Instead, he sucked, moving his head up and down, and put one of Carleton's hands on the back of his head.

Carleton was reeling from the hot, wet, teasing mouth. "Oh, little brother!" he exclaimed. "Where'd you learn to do that?"

"So you like the way I suck your dick?"

"I'll give you about five years to stop."

The next time Moss stroked Carleton below his dick, there was no negative response. It seemed to be okay to stroke the sensitive tissue as long as there was no penetration. "Stick your fingers up my ass," Carleton gasped. "Fuck me in the ass while you suck my fuckin' dick, man. I'm so close to coming. Please, I need it really bad."

In a trice, Moss's left hand was lubed up and working its way home. Index and middle finger found ample room for their invasion. How hard would Carleton want it? Moss settled for a slow, steady in-and-out beat that was not likely to make Carleton's ass push him out. He was rewarded with an even bigger package in his mouth and two hands on his head, holding his tongue on its rigid and yearning target.

"Oh, yeah!" Carleton yelled, and bucked into Moss's mouth, his ass contracting around his little brother's probing digits. It was a good orgasm that left Carleton feeling sleepy and drained. Moss withdrew, and they cuddled on the bed together. Carleton pillowed Moss's head on his shoulder. "You're a treasure," he said fondly. "Wish I could feel your dick up my ass."

"Next time?" Moss asked.

Carleton answered him with a kiss. When a tongue went into Moss's mouth, he decided to allow it. Normally this was where sex would end, and he would pull away to allow his overheated body to settle down. But Carleton seemed determined to keep him turned on. The kiss was so exceptional that he barely noticed Carleton unbuttoning his jeans and sliding them down over his hips.

"Lie on your belly," Carleton ordered. "I want to take you from behind."

"Say what?" Moss protested.

"Come on, little brother, let me get some of my own back. I want you. There's no stone butches in this bed, just hot dudes who need to get done." His hand slid between Moss's legs and his fingers played with the moisture and the inflamed flesh that they found there. "If you tell me you want to stop I'll know you're lying, man. Don't you want to be my pussy boy?"

Moss giggled into his folded arms. His bare ass felt cool, and Carleton's hands were practiced and delicious. His body wanted more. And for some weird reason, sucking Carleton off had not been like making love to a femme. "Just make me the same promise that I made you," he told his tutor.

"I will," Carleton said, and meant it. "I won't think you're a girl if you let me fuck you, Moss. But this is the only body you have, and it doesn't deserve to be ignored. Sex can mean whatever you want it to mean."

He was rubbing Moss's clit and using his thumb to separate the folds that guarded the entrance to his wet hole. There was plenty of hip motion to urge him forward, and Moss uttered small cries of pleasure. "Get your hands down here," Carleton urged him. "Stick your hands in your pants and jack off for your big brother. Jack off to show me how much you love to get fucked."

There was something very sexy about rubbing his clit with his hand behind the packer. Moss could lose himself, if only for a few minutes, in the fantasy of jacking off his own cock. Then Carleton was inside of him, filling him up, and it felt absolutely right. "Give me more," Moss snarled, and fucked himself on Carleton's sure and steady hand. "Oh, God, you're so good, it's so hot, please don't stop. Don't stop! Don't stop!"

Carleton was happy to oblige. He fucked Moss until "little brother" came with his own frantic finger agitating his slit. "You're doing good," he encouraged, and kept on going. "Do it for me again. I know you've got more than one shot in you. Come again for your big brother. Let me see how much you want me inside of you. Oh, God, Moss, I love fucking you. I don't think I'm ever going to be able to stop."

But eventually he had to, because Moss begged for a break. By then Carleton's cock was up again, and he quickly got Moss busy at his crotch. "See what you do to me?" Carleton hissed. "I'm going to come in your mouth, boy. Fill that sweet sexy mouth of yours up with my come. Do you want it? Do you want my come?"

When Moss made a garbled noise of assent, Carleton grabbed him by the ears and fucked his face. "Suck harder," he ordered, and Moss's obedient mouth gave him just the right amount of pressure to tip Carleton over the edge and into a hot rush of very satisfying pleasure.

Finished, they spooned one another, both needing to pee and reluctant to get up to do so. Carleton experienced the usual quiet melancholy he felt after sex. It was good to come, good to be touched by someone who understood that you could be a guy and still have girl parts, but this intimate act reminded him again that his body was not perfectly and entirely male.

"Are you okay?" he asked, and kissed the top of Moss's head.

"Mmmm. Dreamy," Moss replied. "I feel so amazing. I don't want to stop."

"You don't have to," Carleton told him. "You're not a bad person. It's okay to be a tranny."

"Is that what I am?" Moss wondered. "Or am I just a butch dyke who likes to dress up and pretend to be a boy?"

"What's the difference?" Carleton asked. "You could sum both of those identities up as forms of atypical gender expression. Oh, hell, why am I lecturing you, of all people?"

"I don't think I want to take testosterone," Moss said, and withdrew from him. He padded off to the bathroom.

Not yet, anyway, Carleton thought, putting on pajama pants and a light cotton robe. As he passed the bathroom, he heard the sound of Moss pulling off the tape, returning his chest to its usual configuration. Carleton put a TV dinner in the microwave and punched in the numbers to heat it up.

When Moss came into the kitchen, he was fully dressed. He had washed the faux-beard off his face. But he came up to Carleton and gave him a loving hug, a grin, and a smooch. "Thank you for going out on a limb for me," Moss said.

"Are you hungry? I can nuke you another TV dinner," Carleton offered.

"No. I have to get home."

They said their good-byes as the microwave beeped for Carleton's Hungry Man fried chicken, and he let Moss out the front door. Before he carried his food out to the TV tray so he could watch his favorite home decorating show, he checked out the bedroom.

Moss had tidied up, putting Carleton's used clothing on the bedroom armchair. But the binder was gone.

"Good for you," Carleton said to his vanished friend, and went back to his meal.

FROM *SEXILE*

Jaime Cortez

In November of 1958, Castro and the rebels, they were fighting their way across Cuba, kicking ass from East to West.

In Camagüey, they burned the sugar mills and even the trains at the factory. The smell of burnt sugar was the smell of change.

Mami started labor during the fires, so going to the hospital was dangerous.

Grandpa went on his bicycle to bring the, what do you call them? The Comadrona? Oh yeah, the midwife. Too old. Too slow. Too late.

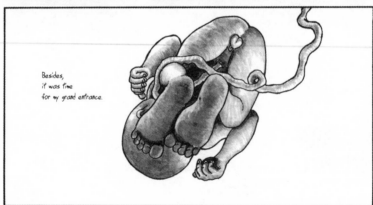

Besides, it was time for my grand entrance.

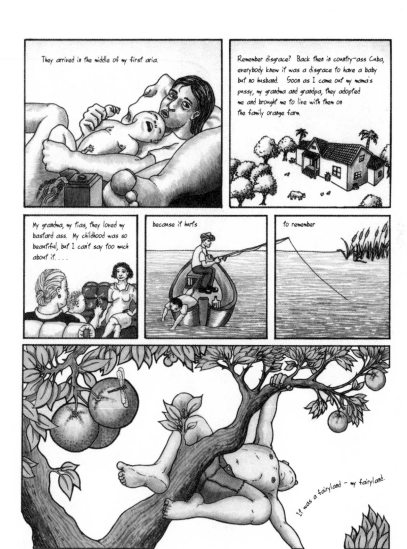

They arrived in the middle of my first aria.

Remember disgrace? Back then in country-ass Cuba, everybody knew it was a disgrace to have a baby but no husband. Soon as I came out my mama's pussy, my grandma and grandpa, they adopted me and brought me to live with them on the family orange farm.

My grandma, my tias, they loved my bastard ass. My childhood was so beautiful, but I can't say too much about it. . . .

because it hurts

to remember

It was a fairyland — my fairyland.

I couldn't wait to grow up because I knew that when I turned 10 ...

my dick would fall off ...

my pussy would grow and finally I'd become a complete girl.

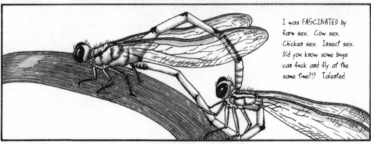

I was FASCINATED by farm sex. Cow sex. Chicken sex. Insect sex. Did you know some bugs can fuck and fly at the same time?!? Talented.

Oh my god, I was the most horniest little kid. I used to fuck this one banana tree. I carved a little round hole in the trunk and child, I hit it HARD!

In the hole, it was warm and wet and nice like inside of a body. It was very tropical, okay? Thank god the banana tree never pressed charges.

I was a baby queer and some people were so mean. I didn't even understand what I was yet, but the the other boys knew. They used the truth like a club, and taught me all my dirty names.

PUTO! Pajaro Pervertido Pato! Maricon

I escaped and started to read my mother's fashion magazines like bibles, and I learned all about couture, makeup and glamour, the fabulous glamour, of America. I knew Americans had cars shaped like women. That even farmers or plumbers can buy them. That you could open a can of soda and it was cold. That you can go buy a pill to make your mustache disappear! That they sent a motherfucker up to the motherfucking moon, okay? That the country is so big that they have to have different times in some states, which is strange from little Cuba. That all countries have their stars, but only the U.S.A. has STAR STARS that eskimos and geishas and pygmies know and want to kiss their feet and their ass if they ever get a chance.

This is a big deal
when you are a girly boy
in a place where people can't remember steak
and people aren't supposed to want special shit
if it's only for themselves.

But back to the sex. Yes, mama had plenty, thank you very much.
I had sex with schoolmates, teachers, cousins, truckers, soldiers, etc., etc.

But do NOT call me gay. I never had gay sex. Never will. I'm always the girl, he's always the man. Even when I'm fucking him.

At 11, the revolution did me a big favor. They sent me to boarding school. By that age, I'd lost all my baby fat, so mama was looking real cute. Me and five hundred boys. HELLO! They all knew about me, and they wanted me. The students, the teachers, you name it. I fucked with them all, and that was how I learned that sex and beauty were power. My power.

If a bully was harrasing me, I'd seduce him . . . .

Then blackmail his ass. Worked every time.

I did the same thing to the teachers. They were extra nice to me after that.

I had these fierce black girlfriends, and they helped me to take apart a coffee sack thread-by-thread to make a fabulous weave.

When I stepped out on stage, all my classmates got real quiet. My shit was too real for them.

Hair. Body. Face. Mama let them HAVE IT!

I took second place to a boy in a pregnant suit, but no matter...

I got a shot of girl power and it left me high and mighty.

Cuba is hella complicated, you know? Dressing as a woman was illegal, and there I was doing it for a school event. Cuban people, we're a great people. We have this flava, this sazon, that is amazing. The beautiful coast. The sound of our rhythms. We're so mixed and gorgeous. It should have been heaven, but Cuba had no place for MY revolution. Only rules and closets and traps for the freaks. I met queens who were captured in the 60's and forced into labor camps to get "fixed". Riiight. Fundamentalists do the same shit everywhere, no?

Funny. The woman I was going to become has been with me all along. She was there when I got my national draft notice from the army. Ms. Thing took charge of the situation right away and saved my life.

Me in the army?

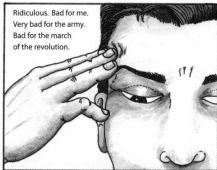

Ridiculous. Bad for me. Very bad for the army. Bad for the march of the revolution.

I'll have to go

deep into the closet

and find the perfect military ensemble.

ATTENTION RECRUITS! THE MINISTRY OF THE REVOLUTIONARY ARMED FORCES WELCOMES YOU TO THE NEW RECRUIT INTAKE.

REMOVE ALL CLOTHING FOR THE PHYSICAL, AND WAIT TO BE CALLED.

One thing about the revolution, they were serious about education. I got to study at the Destacamento Pedagogico Manuel Escunze Domenech for my teaching degree. Baby, we worked like speed freaks. Thirteen months with no breaks, no vacations and you're supposed to learn the latest Russian and Cuban teaching ideas. Mama graduated and I didn't waste no time. I went to work right away.

I was 18. Funny as hell and very for real. My students adored me.

I prepared carefully for classes every day. A little foundation and some tasteful rouge. Nothing wild. I was a teacher, after all.

For all this, I would pay.

Your reviews are excellent. Your class is the most improved in all the city.

Thank you, Direc-

BUT...

As your boss and friend, I must urge you to resign, before I have to ask you to leave.

I think you know why...

I quit. I had no choice.

No one ever forced me to wear makeup to school.
And no one was gonna stop my ass from doing it.
All the womens in my family, we're stubborn.
My mami, my grandma. Large & in charge.

I just felt like I had a right to be
whoever I wanted to be.

Punto.

BEST FRIENDSTER DATE EVER

Alexander Chee

In his profile pictures, he looks like a dirty-minded angel, blond hair sticking up, electric blue eyes, and a pink mouth that pouted beautifully. He was biting his finger, teeth bared, in one. It reminded me of an incident a long time ago, a day when I ran into an old boyfriend's old trick with said boyfriend, and while we were talking the boyfriend turned his back on us. The trick smiled at me and slid a finger up the leg of the boyfriend's very short shorts, pushing in visibly past his ring. I could see the finger slow and then slip forward. When he pulled it out, he looked at me and ran it under his nose with a grin.

The old boyfriend whipped his head around, uncertain which of us had just defiled him there on the street. I was upset for a moment, but also completely turned on.

It was, after all, a championship piece of ass.

This boy, he reminded me of both of them that day.

I found him on Friendster, the giant electronic yearbook for the never-ending high school that is life in the United States. On the outside chance you've no idea what I'm talking about, you join the site, link your page to your friends' pages, and soon you can follow a network out to, in my case, 156,550 people.

I was living in Los Angeles in a sublet with friends in a four-thousand-square-foot, four-bedroom apartment, where we could be home and never see each other, in a build-ing that looked so much like a New York building it was constantly used for location shots. In L.A., people took the Internet really seriously, and my first summer there was the first time I was ever getting hit on over the Net. I decided to hit back. It hadn't been a very romantic summer. The best I'd done live and in person was get blind drunk on vodka and Red Bull at a West Hollywood bar, like a sorority girl, and I bought someone a rose off one of those people who wander through bars with buckets of roses. Said recipient was said to be charmed, a friend of friends, and represented as such on Friendster, with some fairly amazing naked pictures of himself on his Friendster page. My birthday was coming up, I was single again, and while it was too gruesome to contem-plate writing to the man from my blackout, I began paging through the pages and pages of strangers with their brightly colored snapshots and their witty or not so witty profile one-liners, until I saw this one. I sent a very casual note and said something stupid and low-key, like, *This is just a fan letter to say, You're hot.*

A friend of mine has a theory about corny lines from guys.

You see it in movies all the time, guys saying, *Hey baby, show me your tits,* or something really beautiful like that. And the girl gets all mad, etc. But we figured out the reason it doesn't work on girls is because guys like it. It works on *guys.*

Sure enough, the guy with the pout, the guy this story is about, wrote back. He was completely inappropriate: twelve years younger than me, just out of college in New York, but he was smart. A California Rimbaud, skinny and perhaps tall in the photos.

He ended up agreeing to meet me while I was celebrating my birthday at the Silverlake summer street fair. *Sounds like my kind of tragedy,* he said.

Fair enough, I thought.

We exchanged numbers for meeting up that weekend, but he became a little hard to find. We kept missing each other. By the time I met him I was annoyed by the seven calls exchanged, and no longer particularly interested. I found him across from an enormous inflatable ride, the kind kids get inside of and bounce around, a Moonwalk.

In person, he looked like another kind of boy altogether. He was a little taller than me, probably about 6'1", and had glasses, and was dressed like the sort of boys I used to meet back in New York. From his appearance I was fairly sure there was an ex he wasn't over, that he read the *Economist,* and had intimacy issues, especially after I saw the rock-climbing shorts. I was about to give him the brush-off, but a flash of something in his eye caught me—a fishhook notion. And his skin was a miracle of smoothness. He had the kind of perfect, slightly golden skin of some blonds. It was a bit Nordic, but he looked like a child of Great Britain, the bastard of a Viking and the one the Viking found when he got off his Viking ship.

I had friends with me, he had friends with him. It was my birthday, after all. *Let's get a beer,* I said, and we walked. The street fair had seemed like a good idea in theory, but now that I was there I found the bands dull, the people uninteresting, and the goods for sale unappealing. It was like the ugly step-child of a really cool street fair somewhere else in time and place, just not here. His friend group vanished, at which point he admitted one of them was an ex-boyfriend who wasn't over him (check, I thought). My friend group said they were going off to look for a present for me.

We were alone. The beer was almost good enough to stay.

We ran out of things to talk about fairly quickly. He mentioned a pilot show he was writing. I listened, the idea was pretty good. He seemed nervous and a bit abrupt.

My friends returned. With wicked smiles they tossed a paper bag onto the table.

The friends in question were my three roommates, and the subject of how I'd not gotten laid that summer had come up a few times. As had the last, most inappropriate relationship I'd just gotten out of. In a kind of emergency conference, we'd decided *Appropriate* would have meant twenty-eight or older, and this date didn't qualify on that score. Wouldn't for about three years. I pulled out the contents.

Lube, single-portion size. Rubbers. Restraints, made of nylon, clasps from a backpack, and Velcro. A few porno mags. Absurd enough to make it sexy. I laughed. It was a fairly direct editorial comment.

Thanks, I said.

The roommates laughed and removed themselves to another table.

The date reached over for the restraints. He tentatively put one on his wrist. *Hunh,* he said. He seemed blankly quizzical, and I wondered what was going through his mind. I didn't know him well enough to know if he was hard to read.

All I was thinking was, *The real bottoms, you don't actually have to tie them up.*

I looked at the Velcro snaps and plastic hooks. Perfect for hiking and tying up vegetarians. Waterproof.

The night dragged after that. The fair mercifully came to an end, a nearby party was suggested, and we went. There was a liquor store stop, where it seemed one of my roommates was about to make a move on my date. I let it go, wanting to see how it would play out in the gray-white light of the store. There wasn't anything he wouldn't hit on if it was young and smooth, and he could likely sense I was almost abject about the state of the conversation. It wasn't that my date was stupid; we just were interested in very different things. And there were the climbing shorts.

When I really think about it, several things were in play. I was on a date I knew had no future. I had just gotten out of a relationship with a closeted man so frustratingly asexual in its nature, and so tortured, I was a bit like a man on a fast, who didn't know how to start eating again. I was uncertain, but the terms of things around me were not. At the party I watched the boy come in and out of view. I drank a bit, he got more interesting, but noticing this, and remembering the earlier disaster of the summer, I watched myself. He eventually vanished into a crowd of men doing blow in the other room, which wasn't even as interesting to me as a pizza. People were boring on drugs. At least in L.A.

And then when I least expected it, in the light of the garden, he sat down near me and we each smoked a cigarette, he offering that he didn't normally smoke. *Check,* I thought. Economist, *climbing shorts, ex-boyfriend, in denial about smoking.*

If this wasn't boring enough, he was nervous again, or perhaps it was the blow. I had thought him indifferent to me by now, as I was to him. I think we both knew enough to know it wasn't a love match. He was sexy and I was thinking right at that moment how in order to have sex with him I was probably going to have to endure weeks of dull conversations. I was probably going to have to know everything I didn't want to know about him before we got there. I dreaded the ex-boyfriend story.

I really wanted you to have a good impression of me, he said.

What are you talking about, I said.

Well, he said. *I just. I just did a bump.*

Hunh, I said. I shrugged.

I just... he said. *I do this.* And he made some kind of sound, like a child makes, and shrugged into himself. It was sweetly awkward.

What, I said. *Don't worry about it,* I said. *Whatever it is, just say it.*

You just got restraints for your birthday. Do you want to just go home and have a lot of sex?

I laughed. *Let's go,* I said.

As I said, only guys like lines like that.

The first person I ever tied up was my old boyfriend from the beginning of this story, who asked for it. He was wanting me to be someone dirtier and more aggressive than I was then. He wanted me to be the person I felt myself to be in relationship now to my birthday date, who was about to be the second person I was going to tie up.

Twelve years had passed since that first time. The exact age difference between him and me.

My hideously large apartment's layout matters to the story. For this to really work you have to understand that my three roommates and I had taken rooms all on one side of our four-bedroom apartment, while on the other side off the kitchen were former servants' quarters: two smaller bedrooms that doubled as offices. We had a library, a dining room, a living room, a butler kitchen, and pantry. Each bedroom had walk-in closets, and the West Wing, as we jokingly called it, had its own bathroom. We could easily have had a guest there and not known. We usually never heard each other, even with our rooms, which were technically suites, I guess, right next to each other. It was an incredible apartment, and I don't know if I'll ever live in another as odd and amazing in sheer spectacle.

I showed him around. The roommates were still at the party. I took him into the West Wing last, and in the room at the end of the hall, which I used as an office, we realized the tour was over.

We stood for a moment in the dark room. A futon was on the right, a desk on the left, books stacked on the walls where bookshelves should be.

I understood something there in the dark: I realized he was waiting for me to take control. That there was someone each of us didn't normally give ourselves permission to *be*. And that here was where they'd meet.

Take off your clothes, I said.

He blinked and began immediately in a way that was touching, for how quickly it happened.

Turn around, I said. He had a slim body, angular but athletic, almost completely hairless. His skin glowed blue in the sodium-vapor light from outside the room.

I fastened restraints to his wrists behind his back and raised his arms lightly, to make sure they were loose enough to allow him to move. I turned him back around to face me.

His dick was already hard. I tapped it with my finger and watched it bounce. His breathing was already rapid, from the calm of a moment before.

Close your eyes, I said.

He did. He stood there, chest moving, eyes closed.

I'm not going to fuck you down in my bedroom, I said. *Just in case there's shouting.*

Okay, he said.

I turned and closed the door and went back to him. It was incredibly moving to see him like that. For all that the restraints were ridiculous, they did work. I stood close to him, close enough to feel the heat coming off him, and his breath. I leaned in and ran one fingernail across his nipple. He jumped and gave a huffing kind of cry and I slid the nail down along his skin to just above his pubic hairline, where I pressed in again. *Hu-uh,* he let out. And then I pulled him in against me, reaching around to hold on where his wrists were joined. I hadn't taken off my clothes.

I'm not going to take off my clothes, I said. *At least, I don't think I'm going to. But I don't think that's what you get this time. This time, I'm not sure you even get to touch my dick. We'll see.*

Okay, he said.

I put my face near his, and ran the tip of my tongue gently along his lower lip. His mouth opened with another gasp. His tongue met mine and I pulled the cool wetness of it into my mouth, sucking for a moment. I pulled back slightly so that just our mouths touched. He lunged forward to keep the contact.

I pulled back again and his mouth fishmouthed open. I spat into his open mouth. It was halfway down his throat before he knew. He gasped and gulped on it and his dick banged up harder. He opened his eyes to catch his balance and I said, *Eyes closed,* and knocked him backward onto the futon couch.

I pushed his mouth open and leaned down and licked the lower lip again. The magenta pout of him. I bit on it, lightly. It was the only part of me touching him. He was breathing hard still. I let the lip go, sat back, and from above let the spit drizzle out of my mouth, like a fishing line seen by the light of the streetlamp coming in. He gasped again, *hu-uh,* opened his mouth wider, and I just let it fall for a moment in a straight line, him gulping on it. Drinking me.

He was now completely fascinating. I leaned down and kissed him and he reached back hungrily, noisy. *Uhmmm,* he hummed into my mouth. I sat back and opened a condom, pulled it over two of my fingers, lubed it. He opened his eyes.

I'm sorry, he said.

What, I said.

I'm not usually this turned on, he said.

He was apparently embarrassed of his emotions and re-sponses. It made it fun to play him, then. *Can I have a drink of water,* he asked.

Sure, I said.

I went to the kitchen and looked at the lubed condom on my fingers. I filled a glass in the fridge dispenser and went back to the dark room.

Stand up, I said, as I entered, and he struggled to his feet. He looked expectantly at the glass of water. I held it waist high, so it wasn't too hard to stick his dick into it.

It was cold. He jumped in place. *Fuck,* he said. He almost lost his balance and I steadied him as I thrust his dick deeper into water. He was panting again. I held the glass to his mouth, letting him drink from it. When he was done I put it on the desk. I kissed him hard again and as I did reached underneath his balls and slid my finger back and forth gently across his hole, getting it slick. He was breathing as hard as a runner. I slid my wet hand over his dick, down the shaft and over the knob of it, running the rubber on my fingers across the crown in circles before going back down the underside of the shaft and then continuing, under his balls and back toward his hole. I did this a few more times, luxuriating in the way he shook and shuddered and yelped. I kept him close, my teeth on his underlip, his breath fast against my cheek, and when I had established the back-and-forth rhythm, as I went back under his balls one more time, this time I pushed in.

Aaa-aa-aah. I let his lip go as his head flew back and I thrust inside him, his arms tight against the restraints. I slid out and felt him croon a little, disappointed. I made like I was headed back to his dick and instead returned inside him. He was slick and wet there and it went easily.

He crooned again. It was like feeding him, sticking something in there.

I got him on his back on the futon couch, his legs in the

air, arms behind his back, and as I kissed him I worked his hole open with those two fingers, gently, feeling it push back against me like his mouth did as I kissed him and gently fucked his mouth with my tongue.

His face was wet and his eyes drunk on just plain lust. His face was flushed, I could tell, even in just the blue lights from the street, and his skin had the sheen of his exertions on it. He was the most beautiful thing I'd seen right then, arms behind his back and yet also out of control. I tapped the crown of his dick lightly and he winced, his pouty mouth closing slightly and then hanging open again, his lips the larger from the bruising kisses. We'd been at it now for a while.

It would ruin it if he saw anything coming. I unzipped and his eyes focused. I drew out my dick

I want to see it, he said.

No, I said. *You don't get to.*

I drew the condom on and lubed it and covered his eyes with my hands, tipping his head back and up as I pushed inside him. The warmth of him slid over my dick and as I slid down into him I spat hard again into his open mouth and he gasped. He swallowed and made a kind of low hum as I slid in. I slapped his face with my other hand, his legs falling down around my thighs. *Unnh,* he said. *Hunnnh.* I slid my stubble down over his right nipple as I shoved even further, rubbing against it, and his head slammed back and down. *Oh fuck,* he said. I grabbed his dick, letting the crown circle freehand in my palm as I fucked him and ground on that nipple and he used his head to hold himself in place, pushing it into the couch. *Fuck, fuck, fuck,* he said. And then *Hrnnnh,* like he was in a hard cry, his arms thrashing underneath me, stuck under the weight of him and lashed together by the stupid Velcro and nylon, somehow still holding. *Ah fuck,* he said. *Ahhh.*

I sat back and pulled him onto the floor, onto me, turning him on my dick so that he lay full on top of me, unsnapped his arms into a new position and snapped them back again so they were over his head, arms straight. He lay naked and wet, me underneath him in my T-shirt and jeans still, my fly open, and I thrust up into him. He was groaning now, his hard dick bobbing on his stomach as I shook him. I bent my knees, forcing him into place so his legs fell out to the side in a V. His head tipped back beside mine and he reached for me to kiss him and I spat again, this time not caring if I hit his mouth, and it ran wet down our faces so he could slide his mouth over to mine as I ground into him and he ground back.

I made him cum with me inside him, which he hated once he was done. And so I pulled out and put him over my knee, his cum seeping down my jeans-leg. I spanked him and when I started to get bored I pushed him over onto the bed and stared down at him. He stared back.

It had to be ugly like this. I wondered if he'd ever let me do this again. Whenever I treated people like this they loved it but hated me for doing it and also for knowing it about them afterward, and it wasn't always true there'd be a next time. There was the rich shame and defiance, and it wasn't clear which would win.

I shucked off the rubber and beat off over him like that, letting it splash down his leg when I came. The spell was off after that. I bent down, gave him one last short kiss, but I could tell we both didn't care by now. By now it was just a little more than boys done wrestling. I wondered if he'd mind sleeping in there.

Do you mind if I sleep in here, he said.

I was going to ask you to, I said.

Whatever we were to each other, it was mutual from start to finish, I saw then. We'd been at this for four hours. When I got to the kitchen, I was shaking my head with a smile, headed through the vast apartment to my own cool clean bed.

The next morning I went in to find him awake. I sat down on the bed. He seemed gently friendly. He'd been reading something.

We went to Starbuck's, had coffee, talked a bit. He was meeting friends to continue drinking, asked me to maybe come along. *No,* I said.

I get so crazy, he said. *The first time I did that I went home with some guy who had me in a sling.*

Do you like it, I said.

I do, he said. *But I don't let myself, most of the time. None of my friends know me like this. I freak out. I can't admit it, or something. I run away.*

It was my second time tying someone up, I said, *and I want to do it again.*

The Starbuck's we were at was in a corporate center in Korea-town. We sat outside, the traffic on Wilshire on our right, the corporate park in front of us. It was like we'd wandered into the set of *Office Space* or something and made what he was saying more surreal, like the sunlight hitting his blue eyes.

I knew we would probably try to have sex again, as it had been that good, and that we also probably wouldn't. When someone says *I freak out and run away,* what they are saying is *I am freaking out and about to run away.* Life is easier when you take people at their word.

Also, it's good to be wary of people who are afraid of what they desire.

See you later, I said.

I went in to do the sheets. He had left his pot pipe and an empty cigarette box. As I took the sheets off the futon I noticed the stains from the lube and cum. I saw broken wood strings hanging down from under the couch's front edge.

We'd broken the two-by-four that ran the length of the frame.

The memories and images of that night strobed through my days for a week. I'd be somewhere and see the blue silk image of him, bound and heaving, hard, sobbing. I sent him an email, he sent one back, we ran into each other at the gym. It was hard to speak. We were listless now, like prisoners who'd used each other to break out, and now that we were in the wide world, there was nothing more to say to each other. I knew who I was now, or what I was. I suspected he did too.

At the party that night, after he pulled his face off a plate of blow, I remember how he said to me *This is the best Friendster date ever.* I'd grinned at him then and thought, *Well, maybe for you.* But, yeah. It was.

MARCOS Y CHE

Simon Sheppard

"Like Spock and Captain Kirk?"

"Yeah, like the slash stuff. Fantasies of famous guys fucking each other." Neva smiled.

"You straight girls." Bruno smiled back. "What a bunch of perverts."

Neva took one last sip of her dirty martini. "The greatest Cuban revolutionary gets it on with the leader of the Mexican peasant revolt? Sounds hot to me. But then, once a radical, always a radical." Now it was her turn to smile.

Bruno looked around the bar. It was near closing. They were both sloshed, it was time to go home.

"Yeah, you managed to go to Cuba, I'll grant you that. But honey, nobody even knows what Subcomandante Marcos *looks* like. He's always wearing a ski mask." They were getting up now, heading toward the door.

"But Bruno, that's part of what makes it hot, that unknown...er, stuff." Outside the bar, the late fall air hit them like a mild slap in the face. They strolled unsteadily down a street filled with old shingled houses, student housing now. They were just a few blocks from the college where Neva taught gender studies, where Bruno hung out and cruised the sophomore boys when he wasn't trying to write his first "serious" novel, instead of the pornographic stuff that had been paying his bills the last few years.

Down two blocks and a turn to the left, and they were in front of the house where Bruno rented a room. "So you'll write me something?" Neva asked.

"What it is with straight women loving gay porno?"

"Haven't you heard, cupcake? Sexual orientation is all just a social construct." Neva gave his hand a good-bye squeeze.

"Yeah? Then why don't I hear straight girls talking about how much they want to eat their boyfriends' asses?"

"Go on, write me something about Che Guevara and Marcos doing each other. You know you want to."

"What I wanted was for Che and that other guy in *The Motorcycle Diaries* to suck each other's cocks onscreen."

"See? Just remember, *el pueblo unido jamás será vencido.* G'night, sweetie."

"I'll keep that in mind," Bruno said, and staggered up the stairs.

Bruno had been just a little kid when the '60s happened, though he remembered, or seemed to, the tang of danger in the air. He definitely remembered the fights that had ensued when his much older brother Erik had come home on visits from college. He knew how much easier it had become since then for men—men like him—to be openly queer. He despised what he'd heard about the machismo of New Left guys, though he couldn't help but regret what he imagined was a loss of the feelings of infinite possibility. Back then, the stability of the known world must have seemed to hang by a thread. Now the only people who expected the universe to be transformed were the Christers waiting for the Rapture.

"Subcomandante Marcos stepped into the peasant's hut deep in the fastnesses of the Sierra Maestra," he began to write. It wasn't simply that he wanted to humor Neva, darling Neva with her postmodern jargon and her endless screwball ideas. It was more that he had an idea, an inkling of an idea. Of a story that might work. Call it "romantic idealism." Or just an urge to make a sale.

Subcomandante Marcos stepped into the peasant's hut deep in the fastnesses of the Sierra Maestra. Guevara was already there, his rifle slung over a rickety chair. A withered woman, perhaps seventy years old, was serving him rice and beans on a chipped plate.

"*Buenas tardes, señora,*" Marcos said, courteously, from behind his knit mask. "You're taking care of our Che?"

"Oh yes," she said, her eyes bright among her wrinkles. "As he takes care of the people."

Che smiled. "Would you excuse us for a while, señora? The subcomandante and I have things to discuss."

When the old woman had made her belabored way out of the hut, shutting the door behind her, Marcos walked over to the seated Guevara, putting his hand on the guerilla's muscular shoulder. And Ernesto "Che" Guevara thought back, back to the cold night in the mountains when he and Marcos had discussed Marx, had shared a bottle of rum, and had, at last, crawled into a sleeping bag together. Their lips, still slippery from alcohol, had met for the first time. Che had slid his hand down to the front of Marcos's fatigue pants, where his dick stood at attention....

The story wasn't going quite as well as Bruno had hoped. He'd planned on somehow fusing art and politics and dick, having it all come together in a revolutionary fuck on a peasant woman's worn linoleum floor. But now that he was writing it, he was wondering precisely who would publish a story like that, anyway, in this conservative day and age, when even fags were veering toward the right. Who would want to read such a thing, except Neva?

Well, *he* would. Bruno's dick didn't often get hard while he was writing, but now it was. Just the thought of two sweaty, hard men dropping their machismo in the Cuban afternoon was enough to make him want to quit the writing for a while and jack off. So he did, fetching a bottle of poppers from the freezer, grabbing a handful of paper towels from the roll, and getting into bed. Usually his wanks were kind of perfunctory; he saved his most elaborate eroticism for his boyfriends, the current one being Yusuf, a rangy Palestinian with a perfect ass. But now he took his time, cupping his balls in one hand, squeezing them gently, then not-so-gently, as he stroked his hard cock with his other. He let go long enough to take a few good-sized snorts of poppers, just managing to screw the cap back on before the rush began.

He didn't use poppers all that often, either—the bottle in

question had been left behind by the boyfriend before Yusuf. But now they got him way out there, totally focused on the pleasure he was giving himself. He spit in his right hand and slid it slowly, slowly up the underside of his shaft, tugging on his balls again with his left. When his head had cleared a little, he thought of Che, of Subcomandante Marcos, of them curled together in a revolutionary 69, sucking one another's uncut cocks. For one giddy moment, pre-cum already oozing out his piss slit, he imagined writing an essay on "The Artistic Responsibilities of the Horny Leftist Fag in Times of Resurgent Bourgeois Authoritarianism." And then he came.

Night had come to the Zapatista rebels' camp in the hills above San Cristóbal de las Casas. Subcomandante Marcos stood looking up at the millions of stars above, thinking about freedom. An aide came over to him and whispered in his ear.

"Ah," Marcos said, just that, but his demeanor changed immediately, becoming excited, even agitated, as he walked with the soldier to the edge of the camp. A shadowy figure was standing amidst the trees: Che.

"I'm so glad to see you, comrade," Marcos said, his quiet voice filled with emotion. "I'd heard that you were dead."

"It will take more than the CIA to kill me off, my friend," Che said, smiling. He walked toward Marcos, and the two men embraced in the comforting darkness. Marcos stroked Che's beard and drew his fingers across the Cuban's mouth. Guevara tightened his embrace and brought his lips to the subcomandante's, wet and soft behind the ski mask. As they kissed, Marcos lowered his hands to Che's ass, stroking the guerilla's butt through his khaki fatigues. The two men pressed their hard dicks into one another, their tongues still entwined.

"Fuck, comrade..." sighed Marcos.

"*Si*," agreed Che.

Bruno would have to do some research: Would Che's fatigues have been khaki or green? Was the story, finally, going to be set in Mexico or in Cuba? And, though he was having fun with the time-travel improbabilities of the story, something seemed off. How could he fully capture the myth of the romantic revolutionary without getting purple-prose overripe?

He backed up what there was of the story and decided to phone Yusuf—it had been days since they'd seen each other.

Within an hour, Bruno was in Yusuf's bed. The boy from Palestine liked to be fucked, and fucked hard, on all fours like a dog in heat. And Bruno obliged him, his long cock plunging into Yusuf's soft muskiness again and again, so hard that after a while Bruno half-hoped it hurt.

When they were done with the fucking, lying naked side by side, Bruno told Yusuf about the story he was writing.

"I don't know," Yusuf said. "It seems awfully like novelty-for-novelty's-sake. I mean, using Guevara as nothing more than a character in some porn story."

"But he's already a T-shirt design..." Bruno said.

"Yeah, but...I thought you were kind of into nonviolence."

"Well, yeah, kinda."

"And anyway, isn't the Cuban government antigay?" Yusuf asked.

"Well, if it is, wouldn't eroticizing a queer Che be a cool move, or, like, revenge?"

"Oh, yeah? What next? A story about how Reverend Lou Sheldon is such a stud?"

Yusuf could be argumentative, sometimes, in that college-student way of his, and Bruno figured this was probably one discussion in which he'd come out the loser. So he snuggled down until his face was even with Yusuf's brown hip and then leaned over and put his mouth around his boyfriend's cock. It tasted of cum, and, so soon after orgasm, it was in no mood to get hard again. But Bruno liked sucking it, anyway, even soft. He ran his tongue around the cockhead's ridge while Yusuf went on about politics. After a little while, Bruno didn't even hear him.

Che licked the pre-cum from the tip of Marcos's large, curved dick, then ran his tongue down the underside, down to the subcomandante's dark, hairy ballsac.

Marcos shivered and said, "Lower, Che, lower." And Guevara licked the ridge between Marcos's muscular thighs. The Zapatista raised his legs and Che zeroed in on the newly revealed hole, inhaling its earthy smell. Then he began to move the tip of his tongue around the hot puckered flesh.

"Fuck, that's good," Marcos said, and Che's tongue burrowed deeper. Marcos reached down, ran his hand through Che's thick dark hair, then pushed down on Guevara's head, ramming Che's face against his ass.

"I want you inside me, comrade," Subcomandante Marcos said.

"I don't have a condom," Che said after taking his mouth from Marcos' wet, soft hole.

"There are some in my jacket pocket," Marcos said.

Che reached over and got a rubber. He knelt above Marcos, his cock so hard it stood straight up against his hairy belly, and unrolled the Trojan over his hard-on.

"Lube?" asked Che Guevara.

"In that same pocket."

And in moments, Che was fucking the subcomandante, his revolutionary cock shoved all the way inside the Zapatista. Marcos groaned in delight as Guevara's cock stroked in and out, hitting his prostate with astonishing precision every time.

"Christ, you know what you're doing, Che."

Guevara lowered himself down onto Marcos's body, shining with sweat, and the two men kissed, deeply, heatedly, as though it were forever.

After that bedroom discussion with Yusuf, Bruno had Googled "Che Guevara homosexuality." The first two links were—unsurprisingly—to folks selling Che T-shirts that had most likely been produced in some Third World sweatshop. Then came some links pointing out that homosexuality had been decriminalized in Cuba in 1979, that Fidel Castro had said, "I am absolutely opposed to any form of repression, contempt, scorn, or discrimination with regard to homosexuals." Interesting.

And then Bruno had run across a quote by some Republican senator, Tom Coburn of Oklahoma. "Lesbianism is so rampant in some of the schools in southeast Oklahoma," the esteemed lawmaker had said, "that they'll only let one girl go to the bathroom. Now think about it. How is it that that's happened to us?" Leaving aside the charming semiliteracy of the statement (either the schmuck meant "one girl at a time" or a lot of Oklahoma schoolgirls were peeing in their pants), the quote brought together many of the strophes of classic homophobia. There was the threat to society, the rueful tone of alarm, the whole threat-to-youth thing, the alarm over underage sex, even a hint of rape. And Bruno suspected that Coburn might have jacked off on occasion while fantasizing about the ravening babydykes of Antlers, Oklahoma. Small wonder that homosex had remained illegal in the freedom-loving state of Oklahoma for a quarter century after it was legalized in Cuba.

It just showed how far off the radicals of the 1960s had been when they thought the United States was in a prerevolutionary situation.

And here he was, writing a penis-filled paean to icons of leftist peasant uprisings. Who the hell would publish it?

Oh well, it was mostly done now, anyhow. He only had to finish that sex scene. It was a good time to work; he was hellaciously horny. He pulled down his sweatpants till his half-hard dick flopped free, then grabbed hold of his shaft and began stroking.

With one final cry of triumph, Che shot off inside Marcos, who, without even touching himself, let loose a flood of sperm on his own furry belly. After one final kiss, Guevara rolled off Marcos and the two men lay on their backs, side-by-side, holding hands, looking up at an eternity of stars.

"Che?"

"¿Si?"

"Would you like me to take off my mask? Would you like to see my face at last?"

Guevara looked over at his friend. "Yes...I don't know... no. No."

There was a long moment of silence, only the sounds of the night.

"You know, Che, our enemies will tell many lies about us."

Che squeezed Marcos's hand harder. "I know, I know. But I have faith that eventually truth and justice will triumph."

The full moon had made its way above the mountains. Guevara's face was bathed in silvery light. For a moment, he looked like a man about to profess his love, but all he said was, "My cock is getting hard again."

"So soon?" Subcomandante Marcos said, and laughed. He rolled over onto Che Guevara. "Well, this time *I* fuck *you*."

"*Adelante*, comrade," Che Guevara said, and started to raise his legs.

"How's your boyfriend?"

It had been almost two weeks since Bruno last saw Yusuf, who hadn't even bothered to return his phone calls. But he didn't want to get into that now. "He's fine," he said.

"So..." Neva said. "Your story."

"I wrote it for you."

"I know," Neva smiled. "And for yourself, no?"

"Guilty as charged," Bruno said. "Just don't tell the People's Tribunal."

"Ah, bourgeois individualism!" Neva said, and giggled.

"Did you like it?"

"I did, yeah. Though it lacked a certain political sophistication, it sure worked as porn. Bruno, darlin', I found it hot. Actually, it made me want to masturbate."

"And did you?" Bruno thought back to the multiple orgasms he'd had while writing "Marcos y Che."

"I'll never tell."

"Bitch."

"You bet. Anyway, there were a few things that were

unclear. Did the fuck take place in a Cuban peasant woman's hut or in the Mexican mountains at night?"

"Um…I'm still revising it."

"Good enough. Another mojito? My treat."

"Sure, thanks."

When the waitron had brought a couple more drinks, Neva raised her glass. "¡*Viva la revolución!*" she said.

"¡*Qué viva!*" Bruno said. And he took a long, delicious sip.

GARLIC

Bob Vickery

I remember reading in one of those little "grab bag" items in the newspaper that if you eat a clove of garlic, two hours later your feet will smell of it. I think of that now as I bury my nose in Angelo's balls. Among the pungent, yeasty scents lost in the folds of loose scrotal flesh, I get a distinct whiff of garlic. I roll Angelo's ballsac in my mouth, washing it with my tongue, and yes, the taste of garlic is faintly noticeable to my taste buds as well. I look up at Angelo, grinning. "How come whenever I blow you I feel like ordering a pizza?" I ask.

Angelo laughs, and it's a beautiful thing to see. His dark eyes shine and his expressive face lights up with humor. "I don't know, Aaron," he says. "I've long ago given up trying to figure out how you Anglos think."

Angelo's dick lies hard against his flat belly, thick and dark and roped with veins. I wrap my hand around it and give it a squeeze. The ripe plum of his cock head turns deep purple and a single, clear drop of pre-jizz oozes out the slit. I lick it up and roll my tongue around the sticky drop, savoring its taste as if I were sampling a vintage wine. I give Angelo's balls a gentle tug as our eyes meet. "You got a load in there for me, baby?" I growl. "A thick, creamy wad that you're going to splatter my tonsils with?"

Angelo's mouth curves up into a lazy grin. He's got a beautiful mouth, the lips full and sensual. His grin widens, and his teeth flash white in his dark face. "I got a load for you, all right." he says softly. "A mother lode. But you're not going to taste it." He wraps his legs around me and pivots me onto my back, straddling my chest. "I'm going to fuck you tonight," he says softly, his eyes laughing. "Plow that pretty ass of yours. Squirt my jizz inside you. You'll just have to taste it some other time." I slide my hands up his smooth, brown torso, feeling the warmth of his flesh, the play of muscles beneath my finger tips. A crisp black curl of hair falls against Angelo's forehead, and his eyes burn into mine. I give his nipples a sharp twist, and Angelo closes his eyes. "Fuuuck," he sighs softly. He reaches over to the bedside table for a condom.

Angelo fucks my ass with slow, languorous thrusts, me on my back, him looming above me like an angel of the Second Coming, his gaze locked on mine. Angelo's eyes are as black as Spanish olives, and his skin is the tawny brown of the Tuscan hills in the heat of summer. I feel his hot breath on my face, stinking of garlic, reeking of it, and I breathe deeply, closing my eyes. I push my hips up to meet his next thrust, and Angelo groans his appreciation. He has a lube-smeared hand wrapped around my cock, and I fuck his fist with the same deep strokes that he uses to fuck my ass.

"I'm getting close, baby," he whispers, and the next time he thrusts into me, I wrap my legs around him and clamp my ass muscles *hard* around his thick cock. Angelo gives a long, trailing groan, and his body trembles above me. He bends down and plants his mouth on mine, his tongue thrusting into my mouth, and all I taste is garlic. I feel his cock pulse inside me as he squirts his load into the condom up my ass, and with a few quick thrusts, I topple over the edge too and fall into my own orgasm.

"Fuckin' A," Angelo croons. He pumps his fist up and down, and I shudder as my jizz shoots out, coating his fingers, dribbling down his wrist. Angelo collapses on top of me, his dick still in me. We lie there, in the sweat-soaked sheets, the weight of Angelo's body pushing down on me, his face nuzzled in my neck. Angelo's breath takes on a deeper, measured cadence as he drifts into sleep. I roll him off me, and he stirs awake, kissing me absently and pulling me close to him. He drifts back into sleep, his face up next to mine, and the smell of garlic is so strong it feels like something thick and solid. That night I dream I work in a pizzeria in Little Italy.

A couple of weeks later I take Angelo to the Garlic Festival in Gilroy, about two hours south of San Francisco. The festival takes place on a wide, treeless field, what grass there is trampled down and burnt brown by the summer sun. Fair booths dot the field, with red and white striped awnings, flags and streamers snapping in the wind, and salsa music blaring out of loudspeakers mounted on poles. The mob that descends upon the field pushes through the alleys made by the rows of booths. This is not a crafts fair; there are no displays of tie-dyed T-shirts or agate wind chimes or stained glass medallions. The only thing these booths sell is *food*. Food made with garlic. And kegs of garlic-flavored beer and bottles of garlic wine to wash it all down with.

Angelo and I don't so much walk as let the crowd carry us from booth to booth. Angelo has peeled his shirt off and tucked it in the back of his jeans, and his nut-brown torso gleams in the summer sun. Beads of sweat gather around his nipples, grow to full drops, and then slowly trickle down his smooth, muscled chest. We eat whatever the booth we're at is selling. Angelo buys a bag of garlic fries, and we stuff handfuls of them in our mouths and wash them down with garlic beer. The next booth is selling garlic scampini, and we buy plates of it, which we eat in hurried bites as the crowd carries us off. A new band takes the stage, and instead of salsa, hard, pounding rock 'n' roll blasts out of the speakers at deafening volume. Angelo and I gorge on garlic chicken adobe, garlic spring rolls, garlic calamari, garlic goat cheese, garlic fettuccine, roasted garlic cloves that squirt pure garlic in our mouths when we squeeze the outer husks. We switch to garlic wine and then back to garlic beer, served foaming in tall Styrofoam cups. Angelo bends his head back and gulps the beer down, and it spills out of the sides of the cup, down his chin, cascading onto his pecs in a frothy swirl. He rubs the back of his hand across his mouth, and when his eyes meet mine we burst out laughing. Later, Angelo buys a jar of garlic paste, opens it, and smears the rank, stinking goo over my face and shoulders, grinning. I grab the jar and return the favor, slathering his body with the paste like he's a luau pig being prepped for a roasting. Angelo takes my wrist and pulls my fingers to his mouth, licking off the caked gobs of pure garlic, and then takes another chug of beer. We pass a booth selling garlic-flavored ice cream, and we share a bowl, spooning it into each other's mouths. It's thick and creamy, and in the hard, beating sun, eating it is almost as good as righteously good sex.

By late afternoon we are completely shit-faced. The sun still blazes, human flesh presses against us as the crowd surges down the tent alleys like a sluggish tide, and the music pounds us like a force of nature. We find ourselves pressed against the impromptu stage where the band is playing.

"Fuuck," Angelo says. "I gotta get out of this crowd. It's just too fuckin' much."

We sneak around to the back of the of the stage, and duck under the cloth that covers the scaffolding. Angelo collapses onto the hard ground, and I fall down beside him. The shade is like a blessing from Jesus. Sunlight streams in through tears in the cloth, and I drunkenly watch the dust beams dance in the rays. The ground vibrates under my back from the crashing music above us. Just when I think my skull is going to split open with the noise, mercifully, the band finishes its set. The emcee announces the next act, some blues singer just down from Santa Cruz. A couple of minutes later we hear a voice like sandpaper belting out "A Little Piece of My Heart," with guitars and drums backing her up.

Angelo rolls over next to me and buries his face in my chest. He jerks his head up, and his eyes meet mine. "Goddamn, but you stink," he laughs.

I laugh back. "You're not exactly a rose garden yourself."

"Bullshit," Angelo says, grinning. "That's exactly what I am. A stinking rose garden. Garlic, the stinking rose." He reaches over and pulls my face against his. His tongue snakes into my mouth, and I wrap my arms around him, pulling him close to me. We're both soaked with sweat, and our bodies slide against each other like a couple of otters. Angelo rolls me onto my back and pins my arms down, his face looming above mine. Our eyes lock, and his expression grows serious. I crane my head up, and we kiss again, slowly, all tongue, our mouths working together. I reach up and run my fingers through Angelo's hair, curling them, tugging his head back and forth as we tongue-fuck each other's mouths.

Angelo reaches down and cups my dick with his hand. I feel my cock stiffen and rub against the rough fabric of my jeans. "You got something there for me?" Angelo croons. "Something big and stiff for me to work on?"

"Yeah," I growl. "Come and get it."

Angelo tugs my zipper down and slips his hand inside. He gives my dick a good squeeze. "Jeez, Aaron," he says, all exaggerated innocence. "It feels like you're ready for *bear*."

Angelo climbs to his knees and tugs my jeans and shorts down below my knees. My dick is fully hard now, juiced and pressed against my belly. Angelo wraps his hand around it, bends it back, and lets it slap against my stomach. He does that again, and then once more. "Is that all you're going to do?" I ask. "Play slap-the-dick?"

"I dunno," Angelo grins. "You got something else in mind?"

"Yeah," I say. "Get naked, and I'll show you."

Angelo stands up and pulls his clothes off, dropping them in a pile next to him. A shaft of light shines through an open canvas seam and plays against his chest, making it gleam like fine mahogany.

Come on, come on, the singer above us belts out. *And take another little piece of my heart now, baby....*

When he's naked, Angelo stretches out full on top of me, his flesh pressed against mine, his tongue thrust deep in my mouth. I raise his right arm and bury my face in his stinking pit, smelling the sharp, bitter stench, breathing it in, filling my lungs with it, as Angelo sticks his tongue in my ear. I drag my own tongue across Angelo's torso, tasting the remains of the garlic paste mingled with the salt of his sweat. I break free and look at him.

"Sit on my chest," I growl. "And drop your balls in my mouth."

"Sure, Aaron," Angelo grins. "Anything you say."

Angelo straddles my chest and I suck on his red, fleshy sac, rolling my tongue around it, the scrotal hairs tickling my tongue as I breathe in the pungent ball stink. Angelo takes his hard dick and rubs it over my face, smearing my cheeks and nose with his pre-cum. I lock my eyes on his, my mouth stuffed with his balls, and slide my hands over his torso, kneading the flesh, pulling on it, flicking his nipples with my thumbs. Angelo isn't smiling now. His eyes burn with the look of a man with a serious nut to bust, and his mouth is set grim with lust. He spits in his hand and reaches behind and starts jacking me, his spit-slicked fist sliding up and down my dick shaft.

"Fuuuuuck," I groan, and Angelo keeps on stroking, his eyes burning into mine. After a few moments he pivots around and takes my dick in his mouth. I return the favor, and we fuck face and suck dick with serious intent, Angelo's low hangers banging against my face with each thrust.

I feel Angelo's fingers push into my asscrack and press against my bunghole. I thrust my hips up to give him easier access, and when he finally slides his finger up my chute, knuckle by slow, twisting knuckle, I give a long groan. Angelo's lips slide up and down my shaft as his finger works my asshole, pushing hard against my prostate. The music from the stage above us crashes down around us, the air vibrates with it. The singer is crooning "Turtle Blues," and the sound of her rasping voice penetrates me as much as Angelo's thrusting finger. I suck on Angelo's dick like my life depends on it, working it, cramming it hard down my throat, choking on it. Angelo pumps his hips, fucking my face with a burst of piston thrusts. Everything is reduced to raw sensation: Angelo's dick stuffed in my mouth, his mouth sucking hard on my own dick, his finger skewering my asshole, his hard, sweaty flesh pressed against me, the music beating down, the heat pouring over us like thick, hot mud, and everywhere, the smell and taste of garlic....

Angelo's body shudders. He takes my dick out of his mouth. "Oh, fuck, baby," he gasps. "I'm going to shoot." I quicken my pace, working my lips faster down his shaft, pulling on his balls. Angelo groans loudly, and I feel his load splatter against the roof of my mouth, one volley of spunk, and then another, and another after that. I suck hard, milking his dick of every drop of jizz. I don't swallow, but just keep his spunk in my mouth, rolling my tongue over it, savoring it. Angelo's come is pure liquid garlic, the taste of it sharp and pronounced. Angelo bends down and kisses me, and I share his load with him, my tongue thick with it as I french him.

"Do you taste it, baby?" I ask. "Do you taste the garlic?"

"Fuck yeah," Angelo sighs.

Angelo's fist keeps sliding up and down my hard cock, and when I finally shoot, I arch my back up and squeeze my asscheeks tight. My spunk spurts out, splattering against my belly and chest, caking my torso. Angelo licks it up and then kisses me again. My spunk, like Angelo's, is sharp with the flavor of garlic. Angelo collapses beside me, and we lie there on the hard-packed dirt, listening to the music, feeling the heat, soaked in garlic-scented sweat. I feel like I'm being marinated.

A week later, Angelo's come still tastes of garlic, even though he swears he hasn't had any since the festival. We order a pizza afterward. When the pizza man asks me what kind of topping I want, I tell him anchovies. I think it's time for Angelo to come in a different flavor.

ELECTRICAL TYPE OF THING

Sam D'Allesandro

"There's more to relationships than acquisition." Scott was trying to talk me out of something. I wasn't listening. I was thinking about the different ways a relationship can turn out. A lover can be a best friend, a piece of furniture, or an eternity. My Chris treated people like furniture—jumping from one to the next, rearranging the pieces, tossing out and retrieving. Chris says that he's "a very visual person." That means he doesn't like the way a lot of people look right off the bat and quickly tires of the looks of those he does like. Visual fickleness. He moves from face to face, body to body, from inside of one asshole to inside of another. The whole process takes as little getting to know someone as it sounds.

Chris is beautiful, handsome, sexy. That

means person after person is willing to let him put his cock inside of them, or lick the sweat from his belly, or do whatever Chris decides he wants. He knows just how to do everything so that you're always ready for more. His eyes are brown and steady. Unavoidable. In a bar they look straight into yours from across the room—he's interested in getting your interest going, no matter what he plans or doesn't plan to do about it. But it's the hands you should be watching. He might slip one of them down your pants and tease your asshole while giving you a kiss. Then when your resistance is zero he might give you a nice pat and be on his way. He might. He might do anything. With Chris even a pat and a quick kiss are worth something. That's the way it is with him. And the way he does whatever he's decided to do will always seem okay. Almost respectable. He's never rude. His tone is always friendly. There's nothing you could pin down as deceptive, yet the effect is the same: left alone with your buns in the oven, or your iron in the fire, or your head up your ass. That's how I used to think of Chris. I hated him and I would stay with him whenever he'd have me.

I've known Chris for four years now. I'm the only one that he has continued to see and who has continued to see him for that length of time. We have sex about twenty times a year. Sometimes we do it four times in a month and then don't see each other for four months. And we live in the same city. It's not so big. Usually a chance meeting gets us started. It's always up to him, he knows I'm ready. He knows I'm hooked on him. I know that if we're at the same party we'll end up together. We both know that I'm different than most of the guys he sees. We're on to each other. He wants me in a different way, but almost as much as I want him. We are drawn to each other. We are each the free electron the other's unbalanced nucleus needs. It's an electrical type of thing. A charge.

Once when I was on the other side of the country and thought we'd never be in the same city again I sent him a card telling him he was an asshole and that I loved him. When I came back he told me he loved me too. If that was true, I wondered, then why did I get to see him so seldom? He said that I was the one who never called—then I couldn't get hold of him for a month. Still, he does want me. Just not all the time. He does want me but that doesn't mean he can be around me too much. He's just the kind of guy he is. And I'm the kind *I* am. Everyone that can't have him wants him. I want everyone I can't have.

Over coffee I told Scott and Jeff about the way Chris and I are together. I wanted to hear someone else accept the relationship just as it is, the way I have. Instead they gently tried to tell me about the way loving relationships are supposed to be, always sharing and sensitive, etc. Chris and I are sensitive, only in a different way. Chris and I share some needs and the means to satisfy them. Together we're basically self-contained. Scott and Jeff tell me that there are other needs to consider, that a relationship can't be based on sexual intensity alone. I say if sexual intensity's there, the relationship has already been based.

I don't think we can always be sure what it is we need; that seems to be different for me than it is for Scott and Jeff. Or is it? Maybe Scott and Jeff have forgotten how good pure intensity can feel. Maybe they've never experienced the vulnerability of being spanked during sex by someone they really want. Or known the relief you can feel when someone gets you to forget yourself totally. Someone who helps you to find a sub-human state—no language, no questions, no problems—just a pulsing, quivering slab of sensation. People would pay a guru or a Rolfer to do that. Or Werner Erhard. It's not an unusual desire. It's not an unusual need, letting someone else take the reins once in a while. I'd rather be physically fucked by Chris than verbally fucked by Werner Erhard. I never wanted my parents to spank me but when I can pick who's doing it I can enjoy a good spanking. Skin craves sensation. It's those nerve endings. It's the way we're made.

I wonder if protozoa ever get into a little S/M. They seem to think about sex less and do it more. They do it all the time. One-celled nymphomaniacs constantly going at it in a big way, without the aid of cock rings, lubricants, vibrators, or pornography. That can't be totally unfamiliar to us. It's basic, after all.

I don't think Scott and Jeff quite understood. I needed more of something. Self-awareness alone had become pretty vapid. Everything seemed too neat. I didn't want to be dirty exactly but I didn't want to shave every day either. I didn't want to get hurt exactly but I liked sex rough. I needed some-one who could satisfy urges I couldn't even name. Someone complicated enough to be exciting, primal enough to be effec-tive. For me that was Chris. He hadn't chosen his shape and I hadn't chosen mine, yet all the right barriers were there to create the charge.

I met Jack in L.A. He drove a little red truck with four-wheel drive and a Dolby stereo. At first I didn't want him but his shyness interested me. He was very young and clean. He had hairy legs and arms and a totally smooth chest with large, sensitive nipples. His body seemed so vulnerable, so beyond his control—I could make him tremble in a second just by teasing his tits. Soon he wanted to live in my asshole. If I was standing naked anywhere, like brushing my teeth or shaving, he'd come out of nowhere and have his face between my legs, kissing my cheeks and licking my asshole. He was obsessed. I never stopped him. It seemed like his right. It was so easy to give him so much pleasure.

Sometimes he wanted me to spank him and then fuck him once his ass was red. He'd whimper all the way through it. I could tell it hurt him to be fucked, but he wanted it anyway. I respected his willingness to be hurt a little. He'd dumped his conditioning of not being able to want anything that hurts. It was a spiritualness with him, not a sickness. A respect for his own desires without questioning their right to exist. He was perfect, because he had no guilt.

Some people would have called him a whore. I love the whore he is. For him *whore* means beautiful, means uncalculated, means guiltless and basic—like the angels or the protozoa. When I left L.A. I made him promise to use rubbers. I wanted him to stay healthy. The rubbers won't change things for him, this way he can think he's doing it for me. And he'll like that.

Now I am my Chris for Jack. I am his Chris. Now I understand Chris better. I do love Jack, I just can't be with him all the time. He is different from the others. He's not furniture, although sometimes our actions make each of us seem so. I'm only as mean as he wants me to be. Chris is the same way with me. It's the way we are. None of us knew exactly what we needed, but we each knew we needed something. That's what we got. I'm not embarrassed about it now. Maybe I know something Scott and Jeff don't know. There's more than one way to get and give affection, and to me, at the right time, they are all acceptable. If Jack and Chris and I are furniture than we are very well appreciated furniture. We love our periods of use.

One day Chris and I went to the beach. We thought we should try going on an outing together. We didn't have much to talk about. All I could think about was wanting to have sex with him. Later we did. And then we were happy.

Jack came to visit me and brought his new boyfriend. He wanted me to watch him fuck his boyfriend, so I did. Afterwards he smiled and I could tell he was proud for me to see him take the role I usually took in our relationship. His boyfriend loved him and was proud for me to see Jack wanting him. Jack loved his boyfriend and was proud for me to see Jack want him and have him. Then the boyfriend went out for a while and Jack wanted me to fuck him. So I did. And all of this made him happy.

THE PANCAKE CIRCUS

Trebor Healey

Clown Daddy bused dishes at the Pancake Circus, a tacky breakfast joint on Broadway in Sacramento. I only went there when I was depressed and, in my half-baked noncommittal self-destruction, craving food that would kill me if I ingested enough of it. I wanted a steamy stack of buttermilk pancakes with that whipped butter they use that melts slowly and thoroughly, sort of like my psyche does when it's heading south. (It does not have the same effect on your arteries, however, which slowly harden like dog shit in the sun.) And I wanted that diabetes-inducing syrup, of course. Two or three shots of it—lethal as sour mash—surreptitious, sticky and sweet as it vanishes into the spongy cake, absorbed like a criminal into the social fabric.

Clown Daddy began as a tattoo of a tiger jumping through a ring of fire—a tiger with a pacifier in his mouth. A tiger caged in a mess of plump blue veins—veins like the roots that buckle sidewalks. Straining as they held the pot poised over my cup; straining like my throat suddenly was; like my cock caged in my drawers.

"Coffee?" It was Josh Hartnett's voice.

In an effort to compose myself, I drew a breath and followed those veins up that forearm, down through the dimple of its elbow and up across the creamy white bicep, firm and round as a young athlete's buttcheek, before the blood-swollen tubes vanished into his white polyester shirt, reappearing at the neck and passing the Adam's apple, which was nothing less than a mushroom head pushing boy-boisterously out of his neck-skin like a go-go dancer in Tommies. *God have mercy,* my soul muttered, as my eyes, having lost his veins somewhere under his chin (and damn, what a beautiful charcoal-shadowed chin), proceeded with anticipation up his clean-shaven cheek, savoring the pheromonal (and I mean "moan"-al) beauty of him, dead set for his eyes like a junkie tightening the belt. And bingo, like apples and oranges lining up in a slot—oh my god, I won!

I'm a homo and you know where I'd look for the coins. I felt my sphincter dilate, and my buttcheeks were suddenly like open-cupped palms, holding themselves out to him.

I came in my pants. And then, a bit unnerved to say the least, cleared my throat. I'm not sure I would have been able to even answer him if I hadn't relieved the pressure somewhere. Fortunately, God had mercy after all.

I whimpered, "Yes, please." I couldn't even look at him, so I watched the cup as he filled it to the top, and then some. It crested the brim and ran down onto the saucer—and then I watched the pot move away, off to the next table.

Jesus H. go-go-dancing Christ. My drawers were soaked and cooling. I felt like a kid who'd wet his pants. This had happened to me only once before, in junior high, when Greg Vandersee had stretched, lifting up his arms and revealing a divine cunt of underarm hair that made me lurch forward as my cock emptied its boy-fresh copious fluids into my little BVDs.

Fortunately, Clown Daddy was a busboy and not my waiter. I could handle *yes* and *no,* but *the buttermilk stack, with sausage and one egg over easy* wouldn't have been pretty—or perhaps even possible.

"Hi, I'm Edna. What'll you have?" She smiled.

A bed, some lube, and an hour with your busboy would have been the honest answer. *Or a fresh pair of undergarments.* But this wasn't about honesty, this was about self-destruction. Wasn't it? I ordered the low-cholesterol eggbeaters in a vegetable omelet with whole wheat toast. Say what you will—lust leads to healthy choices. Doesn't it?

What I hadn't realized as I sat back gloating, my penis clammy in my damp, semen-soaked briefs, was that when I'd looked in Clown Daddy's eyes my days as a law-abiding citizen had abruptly ended. Choices? Choices had nothing to do with it.

But ignorance is bliss. While it lasts. And while it lasted, my head wobbled like one of those big-headed spring-loaded dolls that resemble Nancy Reagan, swinging this way and that, watching for him, rolling up and down and around like an amusement park ride, taking in the Pancake Circus as I did so, its paint-by-number clowns adorning the walls, its circus tent decor, its uncanny ambience of a sick crime waiting to happen.

I watched him move about while my fly tightened like a glove over a fist. A wet fist, sticky and greedy for whatever it had just crushed to sticky pulp. My mind played the sideshow song as I imagined Clown Daddy behind the curtain, Edna up front barking for him: "Step right up, see the man who makes you cum in your drawers!"

I gulped the coffee down, which drew him back to my table like a shark to wet, red, bleeding bait.

He didn't look at me until I thanked him, and then it was just a shy, straightboy grin. God, but his features were sharp, angled, and clean. His dark, deep-set eyes, the long lashes, the wide mouth with its full lips, the arresting pale blue-white of his skin and the night-black hair—that goddamn shadowed chin. And his eyes: dark as crude oil, raw out of the ground. He was undeniably, painfully handsome. Pro-zac handsome because he cheered me up. Wellbutrin hand-some because one saw one's sadness disappear like a wisp of smoke—and those pesky sexual side effects? Gone. Every woman in the place blushed when he cleared their plates. I probably wasn't the only one stuck to the vinyl seat in my booth. Thank God my cock has no voice or it would have been barking like a dog.

But I felt the letdown all the same. He's probably straight. Though he ignored the blushing dames. He seemed even a little annoyed by their attention. But we knew who each other were, the girls and I. I eyed them and they me. Did I look as greedy as them? Like there was one cabbage patch doll left and they'd kill to wrest it from whatever fellow shopper had his or her eye on it. Fact was, we all had holes we wanted his cock in. Simple as that. It was like there was one tree left in the world and the ditches yelped like graves to be the chosen one.

I gulped my food like a scat queen falling off the wagon. Delirious, my diaper soiled, I paid my check and left, one glance over the shoulder to see him bend to pick up a fallen fork. Damn, Clown Daddy had a butt like a stallion. My dog leapt, knocking over the milk dish again. Jesus H. cock-hungry Christ. I lurched out the door as my piss slit opened like a flume on a dam.

Clown Daddy sent me home in a frenzy, is what he did.

I rushed home, needing to get naked. Onto my back on my bed, my legs kicking like an upended insect as I pulled like a madman, again and again, on my slot handle, hitting jackpot after jackpot until my bed was plain lousy with change.

From then on, he filled my nights and days like a cup, brimming over.

I went for more pancakes two days later, but he wasn't there. On the third day, he was, with a beautiful zit on his cheek. Clown Daddy looked right through me when he recognized me, and then he pulled himself back out.

I lurched. Shit—I came again.

"Coffee?"

"Uh, yeah," I half-coughed.

"Cream?"

I nodded. The greed. My shorts were already full of it.

"Sugar?" He's talkative today.

I regained my composure. "No sugar—sugar's for kids," I answered flirtatiously.

I don't know why I said it. I had to say something. I wanted to hold him there, even if for only a few seconds.

He smiled the brightest smile, and walked away.

My head swiveled. What was that? Had he flirted back?

While I waited for my waitress, I read the ads urethaned into the tabletop: vacuum repair, van conversions, derogatory credit, body shops, auto detailing, furniture, appliances, and bail bonds. The clues were everywhere. It occurred to me then that he was the only white busboy in the place. The rest were illegal Latin guys who didn't have a choice. What would a citizen take a job like this for? Maybe he was Rumanian or something. But he had no accent. What could he be making?—four, five bucks an hour? Hell, his looks alone could get him ten doing nothing for the right boss. He could hustle at two hundred an hour, do porn for a few thousand a feature; he could wait tables and fuck up and they'd still forgive him because the doyennes of Sacramento would return for the way he made them feel against their seat cushions. *What* was he doing here?

Who *cares*. Just let me fuck him. Shoot first, ask questions later.

He was as aloof as ever when he came back with the coffee. Three cups later, I asked for sugar. He smiled again. "Sugar's for kids. You like kids?"

"Sure, kids are all right."

He nodded and raised his brows with just a hint of a grin as he said, sort of stoned-like, "Kids are all right." And he walked away.

Go figure. I scribbled my phone number on the coffee coaster, with a little cartoon kid, waving.

And he called. But he never left his name.

"This is the guy who likes kids, down at the Circus. I can't leave a number, but meet me at the Circus at three Wednesday."

I jacked off at 2:30, not wanting to repeat my little Pancake Circus habitual jackpot when I sidled up to shake his hand. My knees might buckle, and then what? Would I hold onto his hand and pull him down with me? Would I beg him to clean up my shorts with his tongue? Would he do it?

I needed to get hold of myself. I turned the key in the dead-bolt as I left the house. I pushed the key in hard, my mouth agape. In and out went the key. I reached for the knob. Good god, I've lost it.

I saw him from two blocks away. He sat on the low wall of the planter that had endured, neglected and falling to pieces with its ratty bushes and weeds, between the sidewalk and the parking lot.

He wore black boots, Levis, and a camouflage winter coat. Not a promising fashion statement for what I had in mind.

He nodded when he saw me coming, but ignored my hand when I put it out to shake. He just said, "What's up?" And then, without waiting for an answer, added, "There's a playground about five blocks from here."

"What?"

"Come on, I'll show you."

I feigned having a clue, but I really didn't have one until it occurred to me he might be suggesting a place to have sex—some doorway maybe, or a clump of trees out of view that schoolyards were notorious for. But it was three P.M., school would still be in session.

I could see the schoolyard fence from a couple blocks away as we approached. Stepping off a curb, he abruptly grabbed my arm by the bicep, and my cock leapt like a Jack Russell terrier.

"Stop here," he stated flatly.

I looked at him inquisitively, at a loss. He dropped his gaze and I followed it as, with his left hand firmly in his pocket, he lifted his pant leg slowly to reveal a plastic contraption surrounding his ankle. A small green light pulsed intermittently. He studied it, then, backing up three feet, got it to stop pulsing and simply glow a constant green.

"This is as far as I can go," he stated, matter-of-factly.

It took me a minute to realize he was under house arrest. What does it mean? I didn't know anything about law enforcement. Drunk driving? It must be some kind of probation. He's probably a rapist or a killer, a thief or a drug dealer. Nah, too cute to rape. But if he's fucked up enough, what would that matter? Too smart to kill. Thieves are a dime a dozen and I'm only carrying twenty bucks. Drug-dealing? Humbug. So what. But none of these possibilities were in any way convincing. He was just too sexy to fit any criminal stereotype, which shows you what a dumbfuck I was.

I may have misread him, but I wasn't completely foolish. Not completely. I knew he was a criminal, so I figured I'd need to find out about the ankle bracelet before taking him home. Just in case he was going to murder me or steal my stereo. The logic of queers. On top of all that, I assumed he'd tell me the truth, which was preposterous—except that he did. More or less.

He retired to a sloping lawn in front of a house on the corner, offering, "This will be fine." I was getting more and more confused. Sex right here?

Within minutes, we heard them: the cacophony of tykes, who were now streaming down the street in gaggles. They reached the far corner, stopped, looked both ways, and then proceeded across. Group after group of them: little Koreans and Viets with rolling book bags, Mexican kids burdened by overstuffed backpacks, white kids on skateboards, little black kids strutting.

"Aren't they beautiful?" he said.

"Sure they are," I concurred. "Kids are like flowers."

"Flowers?" He looked at me like I was stupid.

"You know, those colorful things? New life? All that?" He wasn't buying my poetry.

"I mean beautiful like meat," and he ran his tongue lasciviously across his full upper lip as it occurred to me, amidst my throbbing erection, that he was a pedophile. My cock was like a poised spear now, but not because of what he'd just confessed about his sexual orientation—it was his tongue and what it had just performed. Take me, you beast. I must confess, the moral repugnance was not the first thought that entered my mind, nor the second. The tongue being the first, what followed was my sudden disappointment that not only was I possibly the wrong gender, but I was most definitely not the right age. I hadn't a chance. My cock still reached for him, fighting against the binding of my jeans—not to mention the limits of his orientation—like a child having a tantrum, refusing to let go of a cherished teddy bear. But I felt the sweat on my asshole cool.

He lay back, a sprig of grass in his teeth, smiling at the kids— a pedophile cad. They smiled back. Jesus Wayne Gacy, we were cruising!

I tried to get a foothold. "Uh, would you like to go grab a coffee?"

"Nah, I'm happy right here."

I said nothing more, paralyzed with ineptitude. We sat there for just fifteen minutes, until the herd had passed.

"Damn, I gotta jack off. Come on."

Speaking of come-ons—was this one? I'm not sure I was interested anymore, but of course my cock still was, throbbing like a felon in chains. I followed.

Back to Broadway, to an ugly stucco motel-looking apartment building streaked with rusty drain runoff, its windows curtained and unwelcoming. Clown Daddy said nothing. He simply keyed the lock, and I followed him into one of the saddest apartments I'd ever seen. A mattress lay in the middle of the living room, with a single twisted blanket on it. There was an alarm clock on the floor, and in the kitchen, fast food trash in the sink.

The toilet was foul and ringed with dark grime. There were no pictures, no kitchen utensils, plates, or cups, no toaster, no coffee maker, no books, no phone. Other than the bed and the roof and plumbing, there was but one thing that made the place habitable at all: a TV with a VCR.

He pulled a videocassette out of the back lining of his camouflage hunting jacket and placed it in the VCR. He sat down on the bed, suddenly eager and animated. "I just got this from a dude I met. It better be good; it cost me thirty bucks." There were no credits, no title, not even sound. There were a lot of kids though, doing things that got people put away.

"I think I better go," I muttered, when all at once, with his elbows now supporting him on the bed, he leaned back and yanked his jeans down, revealing an enormous marbled manhood that slapped back across his taut belly like a call to prayer. His eyes fixed on the TV, never even acknowledging his handsome cock as he grabbed it full-fisted. *Jesus God,* I muttered to myself, staring at one of the most stunning penises I'd ever seen: nine inches, wired like the backside of a computer with mouth-watering veinage, and nested in the blackest of hair, which right now was casting deep forested shadows as it worked its way under his well-stocked jumbo-sized scrotum. I never had a choice. It was in my mouth before I made any decisions or even considered whether he wanted it there. He didn't protest, bucking his hips and driving into my whimpering mouth as he glared at the TV set. I shot in my pants without so much as touching myself, just moments before my throat filled like a cream pastry, hot gobs of his God-juice leaking from the crust.

I tongued it clean before he quickly grabbed it like a hammer, or anything else I could have been borrowing, to put it away. He didn't even look at me as he hopped to his feet, yanking up his jeans in one fluid motion. It wasn't fear of intimacy like I'd seen with other guys. He was simply done, and more or less emotionless—in his own world. God knows what he'd been thinking as he bucked his manly juices into my craving body, which for him had become just one big hole to propel his antisocial lusts into. I can't call it my mouth; it was just what was available. I'd have torn my skin back like curtains if it were possible and let him drill through whatever part of me got him off.

"That tape sucked," he casually related. I was still sitting on the bed, stunned, not knowing what to do, licking the remnants of his now-cooling semen off my chapped lips. "I gotta go to work," he informed me, pulling the videocassette out and handing it to me, without making eye contact.

"Uh, I don't want this," I said as my hand opened to accept it.

"No? Don't you like kids?"

"Uh, I think you know what I like."

He said nothing. Then: "Keep it for me 'til next time." And he grinned.

"Next time?" I was in a daze, but hope springs eternal.

"Yeah, next time I see you." I lit up even though I was consumed with dread from what, other than the amazing cock action, was a profoundly depressing social interaction.

"I'll just leave it here," I said, balking.

"No can do, guy. I'm on probation. Can't have that here. Keep it for me."

"Uh, yeah, sure, 'til next time."

I didn't think myself an accomplice as I walked home. What did I know about such legal machinations? I only knew I was no longer depressed and had just had one of life's peak experiences. Had his cock literally trounced thousands of years of science that had eventually developed selective serotonin reuptake inhibitors? Imagine the clinical trials. I'd seen a lot of cocks, a lot of naked men, like any fag. But Jesus H. Priapus Satyriasis, I had never seen such a beautiful manifestation of the male organ anywhere—in print, on film, in my bed, even in my fantasy life, which was no slacker when it came to cock. I imagined what it must have been like for explorers coming upon Yosemite, Victoria Falls, the Grand Canyon. Unimaginable and sublime beauty. I leaned against a wall at one point on the walk home, needing to catch my breath, my cock once again tenting my jeans. The fact of the matter was: I was strung out on his cock. And I didn't even have a phone number.

No matter. He called, thank god. It was either that or I was in for a lot of pancakes.

"I got some more tapes. Wanna come over and check them out?"

I didn't hear any of it but the come over part. "When?"

"Now."

"I'm on my way."

The door was cracked when I arrived. When I opened it to step in, I lost my breath. Splayed across the bed was Clown Daddy, his substantial manhood like the clock tower at some university—everything converged toward it.

"Oh baby," was all I could think to say, which was oddly appropriate considering what was happening on the VCR where his gaze was fixed. My brows furrowed. Good god, they can't be more than three.

"Come to poppa," he said with a fatherly grin.

I was like a panting puppy with the promise of a walk. He held the leash. I leapt and was sucking on his teat like a hungry lamb before you could say baahhh, drooling and lapping up and down the hard shaft, savoring the throbbing gristle of his veins, weeping at the sweet softness of the massive velvety helmet. I was aware of what felt like a tear rolling down my inner thigh. My asshole was sweating like a day laborer short on rent: more baskets, more peaches.

I knew I needed to strip but balked at taking a time-out for fear he'd lose interest or lose control. I hopped up and stripped quickly. He didn't even notice, his eyes locked on the romper room shenanigans stage left like a baby enthralled with a mobile.

I knew all I had to do was get into position, and in no time was on my knees, facing the TV, blocking Clown Daddy's view. He didn't miss a beat as he hopped up on his knees and grabbed my waist, answering my plea for "Lube, Clown Daddy, lube," with a hawk into his palm.

I opened like sunrise, pulled him into me more than he plunged. I heard him as he vanished into my sleeve:

"Uuuuuuuuuuuuuuhhh." And I matched him like a chorus: "Aaaaaaaaaaaaahhhhhh." I dropped my face into the mattress as he pounded me, knowing I'd be unable to maintain any balance with my arms, which not only were shaking with excitement, but were seriously challenged considering the slams he was delivering and the fact that my body's focus was pretty much solely directed at the contractions of my rectum as it greedily grabbed at what can only be described as the bread of life. A baguette of it, no less.

He sent me onto the floor by thrust ten or so, and then he emitted an enormous Josh Hartnett "FUUUUCK," as my asshole filled with his ambrosia.

He pulled out with a *pop* and wiped his cock with the blanket and fell backward onto his back. "That's a great age," he wistfully concluded, staring at the ceiling.

I felt a momentary sinking feeling as I looked at the video monitor, realizing all at once the makeover I would need if I was to hold onto Clown Daddy past the duration of his probation.

"I gotta go to work," he stated. I nodded; I knew the protocol. He popped out the tape and handed it to me. I staggered down the walkway of that shitty apartment building past dried-out cactuses in pots and a pair of roller skates— good God, did his or her parents know who was living next door? What about Megan's Law? I was lost in a strange milieu of overarching lust, revulsion, horror, responsibility, and that unique postfuck feeling of *that was great; everything's gonna be just fine.*

At home, I fumbled through my bathroom drawers for the Flowbee and set to work shaving my body clean of hair.

While my mind remained a stew of anxiety, and I winced at the razor nicks I was inflicting on my balls, I reveled in how I was going to finally incite his lust as he had mine.

Next, I got out my sewing machine and set to work on a new wardrobe: a sailor suit, a Boy Scout uniform, a large diaper, Teletubbie briefs.

I put on the briefs and sailor suit, looked at myself in the mirror. Ridiculous. *Don't be so negative,* I self-talked back. I did a striptease, attempting to be convincing. I worked on my little-boy shy look. But when I finally dropped my trousers and gazed at my hairless cock, I was sorely dismayed. I had a big dick, huge really, and the shaving had only made it look bigger. How am I gonna convince Clown Daddy I'm a child with this thing? How many grade-schoolers are packing eight inches? Then there was my chest and arms. I worked out, for God's sake; I was a mess of secondary sex characteristics. I needed to gain fifty pounds, maybe take some hormones. *One step at a time,* I calmed myself.

I'd done what I could and I wanted to see him, to show him how I'd be whatever he wanted me to be. I don't think at that time I was considering saving him and reforming him. I just wanted to please him, make of myself a gift. Woo him.

Chocolate. I bought a box of Le Petite Ecoliers and went for pancakes. He smiled big when he saw me. The hostess looked askance. The crowd wondered. It occurred to me I was exposing him. I blushed red as a swollen cockhead. I left as quickly as I'd come, racing back up the street. Whatever happened, I didn't want to hurt Clown Daddy. Goodness no, I was interested in his pleasure.

There was a message on the machine when I got home: "Nice suit, hee, hee. Eight P.M. Wear it." Click.

The shirt never came off, as Clown Daddy's maleness hovered over me and he ominously climbed up on top of me, his lead pipe of a cock bobbing like a tank gun, my legs held behind my ears like the spring-loaded pogo stick I would soon be playing the part of as he bounced me off the mattress.

"You look fucking great," he smiled, and he kissed me this time, full, his tongue like a tapeworm, bent on my intestines, determined to reach all the way down to where his cock was reaching from the other end to meet it in a hot sticky mess of saliva and semen.

"Daddy, daddy, daddy," I yelped. We growled, we lost ourselves and rode our dicks like runaway horses. His final thrusts were so divine, my hands digging into his firm white buttcheeks like talons holding their kill. He split me like a piece of wood and my cum hit his chest so hard it bounced and splattered like blood would if the axe of his cock had buried itself in my forehead.

I'd brought the diaper in my backpack.

"Daddy...please...diaper me."

He guffawed, and then with an eagerness I'd never seen, yelped, "Yeeeeaaah!"

He diapered me. Patted my ass. Told me to pack up and get out.

My god, I'd done it. I'd seduced Clown Daddy.

He didn't kiss me good-bye, of course, or invite me to brunch. But I walked away without a videocassette this time. Progress.

I guess that's when it occurred to me I could save him. And maybe not only him. Maybe I'd just found the treatment for pedophilia. God knows, no one seemed to give a damn about these people. The last sexual minority. I could rehabilitate them all. My shaved asshole, a rehab center.

That's when I saw the squad car. Parked in front of my house. Next to the undercover white Crown Royal. Three men in dark suits. It was *The Matrix* and I was Neo, standing on a street corner in a sailor suit, my hips bulging from the diaper that swaddled my manhood.

I knew what they'd found. I knew my chances. I ran. It wasn't much of a chase. I had nowhere to go. All I had was a shot at making it back to Broadway where the great voting public could witness four cops tackling a child—a rather large child, to be sure—in a sailor suit.

I felt the tug as one of them got hold of the back of my shirt just as I reached the intersection of 23rd and Broadway. I screamed as high-piercing a preadolescent scream as I could muster.

I was interrogated at length. I assumed they had Clown Daddy somewhere. How else would they have nabbed me? I drank coffee, got knocked around, but through it all I endured by dreaming of meeting Clown Daddy—when I was finally convicted—in some filthy prison cell where we could pursue our love affair in peace—me trading cigarettes and gum for razors to keep my cock and balls soft as a baby's behind for my Clown Daddy and his meat-Eucharist, truly a transubstantiation of all the misery around us into an Elysian Field of bliss.

"Where did you get the tapes?"

I refused to tell. "I found them."

"Where?"

I had to place them as far away from Clown Daddy as possible. "In a trashcan in Vacaville."

"What were you doing going through trash in Vacaville?"

"Someone on the Internet told me he'd put them there." I was indicting myself. I thought I was saving Clown Daddy. If I had to lie, even to the point of destroying my own future, I'd do it for Clown Daddy—blinded by love, or myopia for his cock. Same difference. And to think I didn't even know the details of his crime. We'd never discussed it. I didn't want to know.

"Who?" The cop demanded, but in a boring, annoying, nonsexual way. Why couldn't Clown Daddy be my interrogator?

"It was one of those throwaway names."

"What was it?"

"Bob."

"Goddammit! Bob who?"

"Bob1 at aol-dot-com."

Whack! And he backhanded me across the face.

They threatened me with a stiff sentence if I didn't give them something. I only considered that their sentence could never be as stiff as Clown Daddy's meaty member, so I was unimpressed by their threats.

They gave me five years.

Clown Daddy did not appear in my cellblock, though I looked and waited and pined. It had been explained in my trial that the videos found in my home had been coded with a tracking device, leading the authorities to my house. Not unlike an ankle bracelet such as Clown Daddy wore. It had even been suggested that Clown Daddy was a narc, or had used me as a patsy. The judge put a stop to those conjectures, admonishing the defense: "Whoever gave him the pornography is not on trial today. Another day. Right now, we're trying this man." And he pointed at me like Clown Daddy's member used to do.

Clown Daddy never appeared. Only Vernon. He was my cellmate, and, as a skinny white fag, he informed me I'd be wise to do his bidding. I've done it, though he lacks both Clown Daddy's girth and length, not to mention all the other characteristics that gods wield over man.

Ah, but the gods are kind for they have blest us with imagination. And so when Vernon slicks his member with Crisco I steal from the commissary and mercilessly impales me, I close my eyes and see a circus tent, and the circus music begins, and all the clowns drop their baggy pants, and then the tigers and lions turn, lifting their tails, and the dwarves and ape men offer up their tight behinds, hands firmly gripped to their ankles—and the crowd cheers, and then goes AAAHHH as Clown Daddy in all his naked huge-dicked grinning Josh Hartnett–throated glory comes swinging through on the trapeze spraying his jism all over the clowns and animals, dwarves and freaks, and the whole damn crowd, who bathe in it as in the blessed waters of Lourdes.

And Vernon is proud. He thinks he's made that mess all over my chest and belly. Let him think it. The truth is hardly important at this point. I'm an innocent man doing time for kiddie porn, the police are fools, Vernon's a chump, and my asshole's just a 7-Eleven that he holds up every Saturday night. As for the cash, I hand it right over. In fact, I leave the register open. No way to run a business. But I, unlike Vernon, am not proud. For I have seen God.

I spend all my time with him. Vernon that is, not God. We even eat pancakes together. I stuff my face. I'm fattening up for Clown Daddy, while Vernon goes on and on with his theories.

"The earth is a plate," he tells me. "Mankind sat down and is eating. When he's through, it'll be over."

"Where are we now?" I ask, bored.

"Somewhere deep in the mashed potatoes; maybe halfway through."

"Are you gay, Vernon?" I like to get a rise out of him.

"Not at all," he explains. He tells me men are pigs, and this is why you can't call him a faggot. Vernon says if it were legal most men he knew (and he knew a certain kind, though he always meant every man) would fuck everything in sight, and what's more, they'd never let their sex partners survive to betray them (as they always will, by his reckoning—something to remember when I get out of here). Therefore, he's of the opinion that men "would drill holes in their sex partner's skulls if they could, and fuck their brains out. They'd drill holes in backs and arms, thighs, through the bottom of feet, right through the front of 'em, core the motherfuckers like apples," he says drolly, "leave them like the dough after all the cookies have been cut out of it. But the screaming would be annoying, so you'd do the brain first."

"Do you like the circus, Vernon?"

He shrugs his shoulders. "I don't like those clowns. Creepy."

"I knew a clown once."

"Shut up and eat."

I pour more syrup on my pancakes and watch it vanish, watch it run away and join the circus.

DOGBOY AND THE BETAGOTH

Nadyalec Hijazi and Ben Blackthorne

"Goddamn," says Ben.

"Goddamn," echoes Alec.

On top of the shitty news that Kerry conceded last night, they've just found out that their high school's mock election voted 99.87 percent for Bush.

"Point thirteen percent. That's pretty much us," says Alec. "Pass me a fucking cigarette, would you? God, I wish I had a beer."

Ben passes him a cigarette. They smoke in grim silence.

"Fuck."

"Fuck."

"Let's move to California. Get out of this fascist fucking state."

"Okay. We can steal your mom's car."

"I hear San Francisco's gorgeous this time

of year," says Ben.

"Really? I hear it rains all the time," says Alec. "But I'd rather have rain than fucking fascists." They contemplate this for a moment. "Well, fucking fascists might be okay. It's the celibate ones you've gotta watch out for. You've gotta watch out for the fucking virgins."

Ben feels his ears heat. He focuses on his cigarette.

Alec warms to his theme. "Fucking virgins. Yeah. The problem is they're all tight-assed repressed little virgins who need to be bent over and fucked senseless. Fucked senseful. Have the sense fucked into them. And I—I'm the man to do it."

Ben has no comment.

"What this state needs is more sodomy," says Alec.

Ben has nothing to add.

To his eternal gratitude, the subject changes to the relative merits of the Yeah Yeah Yeahs and System of a Down.

And then it's time for the pep rally. Ben and Alec walk into the gym, take one look around, and walk back out again. The vice principal in charge of discipline is standing outside the door; he scowls and points. They walk back inside and lurk just within the door.

Alec gets a mischievous look. He waits until nobody's looking, then grabs Ben's hand and drags him under the bleachers.

Above their heads people are stomping their feet and shouting. Here under the bleachers, though, it's dark and weirdly quiet.

Alec finishes rolling a joint and hands it to Ben, chivalrously offering it to him first. Ben takes a hit, wondering where Alec gets his pot. Lately Ben's been giving Alec money to buy pot for them both, but he doesn't know where he's getting it. It's one of the mysteries of being a senior—Alec's not a virgin, he's done it with boys and girls, he always has drugs. He's taller than Ben; Ben has gotten used to tilting his head and looking up at him.

"Good shit," says Ben.

Alec nods and takes a drag.

"Man, fucking George Bush," says Ben. Alec says something and Ben doesn't hear it. More pounding from above. He makes a gesture of lack of understanding, wondering how Alec heard him. He realizes Alec's staring intently at his lips. He feels weird, blushes, realizes that Alec's reading his lips. Focusing on Alec's lips makes him feel even weirder. Or maybe it's the pot.

"Fucking George Bush," he says again, and Alec nods, says, "Fuck him." He can't hear it, but he knows that's what he said. Lip-reading is cool.

Alec passes Ben the joint and he takes another drag. "Fuck all of them."

Ben is starting to get stoned. "Why does everybody want me to fucking want fucking George Bush?" he asks. "I don't want fucking Bush. Fuck. Fucking fuckers."

Alec is smirking at him, eyebrows arched. "You don't fucking want Bush? What do you fucking want, babydoll? Or rather, who? To fuck, that is?"

Ben blushes to the ears.

He's saved when somebody above yells, "Bush!" and the crowd takes it up. Soon everybody's chanting "Bush, Bush, Bush" and stomping. Ben and Alec huddle under the bleachers grimly.

"Fuck all of them, too," he improvises, and Alec grins at

him. Alec has a beautiful mouth. Why has he never noticed that before? It must be the pot.

Alec has kissed boys and girls. Alec's mouth—Alec's mouth has wrapped around guys' cocks. He's told him about it, looking amused while Ben squirmed and tried not to blush. Ben has never even kissed anybody. He feels like he has "Virgin" stamped on his forehead.

Alec is smiling at him, though. Alec doesn't look like he thinks Ben is stupid and uncool. Alec looks like he's happy to be under the bleachers with Ben. Has Alec ever wondered— Fuck, why is he thinking this stuff? It must be the pot. It's not the pot. It's the lip-reading. It's Alec's mouth.

Alec pushes his chin-length pink hair back and takes another drag. His hazel eyes are looking right into Ben's eyes. It makes Ben dizzy. Then Alec puts his hand on Ben's thigh.

Ben freezes, then his whole body gets hot. There's a very long moment while they look at each other, Alec leaning forward, his hand on Ben's thigh. Then Ben puts his hand on top of Alec's.

"Do you want to kiss me?" he says, at the same time that Alec asks, "Do you want a blowjob?"

They're both blushing. Ben's mouth has come open. Alec smiles at him, pushes Ben's dirty hair out of his eyes, and says, "Yes." Slowly, so slowly Ben wonders if he's going to die, Alec leans forward and kisses him.

It's 4:30 P.M. and Ben is in his garage, smoking a blunt and thinking. Or at least trying to think through the pungent smoke. But that's the point, right? Blunting the edges so he doesn't really have to think too hard. Like about that kiss under the bleachers. This thinking business is overrated, he thinks.

Alec is on his way over to spend the night and get wasted. Ben's mother is in L.A. on some spiritual Botox retreat. She was *so* very relieved to hear his little friend was coming over to keep him company, as she's been worried about his "lack of social connections" lately. Been hitting the parenting self-help books along with the pills, he thinks with annoyed indifference. Ben's largely absentee dad died in a rather dramatic plane crash, leaving his working class mother and him an unexpectedly large amount of money that they never knew was there.

Ben still wears secondhand clothes, which largely annoys his recently face-lifted mother.

But back to Alec. A year older, decidedly *not* a virgin, and Ben is just sure Alec was talking disdainfully about him this afternoon under the bleachers. *Fucking tight-assed virgins* was what Alec muttered, having the sense fucked into them. Ben blushes in remembered embarrassment, trying hard to sit stone cool indifferent and not let his own tight-assed virginity show through the smoke and shadows under the bleachers. Alec had to know that today's blitzed-out kiss was Ben's first with anyone.

Ben sits and feels vaguely nervous, anticipating how badly he'll probably botch the evening. He'd been thinking about inviting Alec to stay the night for weeks, since he found out about Mommy Dearest's lipo-yoga extravaganza. He'd gotten his cousin Jim to get a six-pack of Guinness and a bottle of Jack for the evening, and had scored a surprise—a full ounce of sinsemilla. He's been thinking nervous exploration, maybe get Alec fucked enough that they could...Ben's brain shuts down there, since he really doesn't know what it would be like at all. Vivid imaginings and a seeekrit stash of Internet porn's been enough to let Ben know he's interested, and given him a vague sense of how the mechanics are supposed to work, but Ben's nervous, and more than a bit neurotic.

Ben up until now has been fairly oblivious. Vaguely interested in big tits because hey why not, no real luck with the ladies mostly because he finds them terrifying. Pot, porn, video games, and skateboarding had mostly kept him shielded from the existential teen angst, the sorry state of the country, and the life with Mother he otherwise found himself tangled in. Until Alec showed up.

Alec. Half his head shaved, the rest hanging in his eyes and dyed pink. Eyebrow ring under thick-framed glasses, tattoo, and tight black artfully shredded and safety-pinned clothes, always smelling faintly of clove cigarettes, atrocious taste in gothcore. Addicted to CNN and constantly depressed over the state of the universe. Ben met him during detention. Ben had been sullenly listening to music and flipping through an old issue of *Thrasher* when Alec had walked into the room, whipcord thin bad attitude with a twisted sarcastic smile. He sat in the empty seat next to Ben, and began whispering made-up stories about the bitchy cheerleader in the front of the room trying to blow the detention monitor and choking on his nasty dick. They were instant friends from that point on. Ben had never considered his sexuality beyond his own hand before Alec had shown up. Now he couldn't stop thinking about it. Alec was queer, a take-no-shit pansygoth, and told Ben detailed stories about blowjobs in back alleys behind leather bars. Ben figured some of it was probably made-up, and some of it kinda scared him too. But they'd get blitzed together, and Ben liked to just watch Alec's mouth as he told some outrageous story.

And then there was today under the bleachers. One minute bitching about the damn sorry fascist state of their school, the next minute that kiss. And Ben was definitely fucked up when he asked Alec to kiss him, but he thought he might have heard Alec ask him if he could suck his dick. Ben hadn't really gotten around to fantasizing about kissing; mostly he'd fantasized about faceless, genderless mouths or holes for his cock. The reality of a kiss had knocked him on his ass. He was secretly hoping but also terrified at the thought that the blowjob offer was still on the table.

The clock strikes 5:15 and Alec saunters into the living room, letting himself into the house left unlocked for him. Ben, already suffering from damn cottonmouth, finds his mouth goes even drier. Alec stands in front of Ben, duffel over his shoulder, thrashed leather coat, thrashed boots, thrashed jeans, tight Pansy Division shirt and spiky dog collar, sneer firmly in place. Ben's eyes go straight for Alec's crotch, at eye level as Alec looms over Ben on the couch, find their way up to Alec's mouth as Alec says, "Dude, you started without me?" and snatches the bong from Ben's hand. Ben just watches as Alec's cheeks hollow out as he sucks in smoke, a blissed-out look crossing his face as he starts coughing. "Aww, honey, you got me the good stuff," he snarks cheerfully, and plunks himself down on the couch next to Ben. "But what's *up* with the music? Dropkick Murphys is *so* Riverdance." Ben scowls, remembering he'd been listening to "World Full of Hate" because it reminded him of Alec for no good reason. Alec pops in his own CD and they settle into some serious smoking.

"Hey Ben," says Alec abruptly, "I know a way to get even more out of this killer weed. You game?"

Ben looks at Alec suspiciously, says, "What were you thinking, bro?"

"You ever sucked smoke outta someone else's lungs?" That could have been a leer if he wasn't trying not to giggle. Ben blushes and takes a long hit, doesn't say anything. Alec leans in, grabbing Ben by the back of the head, pressing his lips firmly over Ben's, and sucks the air out of Ben's lungs. Ben feels dizzy from the lack of oxygen, dizzy from the proximity, dizzy from Alec's smell and taste. Alec breaks the contact, leaning back and slowly exhaling. He shoots Ben a sly sideways look, and Ben Can't. Stop. Looking. Frozen in a sea of dope and hormones, Ben just watches Alec, mouth slightly open and panting, too scared to move, too turned on to talk.

Alec looks smug as he says, "Ya know, you can touch me if you want. You've been staring at me since I got here. Actually, babydoll, you've been staring at me for the past week." Ben blushes even harder, but musters up enough courage to reach a hand out and brush it across Alec's cheek. Alec's eyes close involuntarily and he sighs, leaning into the timid caress. Ben is afraid to move, afraid not to move, focuses all his attention on the feeling of Alec's smooth cheek under his callused fingers.

Alec takes hold of Ben's hand and sucks two of Ben's fingers into his mouth. Ben's eyes go wider as his breath hitches in his throat. Alec's eyes are open and predatory now as he slowly sucks on Ben's fingers, licking between them, taking them deep into his mouth.

The doorbell breaks the mood for a moment, and Ben gets up to retrieve the pizza. Shoving money at the delivery guy, Ben slams the door shut and watches the pizza box jiggling in his shaking hands. Alec, unflappable as always, takes the pizza from him and is sitting on the floor digging in. Ben grabs a slice and begins eating, appreciating the distraction of food to lighten the tension of the evening. Pizza, being what it is, promptly begins dripping everywhere, and Alec leans over and licks sauce from Ben's chin. "Have mercy, boy!" Ben chokes out, "I swear I need to eat first!" Alec just laughs and looks evil, returning to his own slice. Poor Ben is sweating now, having imagined needing to do far more work to get this level of interest from Alec. He thinks of the beer in the fridge and the porno tapes in his bedroom, and realizes he's totally out of his league, but is definitely not minding the direction the evening has gone.

Pizza done, Ben decides to take his turn at aggressive sex-dude, but finds he has no idea how to be suave the way Alec has been thus far. He does the only thing he knows how to do to get male physical attention, and kicks Alec's foot. Alec raises an unimpressed ringed eyebrow at him, and Ben kicks Alec again. "Um, dude…" Alec begins, and Ben takes a flying leap and tackles him, wrestling him to the ground and knocking his glasses away in the process. "Whoah there, sugarplum, do *not* break those, please." Alec tries, but Ben is already on top of him, pinning Alec's wrists as all of a sudden both boys notice their cocks are hard and pressed against one another. Ben freezes and his eyes go wide as Alec starts cracking up. "You are such a puppydog, Ben, I swear to God. You know you fucking want me. But you're fucking terrified, aren't you?"

"Fuck you," Ben growls and pins Alec's wrists more tightly.

Alec pushes his dick up into Ben's and says, "Yes please? Or are you just going to play Wrestlemania 21 with my arms and pretend your dick isn't trying to dig into my hip?" He leers up at Ben.

"Shut *up*," says Ben.

"Ya know, if you want something from me you just have to ask. Or take it. You are the alphadog, I am the defenseless little betagoth, you've proven that, oh large and muscular one," Alec continues to snark, rubbing his hard dick into Ben. Ben, knowing defeat when he sees it, er, feels it, realizes the only way to get Alec to shut the fuck up is by giving his mouth something better to do than talk.

Ben grabs Alec's head, kissing him awkwardly but insistently, and suddenly Alec's arms are freed. Alec flips them over and resumes some amount of control, kissing Ben and grabbing him closer. They writhe against one another, half making out, half grappling, Alec's fist locked in Ben's long hair, Ben's hands locked on Alec's ass. Clothes begin to fly across the living room and suddenly Ben is in his Scooby boxers and socks, Alec in his black boxer briefs and nipple rings, and Ben has a sudden blinding flash of realization that his cock is being stroked by a hand that isn't his. That fact alone is nearly enough to undo him, but when he looks into Alec's half-closed and suddenly serious eyes, looks at Alec's black-painted fingernails on his cock...he comes with a grunt that is nearly a squeak, drowning in new sensations and gasping for air.

Alec's look of smug satisfaction nearly sets Ben to mouthing off until Alec lifts his cum-soaked hand to his own mouth and begins to lick his fingers clean.

Ben is transfixed, and considers being vaguely grossed out, which for some reason turns him on further. He'll be embarrassed later when he realizes what a quick date he is, but for now he's too stunned at just having had his first sexual experience to feel much of anything besides fuzzy *mmmmm* and wow Alec is *hot*. Bolstered by pot, cum, and pizza, Ben pulls

Alec's boxers off and looks at Alec's dick. "Jesus, *please* don't get shy on me now, dogboy," Alec harrumphs, cock hard and purplish. Alec grabs Ben's hand and puts it on his dick. Ben, being a quick study, holds on and starts to stroke Alec, who begins mouthing off instructions.

Ben says in exasperation, "If I suck your dick will you *shut the fuck up*, please?"

Alec just giggles and says, "That might work."

Ben thinks back on porn stories he's read and begins shimmying down Alec's now-naked body. Alec is leaning up on his elbows, watching Ben. "You don't have the balls to..." Alec starts but then Ben is licking him and Alec's hands grip the carpet under him. Ben does it again for good measure and begins exploring Alec's cock with his tongue. He breathes in Alec's musky crotch smell, memorizing it, recognizing its cadence from other wrestling matches and postpunk shows spent with Alec.

He begins tonguing Alec's balls and around the base of his dick, just to see what Alec's reaction will be. Alec gasps and tucks one arm under his head, the other reaching down to touch Ben's hair. Ben grasps Alec's cock and works the head into his mouth, going down too fast and gagging. Alec sniggers above him and recommends taking it slower. Ben mutters that Alec should shut up and begins sucking in earnest, his pace and technique a clumsy combination of slash fanfic stories, porn tapes, and beginner's luck. Alec begins to breathe faster, bucking up gently into Ben's mouth as Ben sucks and pulls, Alec's balls in his other hand. Alec gasps again and is moaning just a little, mumbling something that sounds suspiciously like "Suck me harder, dogboy," but Ben is past caring what the fuck Alec is saying, as he's in the process of discovering exactly how earnestly hot it is to have another guy's cock in your mouth. His whole self focuses down into his mouth as he sucks for all he's worth, Alec's hand in his hair guiding his rhythm. Alec shouts "I'm coming!" and makes a half-hearted attempt to get out of Ben's way but Ben clings with the tenacity of a barnacle and gets a mouth and chin full of bitter, salty cum for his effort.

The taste surprises him, different from his own taste, and he swallows whatever's made it into his mouth. It's his turn to look smug as Alec collapses bonelessly onto the carpet, panting. Ben climbs up Alec's sweat-sticky body and collapses next to him, panting. "Dude," Alec manages to get out, "you fucking swallowed."

"Um, was that wrong?" asks Ben nervously.

"Hell no, baby, I just wasn't expecting it. It was perfect," Alec reassures him, pulling Ben into a sloppy hug and petting down his back.

The boys doze off for a bit until Ben's stomach wakes him. He wanders up to get a slice of now-cold pizza and looks around the room. Clothes and pot paraphernalia everywhere, a thoroughly debauched gothpunk sleeping nude on the floor, cold pizza, a lamp he didn't remember knocking over on the ground. Ben thinks he can easily get used to this. "Any pizza for me?" Alec asks sleepily from his spot half under the coffee table. Ben brings him a slice and grabs a blanket from the couch, wrapping it around himself. Now that the drugs and the sexhaze have worn off a bit, he's suddenly self-conscious about his body, and begins to feel the first onslaught of neurosis and nerves kicking in. He feels vulnerable without his clothes marking him as a skaterpunk. Naked, he's just a teenage boy, skinny and knock-kneed, with a bit too much chest hair. Alec at least has piercings and tattoos, crazy hair marking him as different even without the clothes. Alec seems to sense that the nerves are kicking in and pulls Ben down next to him, curling into the blanket with him. They switch on the TV and munch on pizza in relative quiet.

"Is this weird?" asks Ben.

"Is what weird?"

"Sitting with a dude eating cold pizza naked and watching hockey?"

"Yes, definitely," answers Alec. "Hockey is weird and I have no idea why you want to watch it." Ben sighs and gives up. Everything about spending time with Alec has always been weird, and sex or something like it has not made things different between them in any significant way. Except for the part where they're naked. And Ben is getting hard again.

On screen a bunch of people are singing "The Star-Spangled Banner."

"Fucking Bush," says Ben. The room fills with gloom; the boys proceed to get significantly more stoned, and decide that the occasion warrants the JD as well.

When Alec starts talking, it sounds like the middle of a conversation. "So I was sucking off this old guy—I thought he was a sexy Daddy type but it turns out he was just old—and he starts telling me how lucky us kids have it today."

Ben is still stuck on the sucking-off part of the story; he has a sudden vivid image of what that would look like and it's hard to pay attention to the rest of the story.

"...fucking Gay Straight Alliance, everybody's afraid to go! Last week it was just me and twelve straight girls who are in love with fucking Morrissey...Fuck Morrissey! He's old! He just needs to get fucked up the ass, fucking celibacy...."

Ben's faded out again, watching the porn video inside his brain featuring Alec getting fucked up the ass, looking back over his shoulder and smirking.

"...so fucking great that sodomy's legal, yeah it's legal if you're fucking old, not like that's even going to last long with George Fucking Bush appointing the Supreme Court...."

Ben's stuck on the word *sodomy*. Less and less oxygen is available to his brain to follow Alec's rant. Between the pot, the booze, and his hard-on, he's pretty much given up on it.

"Fuck fucking George Bush," he says.

"Yeah, that's what I'm saying," says Alec.

"Fucking George Bush isn't here," says Ben with stoned, drunk wisdom.

This shuts Alec up. He studies Ben with a concerned look.

"I am here," says Ben. "My dick is here." He flips up the blanket to demonstrate the presence of his dick.

Alec starts to smile. "Yeah."

Alec suddenly yelps, shouting "Fucking *cats!*" as Ben's cat, FuzzMuffin (Fuzz for short), goes shooting out of the room. Ben starts cracking up. Fuzz has always had a strange fascination with butts, and will lick any exposed skin he can get to. Alec shrugs and mutters like a cat himself, trying to reinstate lost dignity with haughtiness.

Ben just snickers and waits until Alec is sitting down comfortably again before shyly putting an arm around Alec's waist. They start kissing at a more leisurely pace and Ben is definitely thinking he likes boys now as his hand snakes back into Alec's lap. Alec stops him and looks uncomfortably serious for a moment. "Look, I don't want to rush you into anything you don't want to do but ya know if you want to fuck me, I'd be kind of into that I mean I'd be really into it but don't feel like any weird pressure or anything, okay? I mean like I brought condoms but not because I was like really expecting, I mean...."

Ben puts a hand on Alec's arm and his eyes glaze over a bit. "You actually want me to fuck you? I mean, is it okay if I fuck you, please? Like I mean you'll actually let me fuck you like for real like you know um...whoa...."

Alec looks confused for a minute. "Um. Yes. I want you to fuck me."

"Does it hurt?" Ben blurts out.

Alec starts snickering, and throws an arm over his forehead, consumptive heroine style. "It's a dirty job but someone's got to do it...."

"And you'll be okay that this is like my first time with a guy and...I mean not like it's my first time of anything you know but I mean, um...." Ben begins, realizing he's blowing his cover as a cool and collected, sexually mature, and experienced kind of a guy.

"Baby, I know you haven't been with a guy before and that's totally fine with me," Alec reassures him. "I'll talk you through it," he says, looking distinctly evil and pulling his duffel closer.

"Oh god, here we go with the talking," mutters Ben, but by then Alec is chewing on his neck and he doesn't say much else for a while. Ben mumbles, "So I heard it's like easier for you if you come first, right?"

Alec snickers again and says, "There is no right way to do this, puppy. Just turn me on first." Ben looks bashful but earnest as he continues to hold and lick and pet Alec everywhere he can reach. Alec rolls over, rubbing his ass across Ben's torso and settling down on the floor. Faced with Alec's ass,

Ben is mesmerized and terrified. He has no idea what to do. Tentatively, he pats it.

Alec looks over his shoulder and laughs. "Jumping Jesus on a pogo stick—it's not rocket science. Fuck me, already!" He takes on a tone of exaggerated patience. "Get your finger wet, stick it in, wriggle it around. Get another finger wet, stick them both in, wriggle them both around. Get your cock wet—" to Ben's horror he starts to sing, shaking his ass all the while. "You stick your cock right in, you take your cock right out, you stick your cock right in and you shake it all about—"

To shut him up, Ben stuffs most of his hand into Alec's mouth. Which mostly seems to stop the singing, but Alec's uncontrollable laughter is beginning to piss Ben off. Ben decides to try and get the show on the road, and replaces the hand in Alec's mouth with his boxer shorts, which Alec seems to enjoy in a way that Ben finds vaguely disturbing.

He tentatively begins stroking Alec's ass, running a finger down his crack. Alec moans and shudders. Ben begins rubbing both hands down Alec's back, up his thighs, across his ass, and slowly begins licking up from the back of Alec's knees. "Shit, you are *not* going to actually rim me, are you? Hot damn, where did I find a beginner with totally no inhibitions!" Alec shouts, pulling the boxers he'd been sucking on out of his mouth and startling Ben.

"Um, well...er..." Ben begins.

"Please, you don't talk, baby, just keep doing whatever it is you decided you want to do back there." Ben continues his timid explorations upward with his tongue, delicately separating Alec's asscheeks and running his tongue experimentally down Alec's crack. Alec is panting now, his cock hard and drooling on the carpet as he lifts his ass into the air. Ben begins licking more vigorously, finding Alec's ass smells similarly musky to his cock and it isn't gross at all, just soft skin stretched across hard ridged muscles. He begins pumping Alec's cock with his hand while tonguing Alec's ass, surprising himself yet again with how incredibly hot he is finding being in the driver's seat. He feels it in his own cock every time Alec moans. "Are we there yet?" Ben asks in a hopeful-sounding voice.

"Okay, no, seriously, we're going to start with some basic ass-structions. First off, this here is lube. Put some on your finger and work it into me, okay?" Alec hands Ben a tube of something clear and slippery.

Ben gently begins pushing a finger into Alec, and is instantly struck with how hot and *tight* Alec is. Some instinct keeps Ben's other hand pumping Alec's cock as he works a first finger into Alec's body. Alec's ass clenches closed, then relaxes and Ben is inside. He adds more lube to his hand and starts working on a second finger, feeling around the hard muscles inside Alec's ass. "Wow, your ass is amazing!" Ben blurts out and instantly feels foolish as Alec loses it, laughing.

"Only you, puppy...only you..." he gasps through hysterics. Ben decides to get back at Alec by pushing a third finger in and out, working Alec's ass rhythmically, faster and harder. This successfully gets Alec to stop laughing as now he's moaning in time to the movement of Ben's hand.

"Can I fuck you yet?" Ben asks, trying to sound sexy and hoping he doesn't sound too whiny. Sexy seems to have worked, or at least Alec is too horny to care about whiny at this point, as he moans out, "Yes, please, now would be a good time." Ben gently takes his fingers out of Alec's ass and

Alec moans at the loss. Ben fumbles with the condom wrapper and finally Alec turns around and puts the condom on Ben for him, sucking Ben through the condom to help things along. Alec gets back on his knees, pulling a pillow off the couch to put under his stomach as Ben starts running his dick up and down Alec's ass.

"Put some lube on that dick of yours, please dear," Alec chirps over his shoulder. Ben drizzles cold lube onto Alec's ass just to be spiteful and rubs his cock in it, teasing Alec's ass with his cockhead. Alec is moaning again and pushing back insistently, so Ben grabs Alec's ass in one hand and his cock in the other and begins to push in slowly.

Alec goes completely still, as his body adjusts to the intrusion, and whispers, "Slowly." Ben freezes, cockhead just inside Alec, as he watches Alec's face in profile, eyes and lips squeezed shut. Suddenly Alec takes a deep breath and Ben slides inside, and the heat and tightness hit him like a train. He's never felt anything like this, the strong rings of muscle inside Alec's body gripping him, surrounding him in tight heat, and now it's Ben who's gasping, gripping Alec's body with both hands as he begins begging Alec to let him move.

Alec pushes back in response and Ben begins to fuck in earnest, trying for gentle at first so as not to hurt Alec but losing himself in the heat and rhythm and wet slapping against his thighs as he thinks that he wants to fuck Alec for the rest of eternity, or at least through the next four years of not thinking about politics. And the speed is increasing, and they're both sweating and swearing and moaning and grunting and Ben notices almost from what feels like a far distance the sound of his own voice chanting something about Alec's ass being the hottest thing in the world and wanting to fuck him forever and Alec is almost screaming as Ben pounds into him and he realizes that this is like riding a bike and kinda like coming home and he's awed by the intimacy of his dick in his best friend's ass and finally Alec starts coming in spurts, clenching his ass hard around Ben's cock. And Ben is coming from Alec's coming, shuddering internal muscles milking the cum right out of him and Ben thinks he's retiring his hand and moving into Alec's ass full time and the world goes tilted and he thinks maybe he's passing out.

And he's lying on top of Alec and they're both sweaty and cum-soaked and exhausted. He pulls out of Alec's still hot, still tight ass, trying to hold the base of the condom like he remembers someone telling him he's supposed to, slips it off and slaps it onto Alec's thigh just to be a brat, and unceremoniously falls asleep sprawled on top of Alec. Alec wrestles himself out from under Ben at some point and manages to grab pillows and blankets on his way back from the bathroom, and tucks back in with Ben on the floor of the living room. And they stay that way until well into the late morning.

Alec wakes up first. He looks over at the sleeping skatepunk curled up next to him and gets hit by a wave of...something. Ben looks ridiculously angelic—face gone innocent in sleep. He doesn't look capable of last night's sexcapades.

Alec has never really been able to figure Ben out. He keeps expecting Ben to freak, but it hasn't happened yet. Alec keeps falling into his defensive hostile-flirtation thing, and Ben keeps surprising him by accepting it all. Nothing seems to faze him.

The boy is tough and cool and keeps showing up with butch injuries from stupid skateboarding tricks; he'd puke to hear himself described this way, but he's sweet. He's got this openness—this friendliness beneath the sarcasm—he's no more afraid of fags than he is of breaking his arm again riding his skateboard down the high school staircase railing.

He's a sweet little daredevil and I'm his latest skateboarding stunt, thinks Alec. Did he really fuck Alec last night? Did Alec push him too far? Is he going to freak out and never talk to Alec again? It wouldn't be Alec's first time. Alec nuzzles into Ben's neck for a moment, Ben mumbles sleepily and throws an arm around Alec's neck. Alec catches himself getting maudlin. Fuck that—if Ben never speaks to Alec again, then Alec had better make it worth it. He smirks, thinking of the one thing that they didn't do last night.... Ben has not yet experienced one of Alec's world-famous blowjobs.

Slowly, so as not to wake the sleeping former virgin, Alec ducks beneath Ben's arm and starts to make his way down Ben's body. He stops at Ben's armpit, deeply inhaling the musky clean scent of sleepy boy. Then he licks his way over to Ben's left nipple. A couple of circles with his tongue and it's sticking up; Ben moans and Alec's suddenly worried that he won't be able to complete his mission before Ben wakes up. Deciding not to waste any more time, he wiggles his way farther south and notices that Ben is already starting to get hard in his sleep. In porn movies guys always wake up hard. Alec doesn't usually, but he's fascinated to see that Ben might.

He gently lifts Ben's cock in his hand and begins licking long comforting strokes from balls to tip, ice cream cone style. Ben starts to breathe more heavily and Alec is suspecting that Ben may be climbing his way up to consciousness. Alec has a moment of self-deprecating panic, wondering who Ben is dreaming about, and glances quickly at Ben's face, still relaxed in the closed-eye lines of sleep. He licks some more, beginning to trace smaller circles around the head of Ben's cock. Ben's weight in Alec's hand, Alec's mouth speaks to Alec of ownership; he can let himself imagine in this perfect quiet Saturday morning moment that this will last forever. Pushing back the maudlin thoughts threatening to kill his good mood, he goes to work for real, sucking harder and stroking Ben's balls, lightly squeezing the base of his cock. He starts to suck more intently, and Ben is fully hard now, ass flexing in an effort to thrust and stay still at the same time. Alec smiles around Ben's thickening cock, feeling his rhythm, knowing that this at least is something he's undeniably good at.

He falls into the rhythm of some song he can't quite remember. How does it go? Something about walking hand in glove, with people staring...wait, wait, he's got part of it. "And if the people stare then the people stare, I really don't know and I really don't care..."

And then there's a bit about probably never seeing you again. What is that song, anyway?

Agh! It's Morrissey! He almost spits out Ben's cock in his horror. But Ben is bucking fiercely into his open mouth and he's too far in to stop, and he notices Ben's moans are more like shouts through the musical nightmare in his head. Ben's coming in his mouth and he looks up and sees Ben's brown eyes locked on him, hands in his hair gripping painfully hard. Ben pulls Alec up by the hair and kisses him as if he wants to swallow him whole, wrapping arms and legs around Alec like some puppydog octopus and Alec realizes he's not going anywhere for a while. Alec realizes Ben is babbling into his shoulder and can only make out a few phrases here and there, "...fucking my dick is in love with you, man...moving into your ass full time…retiring my hand…fucking tidal wave of skaters pouring out onto the street…gahhh….” Alec pats him sympathetically with a sappy grin that he's glad Ben can't see, remembering the way he felt after getting his first blowjob. He's thinking maybe Ben isn't gonna jet after all.

In the background the telephone rings. The machine answers, and it's Ben's fascist grandmother calling from Lake Jackson, Texas. “Hi Franny,” she says, “I'm just calling to see how you're doing. I know that in your misguided Godless way you're probably not excited about the election, but I want you to know that Jesus loves you and we're in for four more wonderful years. Call me.”

Alec pulls away from Ben and hides his head under a pillow. “How am I going to live through the next four years?” he moans, voice muffled by high-quality down.

Ben pulls the pillow off and gives another sloppy kiss. “Every time you hear the word *Jesus*,” he says, “you have to stop whatever you're doing, come find me, and suck my dick.”

Alec starts to smile. “And whenever you hear the word *nucular*, you have to come find me and fuck me like you did last night. Deal?”

“Deal.”

They shake on it.

“…so…” Ben leers, “nucular Jesus?”

FROM
WHAT WE DO IS SECRET

Thorn Kief Hillsbery

*May, 1981, the dawn of the Reagan era and
the beginning of twilight for the hardcore L.A.
punk scene that has provided the only family a fourteen-year-old throwaway kid named
Rockets has ever known. It's six months after
the suicide of his onetime lover Darby Crash,
leader of the legendary band The Germs, and
Rockets is roaming the streets of Hollywood
with Blitzer, another teenage punk who sometimes shares his squatting space in a forgotten
corner of the Jell-O factory just off Santa Mon-
ica Boulevard. They're looking to finance an
escape from Los Angeles, and Blitzer has lined
up prospective bankers in Tim and David, two
gay men from Minnesota on their first visit to
Hollywood after piloting a van filled with popcorn and cosmetics to the Coca-Cola Museum*

in Atlanta, Georgia. Blitzer's plan is to stimulate Tim and David's generosity by feeding them LSD, and after leaving them in the temporary care of Squid and Siouxsie—two punked-out lesbian hookers—Blitzer and Rockets head for the Spotlite hustler bar on Selma Avenue, where they find a trick to earn cash for the drug buy.

Bill's house can't be any farther than the Jell-O factory, just a pricier direction, but Blitzer gets him to spring for a cab by saying I'm meeting my new girlfriend for some underage clubbing action at eleven, and otherwise I'll keep her waiting at Crossroads of the World all by her girlie lonesome. He asks me her name, just being polite I guess, and Blitzer slides me a side of elbow, we're all in the backseat and he's in the middle.

"Nancy."

Blitzer has to cough for laugh camo, and I wonder what his name's supposed to be, and what's up with the AKA action anyways, our names are mostly all made up in the first place, and second and third place too for some of us. Darby went by Bobby Pyn for starters, and then Richie Dagger before he wrote "Circle One" and settled on Darby Crash. Though Siouxsie's comes from the nonfiction list, jacked from Siouxsie Sioux of Siouxsie and the Banshees.

Bill says he doesn't get out on the town as much as he might wish. He's got this way of talking that reminds me of English accents, respectable ones, though without the sound of the accent itself. It's hard to describe. Suave, you might call it. When he pays the fare he says to the cabbie, "And a very pleasant evening to you," like he's cruising into Opera Central in a tux with a babe in a Lucille ball gown on his arm instead of heading for the Betamax and the California king with a pair of punk rock rent boys in tow.

The cabbie just grunts. He picked us up on Selma, after all. I wonder what he thinks we'll do with Bill.

Work him over with our studded belts?

Pee on him in his bathtub?

Force-feed him Milk-Bones?

Those are all Stickboy stories. I've never done anything like that. The closest was last year staying at Skinhead Manor by Hollywood High. It was right after Sham 69 played the Whisky and we all had shaved heads and combat boots, and that jerk Eugene who's in *The Decline* started scoring tricks with Jews and minorities who'd get the kinks out through abuse by skinheads, mostly just verbal, though. And I got in on that sometimes, they'd pay extra for a crew of us, I thought it would be creepy-Crowley, but basically it was Live from New York it's Saturday Night. None of us were even prejudiced, the Stern brothers who rented the house were Jews themselves, so we had to really work it to be all hard and mean, though as long as it stayed at name-calling level with backup spitting now and then we definitely conned the vinces, we got lots of repeats.

But this one black dude tried to get us telling darky jokes and no one even knew any. So he ended up flowing us these astronaut ones himself, with punch lines like "janitor in a drum" and "the jig is up." Then to stay dry any refund demands we made up a song on the spot with Animal Cracker on guitar and Stickboy on bass called "I Hate Niggers," and that was such a hit we did an encore later for this big-time Holocaust movie producer, "Anne Frank Was a Bitch."

It turns out Bill's trip is more like the opposite, after we jam up the walk and he goes inside and closes the door while Blitzer runs it down for me, standing on the porch. But I don't know about "fully" nonsexual, I'll be stripping down to my shorts at least and our buddy Bill will be choking his cheetah like the night before the world's end as long as I stick to the script.

And as long as he does.

So I ask Blitzer why he can't go in too, I mean, how fun, being in a strange house almost naked with a stranger alone in his bedroom.

"He wants one on one. I'll be right here. I told him not to lock the door. If he tries anything weird, just yell."

He reaches for the doorknocker, but I grab his hand.

"Just go in with me, okay? Walk me back to the room."

"What hey, sure. We gotta move, though. You ready?"

"Wait. You didn't tell me. Do I have to get a hard-on?"

"No!"

"And what's your name supposed to be?"

He hiccup-laughs.

"Guess."

With Sid and Nancy taken, I say Johnny as in Rotten.

"Nope."

Then he sings, *I came into this world, like a puzzled panther, waiting to be caged—*

So he's Darby.

Not Crash, though.

"O'Toole," he says, and hiccup-laughs twice, in time with the knocker.

The house smells like lemon furniture polish and jasmine coming in through open windows. No sign of any dogs. Walking down the straight-shot hallway to the bedroom Bill says something about his lover who died. Blitzer says a friend of ours died a few months ago. Bill says we have his deepest sympathy. In the bedroom he lights a scented candle while I settle down on the end of the mattress.

"Have fun," Blitzer says.

Bill shuts the door and says, "Please make yourself comfortable, Sid."

Blitzer's Hermans fade stomping down the hall, and I get a little panicked.

"I want you to feel at home."

That's the hint to show some skin, Blitzer said. So I hunch over and unlace my boots. Then peeling off my jeans I feel in my pocket the folded bills from the feet-ure presentation earlier. Which reminds me of the first rule of hustling, the rule you never break.

Money up front.

Everybody knows that.

But I can't ask him. Not now. I never thought I'd be this spooked. I don't know what to do with my jeans, so I drop them on the floor. I pull off my socks. I wonder what the fuck is wrong with my feet. Why didn't that dude like them?

I sit back up and Bill puts a little pinner joint in my hand. He lights it for me. And it's some raspy shit, it tastes fuckin' awful, but I'm grateful, maybe it'll calm me down. I try to pass it back, and he says, "It's all for you."

So I burn it down while Bill gets comfortable too. He says his dressing gown is silk from Thailand.

"Thailand's a wonderful country, Sid. I think you'd like it there."

Before I remember I'm supposed to be part French I tell him I've never even been to Tijuana and he makes this *tsking* sound and says my whole life's ahead of me and he's sure I'll make something of myself.

Though he doesn't say what.

He's sitting on the end of the mattress too but he swings his legs up and moves closer. He asks if I'd like to take off my shirt.

"Okay."

"Could you use some help with that?"

"Sure."

I raise my arms and he leans in close and pulls my T-shirt up from the bottom. His head follows it and he's breathing in deep from like a weenus-length away. He's wearing some kind of hair cream that smells like walnuts. When the shirt's up past my armpits and covering my face he stops pulling for a moment and my blood runs Slurpee cold thinking *Strangler! Strangler!* and what harsher way than with my own fuckin' shirt. But he's just sniffing me, and I guess I make the grade, because once my Sid Sings is balled on the carpet he fires me another pinner and lets me know he wants me stretched out on the bed while I smoke it, stretched out just so, my chin propped up on one hand, one knee bent out toward him, my foot tucked under my ankle.

Those goddamn ugly feet again.

"And, Sid?"

"Yeah?"

"If you'd arrange yourself down there so you're angling out?"

I reach inside my boxers.

"Ah. Perfect." He takes a deep slow shuddery breath. "Christ, you're lovely. Another young stallion. You Frenchmen."

So he really thinks I'm French, then. Fuck, these guys will believe anything. But I suck on the joint and I start liking the thought of being French like Kickboy, liking it a lot, actually, there's no bigger smartass in the scene, he's wicked ranking.

"I can see you enjoy being watched, Sid."

He scoots even closer.

"Don't you?"

Blitzer said to tell him what he wants to hear.

"Yeah, I do."

"Then we've got something in common, you and me. Because I like being watched, too. Oh, yes. Not because I'm young and beautiful and—virile. Like you. But for—other reasons."

He's breathing harder now, and waiting, and I have no fuckin' clue what to say.

"Would you like to watch me, Sid?"

In theory or in practice?

Or sitting on a cactus?

Jesus.

But Blitzer said just stick to the script. And that must be what he does too.

"Fully. I mean, yeah, I'm looking forward to it."

"Then we're going to have fun tonight, aren't we? Because I like being watched, and you like being watched, and I'll be watching you while you watch me. Doesn't that sound fun?"

"It sounds great."

"All right then. I'm going to play a videotape for us. And while I'm seeing to the machine, I'd like to ask a favor of you. May I?"

"Sure."

"Once my back is turned, I'd like you to remove your undershorts.

So when I settle back down beside you, and the tape begins to play, I'll be seeing you in a new way, just as you'll be seeing me in a new way."

I just push my shades up the bridge of my nose and nod. What-fuckin'-ever. Talk about Fantasyland. Then he sits up and maxes the Beta and next thing you know it's Showtime.

The Merv Griffin Show.

"Here today live from Hollywood with Charo and Charles Nelson Reilly, and welcoming after a word from our sponsor, Bill McDaniel, Dog Groomer to the Stars."

And from now on I do the talking.

"That's you?"

"On *Merv Griffin!*"

"Whoa!"

"Dude, you're a star!"

"You know Bo Derek?"

"Personally?"

"Robert De Niro?"

"Stallone?"

"Damn, I want your autograph!"

"That Charo chick sounds a little sweet on you, buddy."

"Who the fuck wrote your lines for you, I bet it was Chevy, wasn't it?"

"You just thought 'em up?"

"No way!"

"Zsa-Zsa's poodle?"

"Bob Hope's bulldog?"

"Angelyne's whippet?"

"Those guys in Vegas get paid millions for shit like this!"

"Man, Merv is bumming."

"Seriously!"

"You're getting all the laughs!"

"You've got them eating from the palm of your hand!"

"You're funnier than Merv!"

"You should get your own show!"

(Oh most defiantly, not a turd, not a plane, not a tumor or a rumor, it's Here Comes the Groomer! Exclusively on Pay-Perve-View!)

"I mean it, man!"

"Hell fuckin na!"

"Can we watch this again?"

The magic words, Blitzer said, so magic they're tragic, the Everest of octane for the groomin' machine. Because once you know how the tape goes you can time your chatter so it sends him summitwards then and there, and you don't have to sit through the whole goddamn thing twice. But Blitzer told me going into it cold I'd have to live with the rewind, and it's maybe six minutes max so it isn't that bad, since I basically just say what I said before, it doesn't matter if it's word for word, in fact it's better if it is.

The only thing is, about halfway through round two I'm feeling gut-bombed, I guess it's the mix of the nast pot with the smells of the candle and his hair oil and the lotion he's using, and I want to ask him to crack the window more, but Blitzer schooled me hard on facing the screen and talking him up all the way through, nonstop, so even when sweat beads break out on my forehead and this sour spit rises up the back of my throat I keep the Hollywood babble on, and with him panting next to me faster faster faster at least I know we're in the home stretch. Then right after I say he's funnier than Nerve Stiffen'll ever be his free hand vise-grips the back of my neck and pulls my head down towards his crotch while he gasps out "Fondle my balls!" in this strangled wheezy voice and Christ on a cream puff, Madonna on a mattress, I can't help it, I can't hold it, I puke.

All over him.

Right at the magic moment.

No!

Punk rock!

Oki Dog and fries!

He jumps up. Though he doesn't hit me or yell or anything. He must be in shock, I know I would be.

Actually I guess I am. He jams for the bathroom and as soon as I hear water running I start flailing for my clothes to bail as fast as I can before he's finished washing. But hanging my head down lacing my boots I just fuckin' break down, why didn't I up-front him, he'll never pay now, I haven't cried since Darby died but it makes me want to end it all, why can't he live in a condo up high so I can take a dive?

Into Swan Lake.

AKA Death Disco.

I can't face Blitzer.

I can't even face the Dog Groomer to the Stars.

But here he is, welcoming after a word with his wanker, handing me a warm wet towel. I start sniffling out *sorries* but no no no.

"I should be ashamed of myself, giving a drug like that to a boy your age."

"Weed?"

"Heroin."

"Heroin?"

"With the marijuana. You've never done it before, have you?"

"No."

"It makes you sick, the first time. I'm so sorry."

"It's me who's sorry, man. I ruined every—"

"You didn't ruin anything, Sid. You were fine."

He puts two bills in my hand, and a business card. He pats my shoulder.

"You said all the right things."

Tim and David's room is one door down and isn't that amazing smells like popcorn popcorn popcorn and what kind of perfume, Squid wants to know.

" 'Promise her anything,' " Tim sings out. " 'But give her Arpège.' "

"My mama wore that," Squid says. "I'd recognize it anywhere."

She actually has a family that she remembers, and they even sent her a present through Greyhound will-call for her birthday. A dress. Or "sundress" according to Squid. She ended up giving it to Su Tissue of Suburban Lawns, who wore it onstage. Later I heard Kickboy wrote up the gig for *Slash* and said more about the dress than the band.

While we're settling onto the bed and around it on the matted shag carpet David offers us Cokes and I ask if there's Pepsi, not thinking. Everybody laughs but me, and it takes a while, but finally I get the joke. I know one thing though, if I was them I'd have made the switch by now. I'd have switched right there in Atlanta. That fuckin' museum wouldn't even let them in for free.

I don't say anything though. I'm sitting at the foot of the bed, legs stretched out on the carpet, leaning back against the mattress with the cardboard carrier box for the mice in my lap. I feel them scratching around in there, scratching around in the dark.

Tim asks Blitzer about the studs on the shoulders of his leather, the swirly ones.

"They're called chocolate chips. They're from London. This was Darby's jacket. He put them on last year, when he went to England."

It was just a year ago. Right at this time. A year exactly. I remember listening on KROQ to the long-distance interview he did with Rodney. Nobody over there knew who Darby was. He carried the *G.I.* record around under his arm and played it for people.

They all thought it was too fast.

Darby said.

Anybody that wants to get in touch with me can get in touch with me, like, through Michelle. Like, if Rory wants to get in touch with me, or Blitzer, or Rockets, or Tony, if he could get in touch with me before he goes to jail.

And how ranking was that, Darby naming us on the radio to all those jacks and all those jills? Especially since it wasn't that long after Michelle stood in for Tony in that scene for *The Decline.*

Though actually she stood in for Rory Dolores, if you want the whole and nothing but. After Darby decided Tony would make him look bad, he asked Rory to do it instead, and I was over there when Tony found out. Tony laughed at Darby and said, "Oh, you don't want me to be in it, but you want this blond-haired freak to be in it? Not only are you gonna look just as gay as if I was in it, but you're gonna look like a gay dude with a hideous, acne-scarred freak for a boyfriend!" And Tony he actually listened to sometimes, so then he asked

Michelle. But just a few weeks later Darby was namechecking his boys on *Rodney on the Roq*. So maybe it finally hit him.

That you can't keep a secret that isn't one anyways.

David starts station-surfing the radio for punker mood music, and Siouxsie tells him he's wasting his time, real punk isn't played on the radio.

"Really?" Tim says. "But how do you know who the stars are?"

At first we shop-talk Poseur and Vinyl Fetish and Zed Records, then scene-check back in the day at the Masque and the Starwood and Blackie's and the Hong Kong Café till finally Siouxsie says the magic words.

"We know who they are because we know them personally."

And you don't need the Amazing Kreskin to read their minds, if they can't be stars themselves, why not settle for knowing some?

Hell.

Fuckin'.

Na.

Goodbye Judy, hello Darby.

It's 1980, can't you afford a fuckin' haircut?

Only *The Decline* was last year, so they don't just want haircuts, they want this year's model, they want Atlantic Blue like Siouxsie, On Fire Fuchsia like Squid.

"And that boy next door," Tim says. "What were the streaks?"

"Aubergine," Siouxsie says.

"And platinum! I loved his look."

"Among other things," Blitzer mutters. He starts massaging my shoulders.

"Well, it's best to dye—" Squid says, then laughs and tells Tim and David it must be catching, she hopes it isn't terminal, their "to-die" disease.

"Anyway, darlin's, you want to color before you cut, if you really want to color. Poseur's fully stocked, and they're still open."

David asks how far it is.

"Within walking," Squid says.

And Tim's boots, rumor has it, are made for just that.

"So that's just what they'll do!"

After the briefest little visit to the powder room.

When he's finished powdering whatever he powders Blitzer asks if they mind if him and me just kick it here. And Tim and David don't mind at all. Or so they say. From the way they say it I bet they mind, all right. They mind not being here to watch. Blitzer follows them doorwards, though he doesn't lock it behind them, just stands there waiting then walks out too. He's back in three or four. He locks the deadbolt and starts searching the closet. I ask where he went.

"Next door."

"Why?"

"I left something."

"Did you do anything mean to Rory?"

He says he channel-surfed the TV to a showing of a movie called *Shaft*. What hey, how fuckin' appropriate. And how spun is Rory's whirled tonight, anyways? There's the open door policy, what the fuck is up with that? Then there's the deal with his boots. He couldn't get his clothes off and keep his boots on, so he must have put them back on. Maybe for the trick, and whatever his sick little trip was. Or is.

I say maybe Rory was wasted and decided to leave when

the trick went down for the count and he got his boots laced then remembered he was naked and just thought *Fuck it* and passed out cold.

Blitzer laughs and says any which ways we couldn't have planned it better ourselves, getting T and D all riled over Rotten Rory.

"How's that?"

"Because they're thinking one thing right now, and one thing only, we can get them in the groove and hook them up with dudes like Rory."

"But they can't be punks, Blitzer. They're way too big of fags."

"We know that, but they don't. They think the whole scene's one big homo clusterfuck, based on what they've seen."

"But sooner or later—"

"They'll figure it out. Right now they're Silly Putty in our hands. We get 'em frying and point 'em at some punk boys and they'll forget everything, their room, their van, they'll forget—"

What hey.

He shakes something, muffled inside metal.

How fuckin' clever.

He takes a sudden whistling breath.

How fuckin' fuckin' clever.

Traveler's checks in the fake Coke can that's mixed in with the real ones on the shelf in the closet.

Three thousand dollars in traveler's checks.

Three thousand dollars in UNSIGNED traveler's checks.

Not so fuckin' clever.

Just fuckin' fuckin' ranking cool.

He dives on the bed and drops his head down over the edge by mine, then huggy-bears me with his arms and pulls me onto the mattress. He kisses the back of my neck.

"It's the real thing, Rocketman."

I'm still sitting facing away, with Blitzer on his knees behind me. He smells like leather and cloves. He links his fingers in mine and raises my arms over my head.

And who do I think of?

The Dog Groomer to the Stars.

How fuckin' romantic.

He pulls his Circle One up over my head.

But not like you know who.

Faster.

I try to smell myself.

Neutral, I guess. Not bad. A little like Jell-O.

His hands don't shake.

He doesn't hold the shirt with all his fingers so none touch my skin.

His fingers touch me.

Everywhere.

Too gently.

He drops the shirt on the bed.

"Something's wrong," he says. "Tell me what it is."

He moves out from behind me and presses me down on my back on the mattress with his hand on my chest.

"Talk to me, Rocketman."

His fingers.

"They can get those checks replaced?"

Loosen my belt.

"That's why they're traveler's checks."

Work my top button open.

"What's up with V-13, anyways?"

Pop my fly buttons.

"I snaked them for a little Desoxyn, like a quarter, but somebody else snaked them for a lot, like a roll. They must have mixed us up. It's like mistaken identity. Pretty soon they'll figure it out."

Tug my jeans and shorts.

"Is there a scene in Idaho?"

Pull them down my hips.

"If there isn't we'll make one."

His fingers fingers fingers.

Move to where to there and then to.

There.

Too gently.

Lips follow, circle check, left nipple, circle check, right nipple, lips follow, singing.

Sex Pistols.

"Submission."

I'm on a submarine mission for you, baby.

Lips follow, circle check, belly button, lips follow, singing.

I can't get enough of your watery—

Drown, drown, down, down, hands follow, his, lifting me, legs follow, mine, lips follow, his, circle check.

There.

Not gently.

Yes.

Darby said.

And you can swim, and it's so great 'cause it's dark, you know, and you can just swim and it doesn't matter if you live or die or anything.

And it's dark, and it hurts, and I'm yes. The poison in the, yes. The future, yes. What I can't tell, yes. The look on my face, if I could only, yes. I know and I can and I wonder, sex boy, was I ever, the slave, am I still, uncontaminated?

All this started with words from songs.

LIZARD KILLING

July Shark

I have to lie on top of him in the hideout up
under the kudzu. I caught the lizard on a fence-
post coming over here. Now it is pinned in
between us and the drying blood sticky around
it. Hard to keep it pressed there to where it
can't squirm loose but to where it won't get
crushed dead either. I have to grab onto his
hands the way we decided it would work and
shove our palms together around the rocks.
Can smell the dark, viney dirt that ices and
thaws but has never got sun to dry it out all
the way, that scuffs into little clotted balls but
dissolves with spit rubbed into it to be black
mud slicker than you get from other dirt.

We don't have any names when we go up
in the kudzu. What we do there is changing
and names don't account for that. Where any

pieces of sun fall in there they are hot and yellow. They are like candy pulled out of sweat. The shadows don't have any color but everything is the barked and throbbing underside of green. If you move you change in the shadows and have different hollows and different dark parts. So I know. Shadows are what let you see what moves. And just because you are in a body you are like a clock or a stick or closed eyes. You are made of bones and skin and you show something pass.

The trick we are playing has to happen so the ghost will be trapped forever. We did have our ghost, Kovi, caught in a jar. Yelling one way, yelling right, I took off the lid and my friend hollered the other way just right and snapped the padlock shut at the jar's mouth. That was the first trick. Ghost in the padlock. Key we busted, padlock shuttered with blood milked from our fingerprints. Padlock we buried in the river bank and marked it. But it wasn't there when we opened the hole to check. I thought most likely he had dug it up to see what would happen. I didn't act like I thought that. All the things supposed to get fixed when we trapped Kovi got bad again anyway.

Now glass pieces we polished on our shirts will call the ghost. I laid the glass trail out lining right over to where we would lie. We took our shirts off then and draped them over the old thick twists of the kudzu.

Our breath will call the ghost but he can't get between our faces. The lizard is alone, an unpaired, unprotected mouth, and the ghost will go to it. Kovi won't know until the lizard swallows him that blood already protects the lizard. Kovi will die. But the lizard has to die too. This magic scared me to figure out but it is surer than the lock ever was. You can't unlock a lizard. You can't open it, not that way.

A spirit will get stuck in shining glass, colored glass. Hypnotized. Glass like you see dangle off the skinny twigs of the dogwood trees or the sarvice trees or the redbuds out front of some houses. Far side of creeks hung with skewed, swinging bridges. That you see if you ride your bike too far up the crumbled tar roads that pierce the hollers and stall out into dirt. Only, for that trap, the spirit has to possess some glimmer of its own. It has to love the color and the light to get snagged on the glinting edges, to sense in that glass a satisfaction of its aimless hunger. Then it will risk the eternity of fascination and bewilderment in the shards.

The kudzu can grow a foot a day. Stray blind ends grow too far and one or the other of us winds them back so that the place we don't have names in is less of an accident all the time. First day after the hideout was cleared we looked to grin at each other but a fear what next what to do with it now we made it snarled our lips over our teeth. I don't know who jumped first into fist throwing. I kept swinging at him mean and wild, thinking how animals use teeth, while his dirty knuckles blurred right back at me. The air under the vines slipped around us like a river of shadows. Fists skidded off ribs from the sweat but it felt like firecrackers I stole from the convenience store.

Me on my knees and him curled on the dirt and us not hitting now but choking out the last frenzy in dry hitches. I told him, you go to sleep. When he closed his eyes and quieted pretending to do it the shadows stood finally still on him and maybe we were on ground that we had opened now. I drew my fingers over the freckles over the bones on him my hands like shadows or cold like fish in the summer air till he whimpered, shook some. Till I didn't know how to go on. Then I lay down and closed my own eyes not knowing if something would come to me.

I keep hold of the lizard in one hand until it is time, no place else to put it. It can be dusty green or brown but in my hand it doesn't know what color to change to. I rub my finger on the side of its jaw to soothe it.

Kovi is old and ugly and too hateful for glass to do more than lure him. That ghost hates us ever since we figured him out. We fished him out of the tangles of what went on at night in our houses. Fears such as water in the tub, or stove burners, or painted nails. Ghost movies show that haunted can be something you get to the bottom of, and cast out. Power to climb out of your dug grave you rip from the very ground, invent out of chickenscratches, words, and your own flesh and bones. If you make it yourself you will always have your secrets by a choice.

First we pull the blackberry thorns across our bellies and it is easier if I let the whole piece of bramble prick and skip all the thorns across instead of just one. Only a couple times and it gets some scratches to dot up red along their high pink lines. So scared my breath comes light and cold and feels like I draw it by choice and the choice is hooking me and leading me by all the hidden parts, all the skin parts. By the elastic that I know is my skeleton and my will. He breathes shallow too, wild eyes and shadows kneeling right across from me. Quick jerking shudders of his ribs.

One time, I went in the kudzu by myself and I took off my shirt and my pants too and put some new pieces of glass in the dirt. Laid down on my back because that wasn't as dirty as if I laid down on my stomach. I started to think about if he was there too but when I tried my breath stopped at the very edge like somebody punched me in the stomach. I couldn't get past. The glass poked and the dirt squished a little under me. It could never get warm but my skin got cool enough that I didn't feel it being cool. I had to think about something so I thought I could tell what colors glass was just by touch, not the sharp or the slick exactly but something going alongside of that. I guess a piece of my mind got hooked in the glass then just like a spirit would and I was looking up into the mottled leaves all layering each other with coolness. As long as they didn't touch. But I knew up at the top layer the sun was hot on them.

I could feel it all of a sudden like I was in the vines. How they lifted their leaf skin up to the sun and how they wanted it as bad as they wanted shade and they wanted to twine up and they wanted to pull down and all of them wanted to be surface all over to be twined up the highest till they felt like they were drowning. I felt it harder and harder inside my skin how it was to be the vines hard in my throat and shoulders and between my legs just skin-knowledge like water on me to where I forgot I didn't like the way I was down there. Then something broke and my mind came back at me out of the glass pieces but I had already peed all over the ground and I took some sticks and dug at it till you couldn't tell. Even if you couldn't have told anyway. I was crying but I had it figured out, the way I would say, look, you can tell a dog did this, look where you can see the claw marks.

He goes to roll over on top of me and I am rolling under. Where our breath hits together it is salty because the sweat flings off him as we are shoving at each other. Some spit falls out of his mouth to hit my bottom lip. The lizard is the softest thing between us and hard at the same time. Tiny and alive, hotter than my hand when I caught it from sleeping in the sun but not now. I fight and twist so we go over again and again, knocking our chests and hip bones together and grinding the lizard between our bellies. All over my skin a screaming like the pulse of cicadas. So loud it must always be there in the background to tune in to by surprise. I know and he knows when it is time to start yelling.

It is a mess of dirt and slime on me and sticky in my pants but I know it worked. I look at the poor lizard dead and bent all wrong with some of itself coming out its mouth and there is a deep quiet beating even deeper all the time in my ears. It sounds more like something that is gone than anything else I ever heard. The lizard in the dirt is what I see until he grabs it and crawls out between the vines.

Out there in the sun. An old black snake will smell just like a cucumber. There is shade but no shadows in the middle of the day. Bunch grass tall and wavy, the ticks that climb in it, robin's plantain, Sweet William. Queen Anne's lace with a chigger in the middle of every flower.

He says, I ain't coming here again, and I say, uh-uh, and look at my foot where I am fooling with a clod of dirt but I don't mean anything.

TOO FAR

Kevin Killian and Thom Wolf

*Keeekeeekeeekeeekpittarumbapittarumbak-
keeekeekeeek* here the bassline keeps popping
and drilling into Alan's feet through the club's
concrete floor, it hurts to keep still, a positive force for evil, he's thinking, or would be
thinking if any room remained in his brain for
thought but not while the DJ, a dark dervish
ensconced in a booth high above the thrashing crowd, is waving his muscular arms and
dropping needles, remixing, sweat pouring off
him in waves. The light's focused on the DJ's
hands, one after another on a row of spinning
turntables, a ring on one finger flashes a tur-
quoise glint, Alan can't see what he's wearing, just the bare sleek arms and the fingers,
nimbler than eyesight, and the spine-pounding
repetitive dancebeat *keeekeeekeeekeeek,* like

Bernard Herrmann ripping the shower curtain down on Janet Leigh in *Psycho*. The boys on the dance floor go wild, mouths twisting in quasisexual pain, eyes rolling back in their heads under beam after beam of white light that plays on their faces for a moment only, then darts elsewhere. It hurts to stand still but Alan doesn't trust himself to let go, to dance. He lowers his eyelids and feels that *Psycho* screech rip right through the sturdy soles of his shoes, plowing at Concorde speed through the muscles and veins in his legs right into the base of his spine. And that means danger, don't it, Alan, base of spine is not a safe place for you.

Can he see you? Magisterial DJ high in his wooden booth, to him you must be a blip down here on the dance floor, one dot in a sea of writhing bodies. Can he see you standing frozen here like a ninny, afraid to dance? *I've got jet lag,* Alan remembers, soothed by this plausible excuse. The balm of the alibi. It had been a long thirty-six hours since alighting at Heathrow and *I'm not used to driving on the wrong side of the road* and *all the new people* and their *clipped accents* and the *different market conditions.* England is so different from the States and yet it isn't, he is finding, exactly like the Austin Powers pictures, either. Apparently there are only maybe three or four full-size pools, swimming pools, in all of County Durham. So where's the glamour? Nor is England like the sweet dusky glen he's conjured up after years of listening to UK pop music at home on his stereo. Boyband music for the most part crossed with massive doses of Kylie Minogue. Where did they film Nick Cave's video for "Where the Wild Roses Grow" in which Kylie appears, drenched, in water ten inches deep, looking like a corpse, Nick Cave leaving roses on her face like Ophelia? Probably in Australia and yet that glade, that eerie green darkness, is how he has always pictured England. Here in this club Alan's supremely unconfident, older and younger at the same time than the rest of the patrons. He's wearing a shirt, for one thing. Subdued black T-shirt, fitted jeans. Where are the women? He's straight, for another thing. Well, sort of.

Alan's thirty-one years old and lives in Greenbelt, Maryland, a suburb of D.C., in a small house he owns on a busy street near downtown, or what passes for downtown nowadays. It's near a Starbucks, which is the same thing. These guys all look high and it ain't coffee fueling their acrobatics. It's something stronger, in fact you can smell it, a thin, high smell like kerosene or the plastic his suits come back wrapped in from the laundry. Ecstasy? Is this what Ecstasy smells like?

At the office he keeps a photo of Kylie in a lurid pink swimsuit on his desk, his ideal girl, he jokes, and the reason his fiancée left him finally after a futile courtship of several years. She still lives in Greenbelt and their paths cross, over and over. Vengeful bitch who's told everyone at the gym he never slept with her, not that it matters, who'd listen to a demented harpy who's presently, or so it appears, dating a black dude whose ass is bigger than hers? Since the breakup Alan's decided to make some changes in his life, get out of the rut all that dating had thrust him into. With his new, chic haircut he looks pretty good to himself in the mirror. Thought of installing a full-length type mirror in his room so he could admire his body more, but then thought it was too gay. As it is, he must sidle up very close to the mirror and look way down, craning backward, to check on his ass's perfection, in a jockstrap, in gym shorts, rolled down perhaps so he can see the crack in his butt, its very beginnings where the hair trails between his cheeks, he can see his mole, like a tiny brown button of desire. When he does this a hot flash colors his skin, from his brow and temples right down to his groin. He steps away from the mirror with the guilt of one who has seen something forbidden.

That's why he doesn't keep any pets, they might spy him at the mirror and think he was pretty weird.

A shirtless man moves in, takes his hand out of his belt. "A drink, mate?" he hears the man bellowing at him. He shakes his head ruefully, no thanks. Doesn't drink much, afraid of drinking, afraid of blackouts, father a drunk, mother a heavy drinker. The guy moves away, Alan dismisses him, another queer probably. What time is it? At home he'd be running, or down at the local gym. His hobbies include reenacting Civil War battles with former university mates—the good ol' days.

Alan's a white man of 6 feet 1, 180 lbs, dark brown eyes that look black at night, with broad shoulders and a somewhat heavy neck. He has a mole below his belt line, pretty much right at the small of his back. When he's worried he presses it, as though for good luck. His hair is thick and black, almost Latin, were the mole on his face he'd look like Enrique Iglesias, and his body is lightly hairy, his pubic hair the color of Coca-Cola. His hands and feet are large as well, so he feels constantly clumsy, but this endears him to people, that he's not coordinated, that he's awkward. He likes things neat and tidy, a reaction to the sloppy housekeeping of his tipsy mother, and the chaotic conditions of former roommates.

Same man's back again, his shirt on this time. "You didn't say what you wanted," he yells. "So—here, cheers." Alan nods, takes the warm glass, smiles politely, as though they were two strangers on a bus queue, then looks up again at the DJ booth. DJ's pale hand fluttering like an exotic bird across the spinning vinyl. The man's foot is next to his, planted squarely up against his boot. Same smell slides off Englishman—thin, greasy smell of brain cells all dizzy with Ecstasy. "New to town?"

Swimming pool chiefs have sent him to England to a big convention here in Durham, hands across the water, get it? Meet his Euro counterparts. The guys who get out there and deal and make it happen. You've got a half-acre of ground, dig it. New passport—his first—new David Beckham haircut, new luggage even. Convention brochures promise a visit to swimming pools of top UK pop stars. Maybe, he hopes, Kylie's will be among them. She must live somewhere, England's a small island, right? So far they haven't seen shit, just endless meetings and horrid breakfast food and finally a night out. And now a guy a bit older than he is apparently making some kind of pass down among their insteps, nudging his foot, which hurts anyhow with the incessant beat, over which Kylie's angelic voice keeps chirping, *"I'm burning up, I'm burning up...."* Flattering if you weren't straight but he's straight. No really, despite the accusations flung at him by that bitch Charlotte whom he'd once thought, finally *a woman I can trust. But Alan, if you've actually fantasized about men, you must really want them, deep down, face the facts, Alan....* Her voice, understanding initially, and him so grateful, so pathetically grateful he could open up, then her voice becoming a slash, a shriek *keeeekeeeekeeeekeeeekpittarumbapittarumba.* Ever since that terrible night of confidences, the night of their breakup, he's only seen her in traffic. Let it stay that way. Over the years, he's rebuffed a few passes made at him by men encountered during business trips, on planes,

or back in his college days. He keeps these memories in a special place in his mind and trots them out when things get dull.
His boss always sends Alan to visit with the gay customers, as
a kind of bait, because he has the kind of body some men really dig, no sense being modest about it, but Alan acts oblivious,
just treats the gay guys like he would every other customer.
Polite, professional. Let's dig this hole! He has one memory
of waking up in a hotel room somewhere in the West, a room
not his own, his clothes torn, his body a bit bruised, his balls
aching with an indefinable pain, and the bedclothes showing unmistakable signs of—what?—of something having happened to him. So maybe he did have sex, he thinks, but he
doesn't know with whom or how....

"Man up in the booth is having a party after at his place,"
announces the foot guy, cupping Alan's ear. "Come to it,
okay? It's quite nearby, we'll drive you. I'm Fitz," he continues, holding out a beefy hand. Alan looks him in the face and
he's overtaken by a weird déjà vu, for the man beside him,
once studied up close, bears a strange resemblance to a singer
from a long-gone pop band he'd followed in high school. All
right, now a lot older, and chunky all around, red in the face,
but still recognizable.

"I'm Alan," he says, then goes for it. "Are you Fitz from
Making Waves?"

"Oh Christ," says Fitz, his face a big embarrassed grin.
"They still remember!" He introduces Alan to his girlfriend,
Phoebe, a tall, willowy, bored blonde. "But you're an Ameri-
can, how would you know of Making Waves?"

"Are you boys coming along?" intones Phoebe, her hand
dangling a charm bracelet of car keys. "Or are we off on a

stroll down memory lane to Top of the Pops?"

"Want to come up?" Fitz asks. "You see, our DJ, our host—he's Chris, also from Making Waves. He was the cute one."

Alan is amazed. First free night in the UK and he's met a has-been popstar! "Can we stop back at my hotel for just a minute?" he begs. Phoebe shrugs, her eyes rolling. She's a stone fox, even a blind man could see that. Alan feels weak, all his expectations jostled and dumped topsy-turvy. "Hey Fitz, want a laugh? I thought you were a gay guy."

"He's not far from it, if you ask me," Phoebe says. "And if you were to ask his wife she'd tell you the same."

"Women," Fitz sighs. "Can't live with 'em, or maybe not with just one of them." Out in the high street, the air so chill around their mouths, Phoebe and Fitz between them try to explain to their new American pal the strange vagaries of DJ Chris. "It's taken Chris a long time to distance himself from Making Waves," Phoebe says, generously. "He's not a boy anymore, he's a man." "Spent years in the gym, he did, always looking for what he calls solid definition." "And credibility." So, Alan gathered, Chris's membership in Making Waves was a subject not to be alluded to. Fitz laughs and downs a tequila. "His credibility as a DJ will crumble into shit if people make the connection between DJ Chris and his cheesy pop past."

"Everyone knows, of course," yawns Phoebe. "He just acts as though, oh well, being a teen idol happened to somebody else."

"You must come to Chris's house," Fitz begs, "It's my birthday."

"Will Kylie Minogue be there?"

Fitz and Phoebe look at each other briefly, a European kind of look. "She's sure to bob up," Phoebe allows. "Durham is her home away from home and Fitz is one of her dearest amigos, aren't you, Fitz?" Alan feels his face swelling up into the shape of a plastic pumpkin, he's so excited and impressed. But he has to keep his cool.

Though confused and virginal, Alan has huge sex appetites. A compulsive masturbator, he likes to do it while driving, finds a special thrill in going by toll-takers during rush hour commute with one hand on his dick. Almost got caught several times. Has a special G-spot excitement area right under his balls, the narrow channel between balls and asshole, the perineum, which he keeps shaved, lotioned, always smooth. He'd keep a dildo or vibrator or butt plug at home, hidden in a closet or somewhere, but he's afraid his house might burn down while he's at work and some fireman or other rescue worker would find sex devices while he's absent. (No porn for the same reason.) So he's forced to resort to not-so-obvious household objects like cucumbers, et cetera. At the gym he's dangerously attracted, not to any man, but to their body parts, their funky clothes. A few months ago he lifted a pair of boxer shorts instilled with a particular fragrance, sweat, piss, the whole drill. Bizarre.

He's decided he has the Christian Bale, *American Psycho* look. Now he wants the personality to go with it.

"You'll love the architecture, at any rate," Phoebe says in the car on the way to Alan's hotel. "It's a Victorian building, once a police station, now converted to residential flats. When Chris bought the place it was nothing more than an empty shell, with cells. It took nearly a year of work before he could move in."

"Don't worry, Alan," Fitz snorts. "Chris took the cells out."

"And regretted that later," adds Phoebe. "Now tell me again why we're having to stop at the hotel?"

"So I can get changed," Alan says. "Won't take me a minute. And also I have some photos and I hope Fitz can sign them."

"You came here to England hoping to meet the pop stars?" Phoebe marvels, pulling in sharply under the hotel's beige marquee.

"I know," Alan says, hopping out. "How gay."

Up in the booth, enjoying the lordly height and the sweep of the floor, I just nod at Fitz, as if to say, *He'll do*. Pathetic that Fitz thinks he knows the kind of guy I like. Comical seeing this straight man cruise a club for tight asses, he's practically incapable of actually seeing a boy's ass. And all because in a moment of insanity I agreed to let him have his birthday bash at my place, seeing that Fitz's wife doesn't understand his need to scarf down cocaine, and his kids don't like him screwing other women, et cetera. You figure it out, I gave up long ago.

"You haven't told him about me," I caution.

"He knows nothing, nothing," Fitz says.

Fitz and I met long ago, in the 1980s, when we each answered an ad in the Sunday paper, "Make Top Money Now, Become a Pop Star," and attended auditions, mine in Hammersmith, his up in Glasgow. Behind the velvet curtain lurked pop impresario Simon Seymour, a devil in a polyester suit. Out of hundreds of applicants, he picked me, and then Fitz. We didn't have to be able to sing or play any instruments, just had to, I don't know, "be." Whatever was in Simon Seymour's mind, which at that flicker of time was—"A new ABBA would really clean up." "And we'll call them Making Waves." I didn't actually meet Fitz until Making Waves shot its first video ("Sunshine Girl") in Aruba.

Two boys, two girls. The girls did most of the singing. I was the cute one, the one all the fans were supposed to fancy. Skinny and inoffensive. On the surface, anyway. My hair, naturally very dark and thick.

I can't even say the name of the band now without freezing up. I've changed my name, colored my hair, bleaching it blond for the last two years. I look nothing like the wide-eyed fuck-puppy who used to dance around a stage, miming the words to terrible pop songs. A year after our debut we were dropped by the record company. A handful of minor hits, one flop album, and that was it. We were making waves no more, Simon Seymour told us flatly in his voice like an ice cube. Sometimes I'll see a program on TV that asks, "Where Have the '80s Stars Gone?" and sometimes they mention Making Waves. Fitz appears on those broadcasts, but I've instructed him to tell them, "Chris? Went AWOL long ago, man. Haven't seen him since 1989."

Two queens have dug out my *Jaws* DVD and put it on. They're watching the scene where the shark attacks Richard Dreyfuss again and again. When the scene ends they skip right back to the start. The sound is turned off and a hard house-track blasts from my stereo. I've no idea who these guys are. This is my fucking house and I hardly know any of the people here.

The mechanical shark is tearing its way into the cage. "Jaws should eat him," one queen says to the other. "Like in the book."

"Isn't the film better?"

"It's different. In the book Jaws eats Hooper."

"I wonder why they changed it."

"Don't know."

I do. They hired a team of experts to film footage of real sharks in the wild. During the filming one of the real great whites got caught up in the moorings of the empty cage and went into a frenzied attack. The producers were so impressed with this footage that they rewrote the script to incorporate it into the film. Richard Dreyfuss gets away before Jaws goes to town on the empty cage. I can't be bothered explaining this to the two strangers who are making themselves at home with my DVD collection. They're so fucked on E that I doubt they'd understand, anyway. They've grown tired of watching Dreyfuss wrestle the mechanical monster and are arguing about what to put on next. One of them wants to see the water skier attack in *Jaws 2* while the other wants to watch the lapdancing scene in *Showgirls*. I warn them to be careful with my discs and go to get another drink.

More than a dozen people sit round my dining room table; snorting and smoking. Colorful pills are passed around in neat plastic bags. No one cares a fuck about what they're taking. I lean over and take a line that's been chopped on top of a Shirley Bassey photo book. The girl whose coke it is smiles politely. If it wasn't my flat she'd tell me to fuck off. I don't know her name but I remember her from the club. She was dancing on a podium, bare to the waist, her pigeon tits hanging almost as far. Her skin is the color of sour milk. This girl could really do with some sun. "Kris is here!" she cries.

"Notorious DJ Kris."

The coke works fast. Tiny sparks of static electricity dance behind my nose. In no time at all it's tingling in my cock. My erection presses against my hip, inside my favorite white briefs. All my briefs are white. I have thirty-four pairs of the same style and color. These are damp now. I'll change them when I get time. No one believes that a DJ sweats as much in his booth as all those dancers he is mixing into a frenzy.

Someone is playing with my CDs. They've exchanged hard house for disco. "Love to Love You Baby" is greeted with enthusiasm. The kitchen is full and the crowd spills out onto the fire escape. Fitz is doing tequila slammers off the washing machine. I slide over to him.

"Give me one of those."

He giggles, sloshing the gold liquid into a shot glass, slopping a good measure over the side. He moves the glass and licks up the spillage like milk.

"Having fun, Fitz?"

"Yes, cheers, Chris. Thanks for lending me the space."

His new girlfriend, can't think of her name, is slicing limes. The blonde bit. Her name's the same name as his wife, which is typical of Fitz and his distorted notions of loyalty. And handy in bed, he says, seeing as he only has to remember one name when he's shouting it out. She passes me a huge handful of salt and a wedge of lime. The tequila is the best, sliding down my throat like a squirt of my own come.

"You got some dykes fucking in your bathroom," Fitz says. He's finding it difficult to speak. "Had to piss in the garden."

"As long as they stay out of my bedroom." My bedroom is private. There's no need for anyone to go there. In the spare room there's a huge bed, equipped with all the toys, condoms, and lube that any of these freaks could want.

Fitz knocks back another shot and refills my glass.

"How many of these have you had?"

He shrugs. "Twenty? Thirty? I don't know," he replies after a bit.

I knock back the second tequila but refuse a third, pouring a glass of Spanish red instead. I wander back through the flat, taking the bottle with me. In the living room *Showgirls* has won out. Elizabeth Berkley is thrusting her naked crotch in Kyle MacLachlan's face. He has a terrible hairstyle in this film.

There's an athletic-looking guy sitting on the floor beside the armchair, staring at the television screen. His legs are folded under him and he nurses an empty glass. I reckon he'll be a couple of years younger than I am, round about thirty. That's a bit older than my usual type but this fella is worth making an exception for. He has black hair, cut into a neat, boyish style, and he's chewing his fingernails. He's wearing a tight black T-shirt and blue jeans, the body beneath is a result of work and dedication.

I pick my way through the outstretched legs and sit down beside him. "Hi," I say.

"Hi."

I detect an accent. He's American but I can't place the region. "You here alone?"

He looks at me and smiles. He's nervous. His eyes are as black as his hair. "I was at the club with a girl but I think I lost track of her somewhere."

"She could be outside," I suggest. "There's a lot of people in the garden."

"Actually she's not really a friend. I only met her this past week. She and I are on a business trip together. I don't know anyone in England, so she invited me out with her tonight."

I'm already wondering what this guy's face will look like once it's stuffed with my cock. His name is Alan and he sells swimming pools. "I don't think there's much demand for home pools here in the UK," I joke.

His face remains stoic. "I'm here for a convention and meetings with your regional sales teams."

Now would be a good time to shove my dick in his mouth and stop him talking. Instead I offer him a drink.

"No, thanks," he says, clinging to his empty glass. "And then in the club your—friend is he, Fitz?—invited me to this party."

"You have to try this," I say, pouring the wine. "It's good stuff."

I can tell he doesn't care for the taste but he drinks it anyway. "This apartment is awesome," he says.

Alan looks impressed. "Fitz was in a pop group, wasn't he?" For a moment I freeze. He can't have recognized *me*. I've changed so much. Besides, we barely broke the band in Britain and Europe, we didn't get near the States.

I laugh. "Yes, he was. Don't tell me you were a fan."

He too laughs, looking at his feet. "No. I've never heard of them before tonight. I heard a couple of guys talking on the line to the bathroom. What were you called?"

"Making Waves."

"Must have been pretty cool. Being in a band."

"We were anything but cool."

"Tell me." He seems genuine.

"Rather not, if you don't mind."

"What happened?" Alan asks. "To the group? Why'd you

split up? I'd love to hear some of your records."

"You won't be hearing them from me."

"Is Simon Seymour still alive?"

The two queens have skipped further into the film. They shriek loudly and applaud when Elizabeth Berkley shoves Gina Gershon down a flight of stairs. After a lot of clapping and hollering they move the scene straight back to the beginning.

When I turn to Alan I see that he's looking at me. He reacts like he's been caught and moves his eyes back to the television. He's finished his wine. I top it up for him again.

"This is a terrible movie."

"You say that like it's a bad thing." I love the way his nose wrinkles when he laughs. I imagine shooting my load all over his face, smearing it around his nose and lips with my cock, rubbing my juicy head against his closed eyelids.

He asks me if I have any pets...says he has to go to the bathroom. "I'm not used to drinking wine." He gets awkwardly to his feet and stumbles his way over to the stairs. He appears very self-conscious, as though aware that I'm watching him. I *am* watching him. His arse is a piece of perfection, so high and tight. I want to get my mouth in there and lick his crack until he pleads with me to put my cock in him. Until he gets on his hands and knees and shoves his arse at me, begging me to take it. I imagine he'll be a frisky and giving bottom.

Sitting on the floor makes my legs ache. I stand up and head back to the kitchen. It's cooler in here. More of the guests have moved down the fire escape to the garden that looks onto the river. Kylie Minogue is drinking a martini and eating a piece of pizza. She thanks me for the remix I recently completed for her. Fitz is still hammering back shots, though they've run out of limes. It's almost five and things don't look like they're going to wind down anytime soon.

My cock feels wet against my hip. It's not sweat this time but pre-cum. I really need to get out of these pants and into a clean pair. I reckon it's about time I checked on things upstairs, anyway. I take the bottle with me. I decide I'll look for Alan while I'm up there. I've got a gram of coke in my pocket and wonder if he wants to share it with me. Probably not. He doesn't even look like he drinks much, can't imagine him going for the party powder, then.

Two clones are getting a blow job on the staircase from a third. I wink as I step around and warn them not to get come on my carpets. They all have very small cocks. Why is that? I've never met a clone with more than an average-size piece, at best. It completely contradicts the tough, skinhead image. I'll take a well-hung chicken anytime.

They are still queuing up to get in the bathroom. There's a second bathroom in my bedroom but I don't tell anyone they can use it. It's strictly private.

My bedroom is the largest on this level. I chose it specifically for the size of the room and the massive window that looks out over the River Wear and the city beyond. You can see everything from there: the three towers of the cathedral, the castle, the peninsula. It's spectacular. But as I enter the room I'm confronted by an entirely different kind of view.

Alan is sitting on the corner of the bed. He's got his jeans around his ankles and a pair of my underpants over his face. The lid from my washing basket is lying on the floor along with a couple of dirty T-shirts that have been discarded in haste. He's sniffing my used pants.

A spit-lubed fist moves over a modest-sized hard-on. A tight pair of balls hugs the root and bounce against his hand with each tug. From my position in the doorway I can see that his scrotum and the passage beneath, leading to his arsehole, are exquisitely shaved. It reminds me of a boy, not yet developed. But his cock is definitely the organ of a man. It's not that big —I'm guessing just over six inches—but it's got a decent girth and a fat head.

He hasn't realized I'm here. He's too caught up in masturbating with my underwear. The anger I initially felt at the liberty he has taken has all but gone. But he's not going to get away with this intrusion. I'm going to have him. I step inside the room and close the door.

Alan bounds off the edge of the bed, dropping my pants. Panicked, he tries to stand up, reaching for his jeans. He stumbles and sprawls across the bed, face down, arse high. He still tries to pull up his jeans but they are caught around his meaty thighs.

"Stay down," I say. I'm over him, one foot rammed in the middle of his back, forcing him into the carpet. He turns his head, wide eyes looking frightened over his shoulder. The reverence in his face excites me. I apply more pressure. "What you doing in here?"

"I'm sorry," he stammers. His face is flushed, bright red around the brow and temples.

"This is my fucking room. It's private, you bastard." He tries to rise but I've got too much weight on top of him.

"I didn't know. Not until I was in."

"And thought you'd have a party of your own with my dirty laundry. What were you going to do, wipe your spunk up on my T-shirts and shove them back in the basket? Hope I wouldn't notice?"

"I don't know. I didn't think. I couldn't stop myself." I'm looking at his arse, which is just as ripe and perfect as I had imagined it. He has a nest of downy hair in the hollow of his spine that trails into the crack. I'm surprised he hasn't shaved this, considering how clean and smooth his balls are. His cheeks are meaty and round. I want to take a bite. Yeah, quite possibly I will.

I reach down for the pants he's been sniffing and take a hit on them myself. They're funky smelling, stained with yellow smears of sweat and piss. It looks like I've worn them for a gig. He couldn't have found a more unsavory pair if he tried.

I grab his hair, releasing my foot from his back, and haul him onto his knees. He looks frightened. I shove his face against my crotch, letting him feel what I've got there. He tries to pull away but he can't. "Breathe in deep," I tell him. "Get it right from the source." My dick twitches and I know he can feel that.

I push him away. There's a wild, frightened look in his eyes. He's flat on his arse and his prick is jutting up toward his round navel. He doesn't try to get away. Now I know where we stand. I unfasten my jeans and ease my big cock out. His eyes widen. They always do. "Suck me," I tell him.

His mouth moves but it's a second or two before any sound comes out. "I can't...I never...."

I smack his face with my cock. The expression of shock is priceless. His mouth is hanging open so I grab the back of his head and shove my dick inside. Surprise is on my side and I get to the back of his throat before he tenses up. Good, oh, damned good. He hasn't got a clue how to move his lips or tongue around such a big piece but that doesn't matter. His warm, moist opening is all I need. I grip his head and shove deeper into the socket of his throat. His face is scarlet now and his cheeks are wet. I'm not sure if it's sweat or tears.

I move back a little, getting a rhythm going. I can tell how hard he's concentrating. I wonder how much experience he's had with men.

I'm big but most boys get used to me after a while. I fuck his face. He hasn't tried to bite my cock off so he must be enjoying it in some way. I know *I* am.

But there's only so much cocksucking I can stand. It gets boring after a while. He gasps as I withdraw, open mouthed and panting. His eyes are wordlessly asking *What next.*

"Let me see your arse," I say.

Alan hesitates, just for a moment, before turning round and lifting his arse for inspection. He pulls his T-shirt up to his shoulders, exposing a broad, flawless back. I notice for the first time a small mole, just above his right arsecheek. My eyes move lower, into the crack, toward his arsehole. It resembles the mole in many ways, the color is almost identical, only it's much bigger. Its color reminds me of dark honey. I tell him to spread his cheeks a little and he does, stretching the opening. I can see something of the pink interior.

"Where's the girl?" I grunt. "The one you brought to the club."

"There was no girl," he moans. "I lied."

I get down and bury my face in his arse. His whole body jerks when my tongue caresses his hole. I'm certain this is a first for him, he's acting like a virgin. It occurs to me that he might have a wife and family back in the States. Maybe he considers himself to be straight. He wouldn't be the first straight man to drop his pants in my bedroom.

My tongue squirms around his hot opening. His has got a

rich, manly taste. His arsehole quivers around my lips.

"Oh my god," he groans, his voice full of wonder. I'm pretty sure now that he's new to this. It seems strange, most men with any kind of interest in dick would have at least experienced something by his age. I fucked my first man when I was fourteen. He was a student, in his early twenties. He dropped his pants in the underbrush down by the river and let me poke him against a tree. I remember barely getting two thrusts in before I squirted a load in his arse. I was scared afterward that he would expect me to return the favor, but he settled for a wank instead.

And Simon Seymour, sitting with him on his Hollywood poolside, him asking if I wanted to be a star, pointing at his tiny dick inside obscenely tight Speedos, me nodding, and then a half hour later, me choking in the perfect blue water, head in the shallow end, my arse up in the air with Simon Seymour sticking something in me bigger than that tiny little piece of meat, me choking, sputtering, from way above I hear, "That's the, *huff,* price of stardom, *puff.*" Can still hear it in my ears today.

I've come a long way since then and I intend to take more than a couple of strokes at Alan's arse. He is on his knees, shoving his butt in my face, knowing what is coming. I feel between his legs, stroking the smooth path between his balls and his hole. That really gets him going so I back off, not wanting him to shoot before I'm inside. His bud is well soaked with spit so I stick a finger into him. He takes it easily enough. Nothing to worry about.

I think about offering him a line of coke but figure he'll panic. "Get on the bed," I say instead. "Face down."

He kicks off his shoes and wriggles out of jeans, climbs

onto the bed in his socks and T-shirt. He lies on his front, spreading his legs. The guy's a natural.

I put on a condom and a handful of lube—then I fuck him. I climb on his back and slide my cock inside him, slowly to begin with. His body tenses with the introduction of my big head. I put my cheek against the back of his neck, pushing his face into the pillows. I tell him to relax, it'll soon get better. His arsehole is hungry, I know it can take me.

I fuck him hard and passionately, grunting with each stroke. His fists grip the pillows. My thighs slap loudly against the back of his legs. I love the squash of his buttocks against my pelvis when I drive it deep. In and out, in and out, I fuck him thoroughly, feeling his arse with every inch of my dick. I dig my knees into the bed, getting more leverage, holding his arse in my hands so he can't get away. Harder. The bedsprings are screaming.

My orgasm is a long time coming. For ages it seems I am almost there. I keep going, harder, faster. I throw my full weight on top of him, my hips hammering. When it finally comes I roar with relief, squirting gobs of spunk inside him.

I pull out straight away. My cock, his buttocks, the back of his thighs are streaked with blood. Shit. He must have been a virgin after all. He raises himself slowly, testing his body. He's come onto the covers.

"Use the bathroom in there," I say. "There are towels under the sink." Alan nods, climbing off the bed. His steps to the door are unsteady. I grab a handful of tissues to clean the mess off the bedclothes. I go to take the condom off my still-hard dick. Something isn't right. I wipe up some of the blood with a tissue and look again.

The rubber has split right down the middle. There's no

semen in the ragged tip. Must have happened inside him. Fuck. He's left a folder on the carpet, plastic folder he must have dropped in his excitement over my laundry basket. Idly I open the folder, a clutch of 8 by 10 glossies slithers onto the floor. Kylie in a bedsheet, closing a blind from the *Light Years* era. Gareth Gates, his mouth a stuttery pout. And there I am, sliding out, my cheery mug from Making Waves, hideous yellowing headshot of young Chris, hair in tight curls, my autograph sprawling across it from a dozen years ago. No more. "For Alan, who must be my only fan in the USA, cheers, Chris from Making Waves, 1987."

JAILBAIT

Darin Klein

Jailbait wasn't technically jail bait anymore, but he had earned the nickname fair and square working chicken hawks on Polk Street during the years when he really was jail bait, and that wasn't too far in his past. He was definitely still among the youngest of the punks on the scene. Rough around the edges, spiky haired, slightly acne-scarred, skinny, disastrously tattooed, he nonetheless exhibited an endearing child-like fascination for new and exciting experiences.

Barging into the Hole in the Wall one night after last call, eyes wild, he came straight at me and grabbed me by the arm. "Let's fuck," he said. I wouldn't argue with that. We had hooked up several times before and it was always hot. One time he blew me on the front steps of the Mission Dolores, not even bothering to stop when the 22 bus rolled by on 16th Street full of late-night passengers. A friend and I had even tag-teamed him once, tossing his scrawny, hairless body between us like a rag soaked in baby oil. He would ride a cock all night. You could just relax and enjoy his hot hole engulfing you completely, his magic ass muscles tensing and gripping you like there was no tomorrow.

Outside the bar, Jailbait and I braced ourselves against the San Francisco cold and headed into the night. I was surprised when he produced a set of keys and opened the driver's side door of a car parked on Folsom Street. "Borrowed," he said. I didn't even know he could drive. He flipped a reckless U-turn and gassed it in the direction of home. He already had one hand down the front of my pants and was working my boner. He apparently couldn't give a hand job and drive at the same time, because the next thing I knew he ran a red light at full speed, and we were broadsided by an oncoming car. He gave the other driver a fake phone number, showed him a fake I.D., and told him Triple-A would cover the damage. We sped off high on adrenaline.

Back at his place he cranked up the Shangri-La's on some makeshift sound system, muted a hot jail-action porno, and poured us whiskey in a glass the shape of a cowboy boot. To top it off we ate a bunch of the homemade magic mushroom–infused raspberry chocolate truffles he was supposed to be selling for rent money.

When the drugs kicked in I became aware of the intense heat of our bodies. We were like touching machinery, embers, a star. We were passionate and riled up, desperate and tender, maybe even clumsy. We 69'd and somewhere angels were singing *Give Him a Great Big Kiss, Right Now and Not*

Later, The Dum Dum Ditty. We thrashed around and whiskey got in our bellybuttons, I pissed in his ass. We came on each other's faces and chests, slaked the mess with sticky fingers. He rimmed me and I felt that life really was worth living. He sat on my dick in a way that made me curious about where I ended and he began. I flipped him onto his back and pulled out of his ass, shooting come the length of his torso and into his mouth, bull's-eye.

Eventually the sun came up and the TV was reduced to a useless bright-blue electrical hum on the periphery. Any role that music had played in the course of events was relegated to distant memory and we were shaky and weak, crashing in the blank air the notes and melodies had hung in. We took something prescriptive and curled into one another in a destroyed nest of bed sheets. For all I know, we were asleep after that.

DEPRESSION HALVED PRODUCTION COSTS

Sam J. Miller

We're crouched in a pool of darkness, behind a small bush in Madison Square Park, which is nowhere near Madison Square Garden. Eventually I'll have to ask Earl about it, about which one is the real Madison Square. He's fifty-five and has lived like every day of it here in the city—point out any odd building or street name and he knows the backstory. For the moment, though, all I want from him is the fingers down my throat, the face pressing into the back of my neck. I want us totally naked but it's freezing.

Yet when I get Earl's pants down and stick in my face his crotch is slick with sweat, as is my own, from all the layers we have to wear. The cold air invigorates us, excites us, and we fuck as freely and noisily as anybody who had a bedroom to fuck in. No cops come through.

"You tire an old man out," he says, while we lie there balled up together. We breathe heavy, watching it steam in front of us.

"Whatever," I say. "You big baby." He's almost four times my age and has about twice as much sex drive as me.

"That was great, Sol, I'm telling you." My head is cradled in his lap, and I can smell him through all the layers.

For two weeks I've been stuck to him like glue. For a month before that I'd been chasing him through Marcus Garvey Park, sharing cigarettes, making my advances more and more advanced. Now I'm trying to shake this sense of him as a conquest, as something I saw and wanted and went for. Because I'm starting to feel strongly about him and I want him to feel the same, and that might be a tougher proposition.

Afterward we walk through the park, talk, smoke cigarettes, just like any other couple after sex. He points to the Empire State Building: "Did you know they built that in, like, a year? It was all set to start in 1929, but then the Great Depression came, and cut the production costs in half."

"Because they could pay people only half as much."

"Exactly. That was the beginning of New York's homeless problem. It's like the pyramids—this architectural marvel that was totally dependent on the misery of slave labor. Every time I see it I think of all the poor workers whose wives were in bread lines while they were up on those platforms with no safety harnesses. Did you know six workers died in the course of building it?"

We sit on a bench on the north side of the park. It's a Sunday night and 26th Street is quiet, except for one building people keep going into.

"Must be a party," Earl says, pointing up to the fifth floor where people are standing around smoking on a balcony. Or is it a veranda? Earl would know the difference.

More and more people go in, mostly young handsome men. I'm picturing something gay, a magazine launch or a graphic designer ball.

"Let's crash it," I say. "The party."

"Are you kidding? Look at me, I'll stick out like a sore thumb. Not only will I be the only black guy, I'll be the only guy over forty."

"I doubt it," I said. "I think I just saw a South Asian guy go in. It might be more diverse than you think. And I bet there's an open bar, and women walking around with trays of expensive rich food. It'll be nice to get out of the cold for a while."

"Let's do it."

"Good." We get up, cross the street, join a straight couple going in.

"Fifth floor?" asks the girl when the elevator door shuts.

"Where else?" Earl asks, flashing that smile that got my attention right off the bat. The elevator goes up slowly, no one says anything, the couple is well dressed and they smell nice. When the doors swing open on the fifth floor there's such a crush of people no one sees us slip in, hang up our coats, head for the booze.

The macaroni and cheese is crusted in some kind of Gruyere, or Roquefort, or some other fancy cheese I've seen in supermarkets and always wondered about. I've shoveled five spoonfuls into my mouth without chewing when a girl comes up to me and says: "You and I must be the youngest people here."

"Might be," I said. "I'm Solomon." We shake.

"Hi, Solomon. I'm Maggie. Do you work here?"

"No, to be honest, I don't even know what this place is. My boyfriend got invited by somebody who works here."

"Yeah, a friend asked me to come along. What do they even *do* here? She said it was a design firm. Must be a hell of a firm to have a space this big. In a building like this. They must make some kind of filthy money."

"I know, right? What do you suppose they pay in rent?"

"I have no fuckin' idea. I moved to Williamsburg when it was affordable. Manhattan rents blow me away."

"Oh god, yes. I don't know how anybody in this city can afford to pay rent, unless you're making, like, a billion dollars a year."

"I bet you're not even twenty, Sol. Are you even eighteen?"

"I'm eighteen." My age just jumped by two years; this is why I love talking to strangers.

Earl's right; he can't blend. I try not to leave him alone for too long but I'm enjoying the way that I can move into and out of conversations, talk to people, fit in. The last party I went to was for Ortega's birthday, at a bowling alley near our high school, six months back or more. The guy at the bar doesn't card me when I ask for a martini. Something I've never had before—the very name stinks of power. Men cruise me. I'm tempted to try for some phone numbers, just to see if I can.

"We could go all week and never get a chance to use a bathroom like that," Earl says, when he comes out of it.

"Yeah? They got a solid gold crapper and an attendant handing you individual squares of toilet paper?"

"And breath mints and lube and condoms. And a bidet. I'm not joking about the bidet. Puts even Grand Central to shame."

In the back are a series of offices. Earl scopes them out and beckons for me; we find the cushiest one. From the business cards on top of a filing cabinet—whoever thought a mere filing cabinet could be so chic?—we figure out the office belongs to Luccia Stevenson, who's the executive director of Krell & Stevenson, which presumably is where we're at. Luccia has one of those expensive swivel chairs, which I sit Earl in. The room smells like money. I kneel between his legs, unzip him, pull both pairs of pants and his thermals and his boxer shorts down to midthigh. He's only half-hard and I stare until it swells all the way out, pointing lazily past the top of my head. I seize it, I jerk it twice, I guide it all the way into my mouth in one gulp. As he strokes the top of my head I unbutton shirt after shirt, letting him out of my mouth at the end of it to pull my thermal undershirt over my head.

"Wow, we're really going all the way," Earl says when I stand up and take his shirts off too. For a second I'm confused: We've done everything imaginable already. Then I realize we've never been naked together before. Life is hard when you have no private space. "Luccia could walk in at any moment."

"Let her, it's her office."

I sit on him, my back to him, facing the door to the office and the hallway and the party. With his hands on my sides he lifts me up, puts me back down, starts fucking me. His hands hold me in place and his hips dart in and out, in and out. "Lean back," he whispers, and I do, pushing him back, pushing my shoulder to his chin, floating in space in that fancy darkened office, in this ghost world of graphic designers and expensive hors d'oeuvres, where we don't belong, where we are the ghosts that haunt the house.

Earl asks, "What do you think she'd be madder about— that we crashed her party or that we got jizz all over her desk?" I'm wiping it up but I think some got in between the keys of her keyboard.

In all the time it takes us to stop kissing, get all fifty layers of clothes back on, no one even comes anywhere near. I take my martini glass back into the crowd. I don't feel bad about taking advantage of Krell & Stevenson's hospitality; in fact, I'm feeling sort of smug and contemptuous about them. All the money that flows through that office.... Letting me steal their food and fuck my boyfriend is the least they can do.

Earl is in the bathroom and I'm waiting for the elevator. I overhear a queeny boy in horn-rim glasses say to someone else, "Who let the homeless guy in?" My face turns red with shame and then I realize they're not talking about me.

NOW FIX ME

Duane Williams

In his dreams, while he was asleep, nothing could frighten Rayne. Not walking into fire. Not shark-infested waters. Not Dr. Lovely, his psychiatrist, whom Rayne blamed for fucking up his brain with experimental drugs. In his dreams, fear was simply an emotion. In the real world, fear was stalking Rayne, following his every waking thought, ready to pronounce its dire warnings inside his head.

At three o'clock in the morning, in Harold's backyard, Rayne stood naked at the side of the pool, stretching out the silhouettes of his long, swimmer's arms. On the back porch, in his bathrobe and slippers, Harold stamped out his third cigarette and whistled quietly. He'd been watching Rayne glide through the water for the past hour, back and forth, from one end of the pool to the other, the moon's light shimmering in his wake. "How was your swim?" Harold asked as Rayne moved toward him in the dark. "How many lengths?"

"I lost count." Beneath the glare of the porch light, Rayne was dripping a large puddle at his feet, his nipples cold and alert. "It's those stupid, fucking drugs. My brain got distracted."

"Well, it's a beautiful night for a swim," Harold said, scanning the star-littered sky. The moon's face was beaming. "It's so incredibly quiet."

"What happened to the crickets?" Lately, whenever Rayne couldn't sleep, he climbed out his bedroom window and jumped the fence between his mother's yard and Harold's. In spite of Nancy's pleas, he'd flushed the sleeping pills that Dr. Lovely prescribed, claiming the tiny blue tablets would cause his limbs to shrivel up and die like worms on hot pavement.

"I don't know," Harold said. "Do crickets sleep?" This wasn't the first time they were having a late-night encounter in Harold's backyard. It was getting to the point where Harold was lying in bed awake, breathing softly as he stroked his erection, waiting for the splash of Rayne's naked body as he hit the water. "Do you want a towel?"

Rayne looked him straight in the eye for a moment and didn't move. It was the look of a wild animal in a cage. "Will it hurt my body?"

Harold was accustomed to his unusual questions. He held Rayne's gaze, as cold and distrustful as it was. "No, it won't. You're shivering a little. Thought you might want to dry off."

"Are you inviting me in, Mr. Fix-It?"

At first, Harold hesitated. Rayne had never called him that

before. Mr. Fix-It. And why was he scowling? Harold was becoming increasingly uneasy around Rayne, which was only making the sex more enticing. "It would be my pleasure," Harold said. That was the routine. Harold would ask him if he'd like a towel and Rayne would ask to be invited in. Although the pretext was no longer necessary, the routine persisted, unfurling on those summer nights like the nocturnal lilies that filled Harold's backyard with the smell of oranges.

It probably wasn't a good idea to get involved with Rayne, Harold's twenty-year-old schizophrenic neighbor who was inclined to storms of unpredictable emotion. Nancy had cautioned Harold during one of their Saturday morning chats in his garden. Rayne was showing more signs of aggression. He'd been removed from university for throwing a textbook at his psychology professor, whose nose and glasses were broken as a result. Rayne believed the professor had been spying on him for Dr. Lovely. "I'm just not sure what to do for him anymore," Nancy said. "I feel helpless." Her husband was dead; she was raising Rayne as a single mother. For nearly fifty, Nancy was gorgeous, a statuesque redhead with a body she'd developed in her work as a cop. Rayne was her only child, which was just part of the reason his illness was eating away at her heart. "I'm afraid of my own son," she said. "That's the worst part, Harold."

In the two years since he had left Toronto and moved in next door, Harold had become Nancy's confidant. The doctors felt that Rayne was well enough to be living at home, but Nancy wasn't sure she agreed. "Maybe it's best that he's home so I can keep an eye on things," she speculated. She believed that a recent hospitalization had only made Rayne's condition worse. That's all that she could bear to call it: his *condition*. Schizophrenia sounded threatening and permanent. Nancy was drinking alone in the evenings and needed someone to talk to. Harold was a good listener. He was an electronics repairman. He fixed people's televisions and computers. That's how he first met Nancy. Shortly after Harold moved in, she knocked on his front door one evening in a tight blouse to ask if he fixed coffee makers. "I know your van just says computers and televisions, but I thought maybe you'd know how to fix a coffee maker." There was a lonely-widow glint in Nancy's eye. He made haste in telling her that he was gay, which he did the next morning in her kitchen while he was fixing the coffee maker.

Harold feared that Nancy might discover what was going on and accuse him of taking advantage of her mentally ill son. What was he doing? The question kept playing over in his head. He considered the possibility that the two celibate years of his suburban exile, on top of his lingering grief, had produced an insanity of his own. After Sean died, he sold their condo in Toronto and fled blindly to the suburbs, where he could enjoy an uncomplicated, single life, complete with in-ground pool and a garden of wildflowers. After two years, the suburbs were still a complex, alien world of uncertain appearances. Whenever he thought that a handsome shopper might be cruising him at Home Depot, the furtive glances turned into nothing more than masturbation fantasies.

Rayne was stunning, horny, and well endowed. Except for the schizophrenia, he was perfect. The closest Harold would come to heaven was when he was on his knees, worshipping Rayne's body. A sweaty hint of old cheese beneath Rayne's balls. The sharp curves of his hipbones. Like a rare, exotic moss, orange hair grew over Rayne's chest, forming a path that divided his lean torso and disappeared into the overgrown bush at his crotch. Whenever Harold was giving him a blowjob, he liked to watch Rayne's face: his placid, angelic expression, not a flicker of madness. There wasn't a wrinkle anywhere, not like on Harold's face, where wrinkles were encroaching and deepening by the year. When he looked into Rayne's blue, wounded eyes, Harold felt a mix of paternal responsibility and pig desire. It was an unsettling combination.

After his swim, in Harold's living room, Rayne was pacing in a circle, absently tapping his lips with his fingertips. The damp towel was draped around his waist, molding his cock with a thick, cotton skin. It wasn't the first time that Harold was staring in awe. How Rayne's cock could fit inside a little Speedo was a mystery to him. Rayne had been a promising freestyler at university until he received a warning about the murderous intentions of his coach, whom Rayne spat on twice in the face and threatened to drown.

Rayne stopped pacing for a moment to study the framed photos on the mantel. Harold was seated on the sofa in his bathrobe, pouring chamomile tea from a china teapot, the steam billowing. "After your swim and some chamomile tea, you should be able to sleep—no problem." As soon as Harold said it, he knew it sounded ridiculous. Sometimes, Rayne would go days without sleeping. "If that doesn't help, maybe a blowjob will."

"Who's this, Mr. Fix-It?" Rayne was pointing at the photo of Sean, the one Harold had taken at the beach in Provincetown the summer before Sean died. Sean was lying on a chaise longue beneath an umbrella, fully clothed, a stiff, sweet smile across his face. "Your lover?" Rayne asked. Harold was about to take a sip from his cup, but he stopped. "Nancy said your lover had AIDS."

Rayne returned Sean's photo to the mantel and resumed pacing. Harold was cornered. He hadn't realized that Nancy would be sharing their private discussions with her son. "His name was Sean," Harold said after a moment. "And your mother was right." He brought the cup to his lips again. "Why do you ask?"

Rayne looked up at the ceiling, his one hand wringing the other. "Do you have it?"

"No," Harold said in a reassuring voice. "Fortunately, I'm fine. I'm totally clean, if that's what you're concerned about." He extended a cup of tea toward Rayne. "Here. I poured you some tea, if you'd like some."

Rayne took the cup and smiled at Harold. His smile so spontaneous and pure. Without fail, it tempted Harold to fall in love with him. "That's not what I'm concerned about," Rayne said. He tipped back the cup and drained the steaming tea into his throat. "I'm already infected."

Harold suspected that Rayne was testing him, but he wasn't sure why. Or maybe he was trying to shock Harold, which Nancy said he liked to do to people. "What do you mean, infected?"

"With HIV. I've got the virus. It's been inside me since Dr. Lovelips put me in that fucking hospital in Toronto. It's what's making me crazy."

Harold wasn't quite sure how far one should keep an open mind with a schizophrenic. He was doubtful about what Rayne was saying, but he was scaling an unfamiliar cliff. A wrong move might cause a landslide. "Why don't you get rid of that wet towel and come over here," Harold suggested.

"Did you like Sean's cock as much as mine, Mr. Fix-It?" The fact that Rayne kept referring to him as Mr. Fix-It was making Harold a little nervous. Or maybe it was Rayne's eyes, which were blinking at high speed. "Was it as big as this?" Rayne squeezed the fleshy mound behind the towel.

"Come over here and I'll tell you."

"You should have seen me. I was a big, fucking porn star in the hospital. A regular Hollywood celebrity. I like doing videos, man. Hot. Last time I was in the hospital, I was in the shower and who shows up but my buddy Tim. From the varsity team. Do you know Tim?"

Harold shook his head.

"Really hot guy. Scandinavian. Great ass. Anyways, Tim and me were taking a shower together. We were standing under the hot water, soaping up each other's cock and balls, rinsing off and soaping up again until we were both ready to blow some mega-wad. You know that feeling? Staying right on the edge. Awesome. Anyways, I made a thick lather around Tim's butthole and went digging with my fingers. It wasn't long before little Timmy was begging me to give him the old skin pickle. So I did. Right there in the shower. I fucked him. I fucked him hard. And I'm glad I did because after I fucked him, Tim confessed. He was working for Dr. Lovelips. My fucking bastard shrink was watching me bang Tim behind a one-way mirror." Rayne was pacing back and forth over the plush living room carpet, wearing a trail. "Anyways, my buddy Tim, who was my closest buddy on the team, was working for Dr. Lovelips. Can you believe it? I didn't know that, man, when I was giving it to him raw. Next day in the hospital, Dr. Lovelips tells me that I'm HIV positive. Tim infected me. As part of an experiment." Harold had never heard anyone speak with so little sense and with so much conviction at the same time.

"An experiment?" Harold asked.

"They're testing my intelligence. To see if I can figure out how to get rid of the virus."

"You mean like a cure?"

"A cure for what? For schizophrenia, maybe."

Rayne looked around the room before he sat on the couch. He just stared into space. He was close enough that Harold could smell the chlorine on his pale, freckled skin. Rayne's bizarre moments could come and go like trains in a station. Harold hoped that the weirdness was now over and they could get on with their business. He was about to indulge Rayne's nipples, which were begging to be nibbled, when Rayne stood up. Suddenly, the towel was on the floor, wrapped around his feet like an affectionate cat. At last, his beautiful cock was hanging in Harold's face, just an inch outside his tongue's long reach. "Come closer," Harold said, running his hands over the large, powerful muscles in Rayne's legs.

"Mr. Fix-It likes my skin pickle too." A bead of pre-cum dangled off the pink slit of Rayne's cock like the gooey nectar in Harold's lilies.

"No, I *love* it," Harold corrected. After carefully removing the drop of pre-cum with his tongue, Harold said, "Yum. Sweet pickles are my favorite." Then he swallowed Rayne's cock. He went down until the mushroom head was in his throat. He loved every inch of it. There was no other word for it. It was love.

The hungry intensity of Harold's mouth was soon tingling throughout Rayne's body. Getting blown was the only time

Rayne could feel his whole body, all its parts at once. He was lying back on the couch, Harold crouched between his legs in a position he could have taken for a prayer. Harold's mad slurping and the sound of a lone, persistent cricket. Other than that, there was silence. Rayne wasn't much of a noise-maker when it came to fellatio. Some nights, Rayne would still be on Harold's couch as the sun was rising, thirsty sparrows making a racket in the garden, Harold still slurping away, Rayne still hard, still silent.

"Stop for a minute," Rayne said, pushing Harold's head away from his crotch. "I need to piss."

When Rayne returned from the washroom, he was holding one of the German steak knives that Harold's mother had given her son for Christmas. He must have made a detour through the kitchen. Or did he even go to the washroom? He was glaring at Harold, a knife in one hand and a commanding erection in the other. He was sliding the smooth side of the blade along his inner thigh.

"Rayne, are you okay?" Harold's words were delicate. He wanted to avoid anything that might spin this bizarre moment into something...what? Psychotic? Or worse, bloody? "Are you okay?" Harold asked again. Rayne wasn't answering. Inside Harold's throat, fear fluttered its small, trapped wings. "What's the matter, Rayne?"

"I need you to take it," he said, in a voice that Harold was sure he'd never heard before. "If you don't take it, I'll die and Dr. Lovelips will take all the credit. That's what the asshole wants."

Harold wasn't about to ask for clarification or how the knife fit in with Rayne's plans. "Well, Rayne, I don't think it would be even possible to do that," Harold said gingerly, after a moment. "You know, chances are you're probably not even HIV-positive and even if you were, you can't get rid of the virus. You wouldn't be able to give it away to me or anything like that." Harold stopped. He could see by the empty screen in Rayne's eyes that attempting to reason with him would be like trying to pin down the meaning of a surreal painting. "Do you want some more tea?"

"No, I'll just have to piss again."

"Do you want to just call it a night, then?" Harold asked, trying not to sound hopeful. "And get some sleep? How does that sound?"

"I want to fuck you, Mr. Fix-It."

"I'm sorry?"

"That's the only way I can get rid of the virus."

Harold looked at him. Ironically, he'd been fantasizing all summer about getting fucked by Rayne, except that in his fantasy it was happening in the pool one night after Rayne's swim, and there was definitely no knife. He wasn't sure what Rayne was intending to do with the knife, if anything. He was schizophrenic. Maybe its presence was no more relevant than the crystal bowl on the coffee table or the framed photo of Sean on the mantel. Or maybe Harold was kidding himself. There was a phone in his bedroom. That was the nearest one. "I've got some condoms in my bedroom," he said.

"It won't work that way."

Harold had taken several unsafe risks over the years, and still he was negative. He could pray that his luck would continue. In all likelihood, Rayne was not infected. He had told Harold during their first encounter that he was a bisexual virgin. "Never been with a guy before," he said. And that first night, he seemed sane. More sane. Tonight, he was looming over Harold, twisting a steak knife in his hand and wanting to fuck him without a condom.

"I have some lube right in here," Harold said, opening the cabinet beside the couch. "I keep it handy for watching porn." Harold thought maybe he could divert Rayne's attention. "Have you ever seen gay porn?"

"Take off your bathrobe."

Harold reached into the cabinet and grabbed the KY. "This stuff's magic," he said, handing the bottle to Rayne, who studied the label for a moment before tossing it on the couch. "Ever used it before?"

"Take off the bathrobe, Mr. Fix-It."

Harold stood there, mesmerized. It was all too unreal. "Rayne, can you put the knife down, please."

"Take it off."

"Okay, but I'd like you to put the knife on the coffee table, please."

"No. It's a trick."

"It's not a trick, Rayne. I wouldn't do that to you."

"Take off your bathrobe."

Harold tossed the bathrobe on the couch. For a man of his age, his body was strong and quick. Still, he would be no match for Rayne. Even with the added strength of adrenaline, it was unlikely that he could successfully wrestle Rayne for the knife or outrun him.

"Now your underwear." When Harold was completely naked, Rayne said, "Get down on all fours."

Rayne didn't bother with the KY. He was kneeling on the floor behind Harold, the knife in one hand, the other clenching the base of his cock, which he was using to club Harold's ass. After a minute, he dribbled a long string of saliva into

Harold's crack. In one thrust, with the full force of his pelvis, he pushed in. Harold gasped, a bolt of jagged pain shooting from his sphincter, burning the length of his spine.

"Nice and easy," Harold said through his teeth.

Like when he was getting a blowjob, Rayne was completely silent. Not even a blissful grunt or one labored breath. Just the sound of flesh slapping flesh. Harold was silent too, Rayne's cock pounding inside him on a life-or-death mission. Harold's fear was charged now with the unstoppable, hot rush of blood in his veins, his hole giving in, stretching wider to accommodate the full force of Rayne's cock.

"That's good," Harold said. "Nice and easy."

Finally Rayne stopped pounding, his cock still buried inside Harold's ass. Harold looked back over his shoulder. "Now, fix me," Rayne muttered, his body seized, gripped by the power of an urgent orgasm. The knife falling to the floor. His cock exploding, filling Harold's hole with the stuff of his madness.

HALF-EATEN LOLLIPOP

blake nemec

My head is so focused on yours that I bang into a cement block, the kind that lines 24th Street, and I ricochet off it. I crash into a dirt pit, my face hitting hard on the cement edge. Good—something is busting open. I don't care that it's my head instead of yours. I need sound and motion.

You don't laugh at my fall, and that additional silence stirs me because why are you so damn appropriate?

The whiskey and selexa mixture in my bloodstream makes my body vault back up and continue. To once again grab your hand and reach for your face. There are Lego blocks in there, crammed in your joints, and I'm trying to hear the noise they make if I bust them up.

We make it to your doorstop. "Let me pee." You agree, then a stolen kiss breaks the fight tension and we're in your apartment. In the bathroom.

I'm now into your ass that's exposed as you're bent over the porcelain tub. The door is open and you're demanding I close it. I want your roommates to walk in, I want to blush and cut through the San Francisco fog that rolls over our backs every day, turning our words to spit-bubbles pasted on our lips, going nowhere. I want frayed emotion while our flesh turns inside out.

I close the door, spit on my dick, spit hard on your hole, then slide back into your ass-gut. If only acid could come spewing out of your mouth.

I pull your torso off the tub edge and turn you on your back so I can stick my hand down your throat. Your gag reflex isn't working but I've still got your hole full and I am fine waiting to open more. Now I'm thrusting into your asshole: your legs are up acting as springs for my chest and shoulders. We're going, and your face is smashed against the wall, pushed and shoved.

Hand back into your throat: you still don't give me a big vomit, but instead hack and turn red. You're gorgeous blotches of fever: a fucked-up kid flown off his bike, unwilling to admit defeat. Then physical bantering takes us all the way to your bed.

"Jack off," I demand, but you knee me in the face real good. I knee your shoulders to the bed and reach for anything—where is there anything to tie? Nothing but the bed and you lying under me. Beneath you is the fitted sheet. I pull half of it off and wrap it around your face ridiculously. You chuckle and stroke the back of your neck—you're not engaged or engorged—and the room turns into a cooler while my mind scatters. I'm eight years old, leaning my body against a water pump watching Lee fill my brother's El Camino with gas. His wavy hair is slick with sweat and the waves fold with the arch in the back of his neck.

Your hair is thicker, but has the same sweat sheen.

"Dennis, you can't pump gas naked."

You swat the sheet off and tell me to shut up while you throw a big burp. You're getting your briefs.

You respond whenever I shove you up against bathroom walls, whenever I pull you into me, but I'm tired of always moving first. Where are your balls? Mine are so loosely formed most people don't consider them balls. They say they are buns, the way they sit around my dick instead of underneath. Whichever, they're brave.

There must be something I could say to make you stay. I've got the time it takes you to get dressed.

"You wanted Chevron secrets. I got you that placement pumping gas at the D.C. facility, so you could learn blue-collar information of their infrastructure." You respond with a smile, almost dressed, then stand looking at me, scratching your wrists.

I sense I've got a chance. But play with me damn it.

"That site blew up in flames the day after you got me in there." You play.

"Oh, yes. Yes. I recall." I kneel in front of you. "It happened the day after the news broke about Abu Ghraib, and me and Cheney decided some black-hooded terrorist just went crazy." I grab your shin submissively. You shove your leg forward, throwing me off balance, then your sneaker goes down on my neck, my head smacks the floor.

"Wolfowitz, I need the Arctic Wildlife account!" you shout, and jam a dirty sneaker traction into my face.

From floor to closet to pantry I hustle into a suit, douse you with oil, then work your thighs with a spatula. I have somehow ended up with a half-eaten lollipop dangling from my hair. It's fun, and now I really need to cum.

My dick's hard. I think with it and pull you into me, yanking us off balance and running into the bicycle mobiles. Then onto the sweepable carpet. I pull off my pants as fast as I can while our mouths are locked sloppy.

"I know what you want," you say.

"No, I'm just ass sweating and it's annoying."

Your forearm goes up against my throat and my chin falls, my forehead falling against your mouth, and you slide your other elbow down my torso grating my breath and displacing my dick train into my belly, which you're now biting.

Fuck, your bite is clutching and I roll into it, trying to escape it.

You go again and damn, it sucks, coiling my intestines. "Rabid rat!" I say, trying to pull the hair out of your back, but just pulling you off me instead, which is not what I wanted. I don't know what I want to do with your face it's now so sweaty and ripe right here that I want to slice it open. I shove my hand back into your mouth and there's your gag—your tongue falls out—I suck it and think about my little dick.

I grab your head and shove it onto mine. You suck it like it's an eight-inch unwebbed cock and I like it, even though the style is off, and not right for what you're up against. I like it because it's you, you're working hard, there's those deep-set eyes and that possessed look.

You keep on and the surge of blood through my chest and

into my mind clears out urban tension. My dick starts to cock, I grab your head to signal you to sit your open mouth over my shaft without sucking. Your obedience is exact and we lie there motionless for a minute so my thing can stop spazzing. Your mouth slides over my dick again until it cocks back and back, shooting nothing, but I'm cumming sweat out of all my pores and I feel skinned—chilled and shaky.

TROUBLE LOVES ME

Steven Zeeland

Handsome young sailors half my age seduced me, gave me drugs, and pressured me to videotape them performing lewd acts.

I never wanted to make a porn video. It happened by accident. With some help from the ghost of a beefcake photographer....

I know it sounds farfetched.

Running a background check on me will not likely make my claim appear any more immediately credible. My record includes authoring several books that could at first glance be mistaken for porn. Especially *Military Trade*, the cover of which depicts a nude Marine. And in various interviews I've called myself a "military chaser."

But only for want of a better term.

To the extent that I have it in me to be at all

a predator, I have always ended up captured by the game.

Bremerton, Washington—January 2001:
  Navy Stray Cat Blues
"Dude, I really need to jerk off."

I turn my head to meet the sailor's eye. But he suddenly looks worried at what he's just said and doesn't give me a chance to comment before hastily adding, "Hey, you don't mind me calling you 'dude'?"

Pro and I are lying on separate parallel couches, watching DVD porn on my living room TV.

I feign a frown. "No...."

Pro's accent is so subtle I don't really think of him as a Texan. But it occurs to me that back where he comes from young men still say "ma'am" and "sir." And that maybe he just now remembered that the year he was born I graduated high school.

"Why would I mind you calling me 'dude'?"

But before he can open his mouth I tell him that if he wants any lube, in the cabinet next to the TV he'll find three different varieties, and I add which brand I use.

Pro's preferences are not the same as mine. But he doesn't take offense at my using a petroleum-based lubricant.

Pro likes his lube slick and water-soluble. And the skin tone pixels he studies on my monitor are of a different body type.

My own gaze is less focused, intermittently shifts offscreen, and especially during the longer super-slow-mo intervals unabashedly favors his body.

Pro's body is flawless. His face is more handsome than any in my straight-porn DVD collection. He doesn't mind being admired with his shirt off and his jeans around his ankles.

But Pro isn't a hustler. And though the first time he visited me I paid him a respectable hourly rate for a test shoot in my studio, tonight he's not here as a model. We're just hanging out. My high-resolution digital camera is on the coffee table right next to me, and that's where it stays the whole time Pro masturbates. Until, that is, the very end.

"I'm just about there, dude."

"Pro, uh, do me a favor?"

A pause. Then, a low, flat, "What?"

I'm pretty sure I know what he's thinking. Something along the lines of *What the fuck? I should have known.... And just when I thought— Or maybe, God, I hope it's pictures of the money shot he wants.*

But one extraordinary quality I've already noted in Pro is his inimitable knack for shattering the ordinary. At random intervals, sufficiently infrequent to defy prediction yet somehow uncannily precisely timed, he'll do or say something so off the wall as to utterly floor you. But so casually, and so adroit and so fleeting, that in the second it takes you to register and look to his face for some sort of accounting, you find yourself confounded by "the neutral face of the Buddha" (which is far and away the only trait of the insatiably desiring Pro even remotely suggestive of the Buddha). And Pro, for his part, has already declared his admiration for my own offbeat "edge."

"I think we need to do something symbolic to mark this night. Would you mind ejaculating on my TV screen?"

Pro almost manages to not smile. "Are you sure?"

The monitor in question is a new, pricey, flat-screen Sony. A gift from a patron.

"Yes. I want to photograph your semen dripping down the screen."

Pro gives my TV a copious "facial." After he leaves the room to wash up I snap three shots and stare at the screen speculatively, wondering how much this AWOL sailor's spunk would taste of the strychnine-rich methamphetamine he shared with me twelve hours ago (my first experience with street drugs since the 1980s).

Pro steps back into the room.

"Dude, when are you going to finally make a video of me? I'm serious. We need to do this. I wanna be in porn, man!"

I see this anecdote hasn't strengthened my case any. How can I claim to be an "accidental pornographer" when I have all *the equipment?*

The first time Pro visited my studio, he thought out loud: "You actually have strobe lights."

And what *legitimate* business could I have residing in a Navy shipyard ghetto devoid of any diversions save for sailors and seedy bars? It may be possible to accept an author of global ultramarginal cult standing not opting for New York or Los Angeles. But it's rather more difficult to concede much leeway to a vegetarian nondriver who opts to dwell where the only restaurant within walking distance is McDonald's and still claims he's not there for "military meat."

Ah, but here's where my story gains some credibility, if only as a potential insanity defense: You see, I moved to this isolated Navy ghost town—where it rains even more than in neighboring Seattle—from San Diego, California, "military chaser" central, USA. And military porn video central.

And I fled to escape my apprenticeship in military beefcake photography.

San Diego, California—January 1996:
  Pornographer's Apprentice
Rewind five years.

I'm in the passenger seat of a cheap leased car, very slowly puttering through a mountainous stretch of San Diego County east toward the desert. Behind the wheel is a man of advanced years and failing health. His breath is rancid. He's subject to wild mood swings. He recites the same anecdotes and same old jokes with trying frequency, and rarely betrays the faintest interest in listening to anyone else. But for once, I've managed to catch and hold his attention, reading aloud to him from the *New Yorker.*

It's Susan Faludi's "The Money Shot," the part about the porn video former U.S. Marine John Wayne Bobbitt starred in to exhibit his surgically reattached penis.

David guffaws so loudly, is so delighted by the story, that I'm almost stoked. And mistakenly imagine that David might share my interest in Faludi's cultural commentary on how ejaculating onscreen in porn video has supplanted more traditional demonstrations of masculine prowess such as working in a shipyard. Only a discharge of David's intestinal gas prompts me to glance over and realize that he's no longer paying the slightest attention.

"I've decided to send her my galleys for *The Masculine Marine,*" I conclude. "I know it's a long shot. Probably we won't end up meeting over arugula and bottled water in L.A. But a blurb from Susan Faludi—"

David looks at me intently. He nods, indicating the landscape to our left. "I've often wondered," he intones, "how those rocks got there. "

Well, it's less of a non sequitur than it was twenty-four

hours ago, when he made the same pronouncement at the same spot....

This is day two of my new part-time job, assisting David Lloyd on outdoor nude photo shoots of straight military men.

Yesterday the model was a brawny Coast Guardsman named Andy who chattered nervously the entire two hours it took us to reach the desert. On the ride there he was too polite—or scared—to comment on David's failure to observe the minimum speed limit and only once said, "Your turn signal's still on."

He did, however, put his foot down when David at last stopped the car and declared, "This is the place."

David's "ravine backdrop" was directly astride the highway and in clear view of its near-constant parade of retirees in RVs, who, confused by the fork in the road there, drove as slowly as David.

The Coast Guardsman balked.

I suggested, "Maybe just behind those rocks?"

David grimaced darkly. He raised his arms like a Joshua tree and bellowed, "There goes half the day right there!" We climbed fifty paces farther into the scrub.

At the conclusion of the shoot as we were packing up to leave Andy got some horrible cactus thing embedded in his foot and made a big deal of stoically yanking it out, for my benefit.

He was less stoic on the ride home, however, when David, in the thrall of another rambling stock narrative, momentarily mistook the treacherous two-lane mountain highway for Interstate 5 and drifted into the other lane. There were shouts, imprecations, and then apologies from Andy.

"Man! I'm sorry I grabbed the wheel. But you just missed hitting that car! We would have been dead! Man, you scared me!"

David graciously forgave him. Glancing at me in the rear-view mirror, he rolled his eyes at this studly straight guy's nervous-nelly attack.

Today's model is a Marine. Because he's stationed north of San Diego at Camp Pendleton, he drives his own car to a rendezvous point on the edge of the desert.

Kris is of Scandinavian ancestry. He fits certain of my stereotypes of Marines and Scandinavians. Kris is so reserved that even David runs out of banter.

And when David pulls over to his ravine backdrop directly astride the highway, Kris evinces a European absence of inhibition. David hands him the girlie magazine and we simply stand there as Kris casually works up a hard-on. By the second roll Kris has clambered onto a high rock and in plain view of passing cars swings his enormous erection. Chortling, David produces a ruler and measures it. "By God!" he roars. "Eight and three-quarter inches! That's how big Mr. Smiley is!"

Pleased with the $500 he's just pocketed, Kris is slightly less taciturn on the ride back. Thinking of Susan Faludi, I ask him whether he sees any potential connection between having proven his masculinity in the Marine Corps and modeling.

"No. You can get into a lot of trouble doing this."

I realize I'm receiving instruction here: being rebellious and naughty is almost as much reward as money and attention.

As a third-generation Dutch American from suburban Grand Rapids, Michigan, with a Calvinist-cum-fundamentalist upbringing, I am not altogether dissimilar to Kris in terms of social restraint. This, I know, is a quality of mine that David values. To the extent I find the experience of witnessing more or less perfect physical specimens of the U.S. Armed Forces stripping and performing indecent acts sexually arousing, I don't betray it. Still, when David calls me up a few days later and reports that at the conclusion of a second shoot, this time in a studio, Swedish Marine Kris requested and was granted permission to ejaculate, I almost feel left out.

David had no choice but to reshoot Kris—hastily. All eight rolls of film he shot in the desert were overexposed beyond salvation.

Even on his best days, David has to shoot double or triple the number of images any other photographer would, owing to his shaky hands. Tremor is a common side effect of lithium, the medication David takes for his bipolar disorder.

David is puzzled as to why this should be so much more a problem outdoors than in the studio. When I ask him why he doesn't just use a faster shutter speed, he's at a loss to answer. It's never occurred to him to toy with the automatic settings on his Nikon, he confesses.

"I don't have time!"

David earns upward of $100,000 a year from his photography. His work has been published in virtually every gay skin magazine at home and abroad and is endlessly recycled in phone-sex ads and other second-use outlets. Who am I to tell him about f-stops?

"The shoot was a total loss!" he thunders, with such outrage and wonder you'd think he'd just witnessed a cloud of locusts descending on San Diego specifically intent on devouring his Agfachromes of the Swedish Marine's "Mr. Smiley." "But I still had to pay Kris the same money again. *In cash!*"

In a quieter tone he thinks to add, "And of course you'll still get your check."

I know that when David does pay me it's as much for my company as anything. And he knows that I wouldn't help him sort through slides or type up correspondence for fifteen dollars an hour if I didn't enjoy hearing his stories.

And as outrageous as his demands sometimes are, I somehow still feel terribly guilty when I nervously announce to David that my roommate Alex Buchman is thinking of moving to Seattle.

He sees through me in an instant. "You are not seriously thinking of moving to Seattle!"

He looks more crestfallen than I anticipated. Given the one-sidedness of our exchanges, I don't like to think that David sees something of himself in me. It's easier to focus on his sighs about how hard it will be to find another assistant like me—someone he can carry on a conversation with *and* who "doesn't drool" over big-dicked Marines.

David grew up in Seattle. His final word is, "I give it two years, three at the most. You're not a Seattle kind of guy." Nodding with conviction he turns his head away and pronounces, "You'll be back."

Bremerton, Washington—January 1999:
Stiffed

Two years later *Military Trade* is almost off press. David is one of the "military chasers" interviewed. One of his naked Marines is on the cover.

But David suffers a massive stroke and dies some months before I write my English friend Mark Simpson that I've realized I'm not really a Seattle kind of guy. "Since I can't seem to face returning to San Diego, I think I might as well take advantage of being perhaps the only person in Seattle who can move to Bremerton without losing face."

Bremerton, Washington, is a downscale Pacific Northwest town located between the similarly depressed hometown of Kurt Cobain (Hoquiam/Aberdeen) and Seattle, with no Starbucks and only one employer, the U.S. Navy shipyard.

I'm drawn to an old brick apartment building of institutional appearance. Only after I move in do I learn that it was constructed during World War I as an annex to the Navy Yard Hotel.

The last time Bremerton flourished was World War II. Most of the storefronts are boarded up. But there are a lot of churches. And taverns.

Bremerton is notorious for its population of sexually aggressive women—"Fat chicks chasin' fellas in the Navy," in the offensive words of Seattle rapper Sir Mix-A-Lot's 1987 song "Bremelo."

I've never lived "on the wrong side of the tracks" before. By the end of my first week here I'm starting to feel a little creeped out. Walking through town I'm struck by the number of burned-out houses posted ARSON. REWARD. I pick up the local paper and read that a woman was raped in the parking lot below my bedroom window. A Friday evening crawl of waterfront bars leaves me struggling to picture myself fitting in here at all.

I'm about to give up for the night when I pass by a derelict tavern and notice that there are lights on inside. The door is open. I walk in and am immediately greeted, "Steve!" A gay submariner recognizes me from a book reading.

The Crow's Nest dates back a century. Knowing that

Bremerton is too small and too working class to sustain a gay bar, the new owner aims for an unobtrusively gay-friendly mixed bar. Reopening night, the crowd is engagingly motley. There are more gay submariners, there are Bremelos—and on the barstool to my right there is a drunken bug-eyed misfit who announces that he is self-publishing a chapbook of poems about crossing Bremerton ferry.

"Steve writes about fairies too," remarks my submariner friend.

The DVD plays George Michael's "Outside" video. Just below the monitor, an old wooden placard reads:

WELCOME ABOARD.

THE LORD TAKES CARE OF DRUNKS AND SAILORS.

I find myself making eye contact with a sailor. When he goes to the men's room, I follow. But I don't get to stand next to him at the awkwardly intimate urinals—someone else beats me to it. Peeing next to the sailor is a thirtyish man sporting short hair and a golf cap. With aching clarity I overhear him inquire, "So...are you in the Navy?"

When the sailor leaves the bar, I somehow feel obliged to sidle up next to the luckless chaser.

He's startled, even shocked that I've pegged him. Buddy tells me that he doesn't like gay culture, he just likes guys. I mention an English writer friend who's edited a book called *Anti-Gay* and his invitation to take me to Plymouth.

"Oh. I've been to Plymouth. It's like Bremerton. I mean, it's a lot bigger. But," Buddy shakes his head, "they've got the same Bremelos."

I become a regular at the Crow's Nest. A sailor I meet there becomes something of a boyfriend. When he's out to sea, I hang out with Buddy. By summer we're drinking pals.

And what a summer it is. Weekend nights the bars are packed with sailors off the USS *Abraham Lincoln,* an aircraft carrier in town for a six-month overhaul. Buddy and I make a game of compiling weekly top-ten lists of our favorites. Even though—he is anxious that I understand this—he cannot himself be termed a military chaser. He's not a predator. "And," he reasons, "I also like firemen."

I don't disabuse Buddy of his conviction that he doesn't fit any stereotypes. And indeed, it seems that the only people who perceive Buddy as stereotypically gay are visiting urban gays.

I accompany Buddy on his nearly nightly rounds of the roughest dive bars on the waterfront. Buddy plays pool with sailors. I sit on bar stools and listen to career Navy alcoholics' sea stories.

These guys tend to come from small towns in the southern United States—or neighboring Idaho. Young men who never once jump on the ferry to Seattle by themselves, because they never have. Instead, they booze and brawl alongside the Bremelos.

Buddy takes to introducing me to local people as a "famous author"—a title that calls for too much explanation. One night I adjure my drinking pal, "Don't tell people I'm a famous author. Tell them I'm a famous photographer."

I'm half-joking. The only photos I've had published are in my own books. But among the thousands of *Lincoln* sailors, a half dozen or so who have become "downtown" regulars exude indisputable star quality, and one night it becomes more than I can bear.

We're in Buddy's favorite bar. I'm entertaining an out-of-town dignitary, a professor at one of the military academies. The prettiest of the *Lincoln* boys is there—drinking Bud by the pitcher, playing pool, and stealing the hearts or at least admiring glances from everyone present. He's winsome beyond measure, from his disarming constant grin to his tight Wrangler jeans to the heavily autographed cast on his broken arm. An inscription jumps out at me:

DON'T JERK OFF SO HARD

Buddy and the professor are merely charmed. And as for me....

When yet another young sailor staggers in, spots Castboy, and with unstudied passion immediately throws his arms tightly around him, I get all misty-eyed, struggle to recite Whitman, and drunkenly vow that I will not return to this bar without a camera because "That picture would have been worth more than all of my books put together."

Buddy is keen on the idea but cautions me that before I start taking any pictures of sailors in the bar a protocol must be devised. I should wait until the hour when everyone is a little drunk but not yet sloppy drunk. The first pictures must be of people we know—say, Buddy and a woman, and then with some other guy. And only then take pictures of a sailor, but still only with a girl.

"If anybody gives you trouble, I'll back you up."

There was trouble, all right. But not like Buddy expected.

The first night I worked up enough nerve to pop my electronic flash in a waterfront pool hall a sailor angrily confronted me: "Why are you taking pictures of him instead of me?"

Of course I obliged him. But this angered the sailor I had

been taking pictures of. Losing the spotlight, he sulked. Seeing this, I reassured him, "Well, don't let it go to your head, but you definitely have the most potential as a model." That was Mike, the sailor with the cast on his arm.

When his best friend from the ship walked in, Mike proudly repeated my appraisal.

This sailor in turn took me aside and demanded, "Him? You're wasting your film. Dude! His ears are too big!" And that was Packard, the sailor who would end up starring in *Out of the Brig,* the porn video I made by accident.

Bremerton, Washington—Summer 1999:
Trouble Loves Me

As with any accident, memory blurs. This much is known:

That summer *Honcho* ran an interview with me to promote *Military Trade.* When I e-mailed the editor my thanks, I attached some JPGs of sailors drinking and playing pool. Doug McClemont wrote back that he liked the pictures. He invited me to shoot a few rolls of slide film for publication in his magazine.

At the time, I didn't own any strobe lights (much less any video equipment).

Of the three USS *Lincoln* sailors who'd fought over who was the most photogenic, one was in the brig and another was in a military treatment center for substance abuse. When I relayed *Honcho*'s invitation to Packard, he expressed skepticism. "Yeah, but how much would it pay?"

I told him how much.

Packard may or may not have dropped his pool stick. It seems like it was only a matter of hours before I'd shot enough rolls of Kodak EPP to FedEx to New York and woke up to a voice mail from Doug telling me the pictures were okay—only, "They're a little dark. If you can, try to get just a basic monolight."

For once, I wasn't "in between books." I had the money, but what motivated me to spend $1,000 on basic studio lighting equipment was not the promise of selling more layouts. I wanted to spare my models the shame of telltale amateur shadows.

That summer the (beefy but reclusive) Navy master-at-arms living next door to me vacated his one-room apartment. I toyed with the extravagant idea of renting the "studio," but not seriously—until the building manager accepted a rental application for the unit from a Bremelo with two small children.

"Well, I'll have the linoleum replaced for you." My landlady was perplexed but also impressed at my renting two apartments. "And about the cracks in the walls—"

She didn't argue when I told her I liked the room exactly as it was.

I had sense enough not to gush about how especially fond I was of the vintage Murphy bed and its stained mattress. Instead, I asked her what she knew about how the building had been furnished during World War II when it served as officers' quarters.

After I dragged up from the basement a battered chair and matching nightstand, my studio was ready. In the thirteen months I rented it I didn't change a detail.

That summer I was prescribed Paxil (paroxetene), an antidepressant/anti-anxiety drug in the same family of selective serotinin reuptake inhibitors as Prozac. Overall, the medication made me more self-assured and confident. Bold, even. I would not have dived into neophysique photography without it.

Paxil also abated some of my anxieties about turning into David Lloyd.

But one side effect of Paxil resulted in a new and unwelcome physical resemblance to David. From my first video recording made in the new studio:

PACKARD: I can see why you like the "steady shot" feature so much.

ZEELAND: [mock confrontationally] So what are you trying to say?

PACKARD: I can see your hands shaking right now.

ZEELAND: [Remains silent]

PACKARD: [Coughs and looks away]

The camcorder was an impulse purchase, prompted by cues from sailors I spoke with about modeling. The most succinct and memorable:

"So...you only take *still* pictures?"

It was in answer to another magazine editor's invitation that I became acquainted with videomaker Dink Flamingo of ActiveDuty.com. At the close of my interview with him for *Unzipped* Dink confided that he'd never aspired to become a pornographer. His ambition had always been to be a journalist.

We agreed to "trade places for a day." Dink promised to contribute some authentic accounts of erotic liaisons with "barracks bad boys" to Alex Buchman's nonfiction anthology in progress. I pledged to try my hand at playing auteur in his scandal-ridden, sordid "adult amateur video" subgenre.

After patiently bearing with me for nine long months, Dink

breathed satisfaction and relief upon receipt of the labor of love I finally delivered.

My timing, however, could not have been worse. The scheduled release date for my video celebrating real-life military deserters coincided with the bombings of the World Trade Center and the Pentagon.

Still, my three masturbating sailors cannot really be accused of "disgracing the military." The title *Out of the Brig* is no fantasy; it's documentary. The sailors in it are real-life tattooed Navy "bad boys" who really have broken the rules, have done their time, and are no longer on active duty—are no longer answerable to anyone. (Even if at the scheduled release date one of them had not yet turned himself in. Had Congress officially declared war, and had he been arrested, he could have faced the firing squad.)

Barracks Bad Boys:
The Movie

The style of my directorial debut is a cross between early Dirk Yates and early Andy Warhol. With, I'd like to think, a human face.

But not mine.

FIRST SAILOR: Approximately three minutes into the opening sequence, which stars Packard, you can hear me say: "You know, you could even sort of self-direct this" (as I hand him a second remote, and flip over the camcorder viewfinder so that he can zoom in and out to...self-direct).

SECOND SAILOR: After a short introductory scene (unscripted and shot in one take at a retro adult video arcade just outside the shipyard), I don't do much "directing." This one stars Pro. He masturbates watching DVDs on my living room TV.

THIRD SAILOR: The first two sequences are exactly twenty minutes long. The closing sequence is a film within a film, and a full hour long. It's an essay by itself, too. For my purpose here, it's enough to tell you that I miscalculated in thinking that for this shoot I had an assistant who would effectively play "Steve" to my "David." But when the door to my own studio slammed shut with me locked out, I was surprised but not altogether displeased.

And when an hour and a half later I was allowed back in the room and rewound through some of the tape, I knew that this was it. My "sailors gone bad" had given me enough "raw footage" to meet the basic requirements of the amateur military porn video idiom. Now I could give myself over to endless hours lovingly *editing*.

Bremerton, Washington—January 2003

By the time you read this I will no longer be in Bremerton, Washington. Every last one of the active-duty sailors I photographed has long since departed. Two or three of them transferred to distant duty stations; two or three received honorable discharges. Between twenty and thirty were kicked out of the Navy for "unauthorized absence" and/or drug use. In February 2002, the Navy announced that all of the ships currently homeported in Bremerton would be moved elsewhere. Also, that the block of 100-year-old buildings adjacent to the Navy shipyard—including the historic Crow's Nest tavern—would be demolished to provide a "security buffer" against terrorist attack. But the bar shut down even before the wrecking ball hit, after the thirty-seven-year-old owner was found dead under mysterious circumstances.

Pro has long since moved back to Texas. But he's kept in

touch. And at one point when I was too long in replying to his e-mail he left me a voice mail:

"Steve! Come out of your fucking Pax-hole!"

Actually, I'd quit Paxil and sworn off maintenance drugs of any sort just before September 11, 2001.

"Are we still friends or what? Dude! *I shot my seed on your TV!*"

It isn't very often I turn on my TV, and almost never when I'm alone. But one special occasion was the day I opened a package from Dink Flamingo, stretched out on the couch, hit the remote, and watched *Out of the Brig.*

And noticed I had missed a spot when I cleaned the monitor.

ABOUT THE AUTHORS

RALOWE TRINITROTOLUENE AMPU is an annoying black homosexual asshole living in San Francisco. When not cruising bathrooms at chain department stores and college campuses or watching porn, she raps, kind of. She's also an instigator of Gay Shame. If you're severely bored, check her website, where you can taste one of more than 150 free MP3s: www.ralowes-confusedsuburbanlaughter.com.

BEN BLACKTHORNE collects Thundercat action figures. He has every issue of *Thrasher* going back to 1988 and frequently fantasizes about being Tony Hawke's bitch. He enjoys sunsets, romantic walks on the beach, and public restrooms. Blackthorne lives with his partner and five cats, and is old enough to drink.

PATRICK CALIFIA is the author of twenty books, including five collections of BDSM fiction, *Boy in the Middle, Macho Sluts, Melting Point, No Mercy,* and *Hard Men,* as well as a novel, *Mortal Companion,* and the classic introduction to BDSM, *Sensuous Magic: A Guide for Adventurous Couples.* He is the author of the seminal texts on sex and gender politics *Speaking Sex to Power: The Politics of Queer Sex, Public Sex: The Culture of Radical Sex,* and *Sex Changes: Transgender Politics.* He lives in San Francisco.

ALEXANDER CHEE is the author of *Edinburgh.* He is the winner of a Whiting Award and an NEA Fellowship in Literature. His stories and essays have appeared in the anthologies *Men On Men 2000, Boys Like Us, Loss Within Loss, Best Gay Erotica 2002,* and *The M Word.* His new novel, *The Queen of the Night,* is forthcoming from Houghton Mifflin.

DENNIS COOPER's most recent novels are *God Jr.* and *The Sluts.* He is the author of The George Miles Cycle, five interconnected novels: *Closer* (1989), *Frisk* (1991), *Try* (1994), *Guide* (1997), and *Period* (2000). The cycle is published by Grove Press and has been translated into fourteen languages. He lives in Los Angeles.

JAIME CORTEZ is a cultural worker in California. His writing has appeared in a dozen anthologies, his visual art has been exhibited at numerous California galleries, and he edited the anthology *Virgins, Guerrillas & Locas.* Cortez has worked as a high school teacher in Japan, at the AIDS Memorial Quilt, and at Galería De La Raza, and has lectured on art and activism at Stanford, Berkeley, UC Santa Barbara, University of

Pennsylvania, and the Yerba Buena Center for the Arts. He is pursuing his MFA in art at Berkeley.

SAM D'ALLESANDRO studied at the University of California, Santa Cruz, and came to San Francisco as a youth in the early 1980s. He was handsome and charismatic, the man who'd turn your head at a hundred yards. He died of AIDS in 1988, leaving behind a brilliant body of work that ranges from stories of only one paragraph to fully developed novellas.

TIM DOODY has organized political actions to challenge the policies of governments and corporations from the East Coast to the West Bank. ABC-TV's *Nightline* listed him as one of the nation's most dangerous radicals during its August 31, 2004, broadcast. He has been published in *Topic Magazine, The Earth First! Journal, XY, The Indypendent,* and two other anthologies: *That's Revolting! Queer Strategies for Resisting Assimilation* and *Dirt Road: Transient Tales.* Doody can be reached at query@riseup.net.

MARCUS EWERT met Allen Ginsberg while still in high school, and the two became boyfriends. Ewert is currently writing about this exciting time in his life in his memoir-in-progress, *Beatboy.* He also writes science fiction and children's picture books, and is the cocreator of the animated series *Piki and Poko: Adventures in StarLand* (www.pikiandpoko.com).

TREBOR HEALEY is the author of the 2004 Ferro-Grumley and 2004 Violet Quill Award–winning novel *Through It Came Bright Colors.* His work has appeared in *Best Gay Erotica 2003* and *Best Gay Erotica 2004.* His erotic poetry collection, *Sweet Son of Pan*, will be published in spring 2006. He lives in Los Angeles. www.treborhealey.com.

NADYALEC HIJAZI is a poseur who buys all his cool clothes at Hot Topic. He has every issue of *Propaganda* magazine going back to 1988, and frequently fantasizes about being Poppy Brite's bitch. He's been published in *Hot Off the Net* and *Trikone*, and online in *Bint el Nas* and the late great *Roughriders*. You can read more of his work on his website at www.nadyalec.com.

THORN KIEF HILLSBERY is the author of *War Boy*, described by one critic as "the most exciting gay novel in a decade" and translated into German, Spanish, and Catalan. A former columnist and editor at *Outside*, he has written feature articles for *Rolling Stone* and many other magazines on mountaineering, skateboarding, and surfing, as well as the punk rock subculture featured in *What We Do Is Secret*, his second novel. He lives in Manhattan and teaches at Columbia University.

KEVIN KILLIAN is the author of *Shy, Little Men, Bedrooms Have Windows, Arctic Summer, Argento Series,* and *I Cry Like a Baby.* He lives in San Francisco, where he is writing a book about Kylie Minogue, a pop singer born in Australia and currently living in London, who appeared in the film *Moulin Rouge.*

DARIN KLEIN is an artist, curator, and small press publisher. His artwork and writing have been included in independently published projects including Angry Dog Midget Editions, *Bedwetter, Incredibly Short Stories,* and *Poorly Rendered.*

He resides in and has erotic encounters in Los Angeles. www.darinklein.net.

Sam J. Miller is a community organizer. He lives in the Bronx with his partner of three years. When he's not writing or organizing poor people to fight for social justice, he's binging on silent movies and punk rock. At present he's working on his first novel, of which "Depression Halved Production Costs" is an excerpt. Drop him a line at samjmiller79@yahoo.com.

BLAKE NEMEC is a working-class phlebotomist, HIV/STI counselor, performer, and former hustler who lives in San Francisco. His writing has been included in the anthologies *That's Revolting! Queer Strategies for Resisting Assimilation*, *From the Inside Out: Radical Gender Transformation*, and *FTM and Beyond*, as well as the magazines *Spread* and *LIP*. He has published in self-sufficiency zines focusing on sound/radio and repetitive stress injuries. He can be contacted at aorticvalve22@yahoo.com.

Kirk Read lives in San Francisco, where he is getting his MFA in creative writing at San Francisco State University. He is an HIV counselor and phlebotomist at St. James Infirmary, a free health care clinic for sex workers. He is the author of *How I Learned to Snap*, a memoir about being out in high school in a small Virginia town. He tours as a storyteller and produces literary/performance events, including the Castro's monthly open mic Smack Dab, which aims to force-feed the culturally anorexic gay financial district. He can be reached at www.kirkread.com.

JULY SHARK is a displaced Appalachian transsexual who now lives in Oakland, California. Shark works odd jobs for a living and haunts wastelands in the off time.

SIMON SHEPPARD makes his eleventh appearance in the *Best Gay Erotica* series, with thanks this time to Neva Chonin. He's also the author of the books *Sex Parties 101, In Deep: Erotic Stories,* and *Kinkorama: Dispatches from the Front Lines of Perversion.* His writing has appeared in more than 125 other anthologies, and he writes the columns "Sex Talk" and "Perv." He's at work on a historically based anthology of gay porn—anyone with vintage smut is encouraged to get in touch at www.simonsheppard.com.

ANDREW SPIELDENNER has lived in New York, Oakland, Saigon, Bangkok, Los Angeles, and Miami. His essays and stories have appeared in *Best Gay Asian Erotica, Corpus, Names We Call Home,* and *Doi Dien* magazine.

BOB VICKERY is a regular contributor to various websites and magazines, particularly *Men, Freshmen,* and *Inches.* He has five collections of stories published: *Skin Deep, Cock Tales, Cocksure, Play Buddies,* and most recently, *Man Jack,* an audiobook of some of his hottest stories. Vickery lives in San Francisco, and can most often be found in his neighborhood Haight Ashbury cafe, pounding out the smut on his laptop. He can be reached at www.bobvickery.com.

DUANE WILLIAMS lives in Hamilton, Canada. His short fiction has appeared in anthologies across North America, including *Queeries, Quickies, Queer View Mirror I* and *II, Contra/*

Diction, Buttmen 2 and *3, Full Body Contact, Friction 6, Love Under Foot,* and *Boyfriend from Hell,* and in *Blithe House Quarterly, Harrington Gay Men's Literary Quarterly, Velvet Mafia,* and *Suspect Thoughts.* He can be contacted at duanewilliams@cogeco.ca.

THOM WOLF has been writing erotic fiction for more than a decade. He is author of the novels *Words Made Flesh* and *The Chain.* His stories have appeared in numerous anthologies, including Alyson's *Friction* series, *Just the Sex, Bearotica,* and *Twink.* He lives with his boyfriend, Liam, in County Durham, England.

STEVEN ZEELAND is the author of five books on homoeroticism in the military: *Barrack Buddies and Soldier Lovers, Sailors and Sexual Identity, The Masculine Marine, Military Trade,* and, with Mark Simpson, *The Queen is Dead: Jarheads, Eggheads, Serial Killers & Bad Sex.* www.stevenzeeland.com.

ABOUT THE EDITORS

RICHARD LABONTÉ, editor of the *Best Gay Erotica* series for more than a decade, writes a fortnightly syndicated book review column for Q Syndicate and the monthly subscription newsletter *Books To Watch Out For* (www.btwof.com), published by Carol Seajay. On a good day, he reads a couple of books; on a bad day, at least part of one. After more than twenty years of a gay bookselling career in Los Angeles, New York, and San Francisco, he now lives with his partner Asa and their dogs Percy and Zak in a Perth, Ontario, apartment and on a Calabogie, Ontario, farm. Life is good in the slow lane. Mail: tattyhill@gmail.com.

MATTILDA, A.K.A. MATT BERNSTEIN SYCAMORE is a prancer, a romancer, and a fugitive. She's the author of a novel, *Pulling Taffy*, and the editor of three non-fiction anthologies: *That's Revolting! Queer Strategies for Resisting Assimilation*, *Dangerous Families: Queer Writing on Surviving*, and *Tricks and Treats: Sex Workers Write About Their Clients*. Mattilda is an instigator of Gay Shame, a radical queer activist group that fights the monster of assimilation. *BUTT Magazine* calls Mattilda "one of the 100 most interesting people on Earth," and the *Austin Chronicle* calls her "a cross between Tinkerbell and a honky Malcolm X with a queer agenda." Mattilda's new novel, *So Many Ways to Sleep Badly*, will destroy writing as we know it, but her sex life is terrible right now—if you want to meet in a park some time, contact Mattilda via www.mattbernsteinsycamore.com.

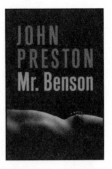

Ordering is easy! Call us toll free to place your MC/VISA order or mail the order form below with payment to: Cleis Press, P.O. Box 14697, San Francisco, CA 94114.

ORDER FORM

Buy 4 books, Get 1 FREE*

QTY	TITLE	PRICE
————	————————————————————	————
————	————————————————————	————
————	————————————————————	————
————	————————————————————	————
————	————————————————————	————
————	————————————————————	————
————	————————————————————	————
————	————————————————————	————
————	————————————————————	————

SUBTOTAL ————

SHIPPING ————

SALES TAX ————

TOTAL ————

Add $3.95 postage/handling for the first book ordered and $1.00 for each additional book. Outside North America, please contact us for shipping rates. California residents add 8.5% sales tax. Payment in U.S. dollars only.

* Free book of equal or lesser value. Shipping and applicable sales tax extra.
Cleis Press • (800) 780-2279 • orders@cleispress.com
www.cleispress.com
You'll find more great books on our website